# NOCTURNE
## WITH
## GASLAMPS

MATTHEW FRANCIS

# NOCTURNE
## WITH
# GASLAMPS

## MATTHEW FRANCIS

NEEM TREE
PRESS

Published by Neem Tree Press Limited, 2024

1 3 5 7 9 10 8 6 4 2

Neem Tree Press Limited
Hamilton House, 4th Floor, Mabledon Place, London, WC1H 9BD
United Kingdom

info@neemtreepress.com
www.neemtreepress.com

A catalogue record for this book is available from the British Library

ISBN 978-1-915584-23-6 Paperback
ISBN 978-1-915584-24-3 Ebook UK
ISBN 978-1-915584-38-5 Ebook US

Printed and bound in Great Britain

The City is of Night; perchance of Death,
But certainly of Night

James Thomson,
*The City of Dreadful Night*

HAM: What, frighted with false fire!
GER:          How fares my lord?
POL: Give o'er the play.
CLA:          Give me some light: away!
ALL: Lights, lights, lights!

*Hamlet*

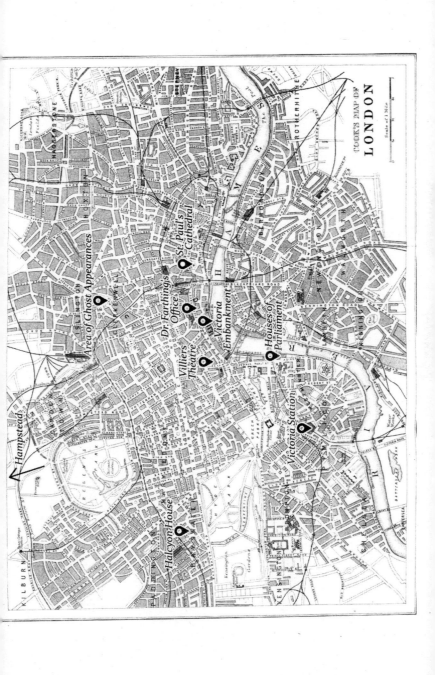

COOK'S MAP OF
LONDON

Scale of 1 Mile

Hampstead

Area of Ghost Appearances

St. Paul's Cathedral

Dr. Farthing's Office

Villiers Theatre

Victoria Embankment

Houses of Parliament

Victoria Station

Halcyon House

KILBURN

ROTHERHITHE

*April 1883*

# Prologue

A pedestrian has just turned the corner from one of London's great thoroughfares into a smaller street, little more than an alley, when the lamp in the middle, some fifty yards in front of him, goes out.

The city has not known real darkness since the beginning of the century; the gaslamps in every street give a purplish glow to the night sky that seems part of the texture of the air. Now this purple has turned to black and it is as if the man has been plunged into the depths of space. A spontaneous noise seems to arise behind and all around him, a sort of gasp, as if the entire population of the city is catching its breath. He hears the whinny of a panicked horse. Without turning round, he knows it is dark on the main road, too, only the lamps of a hansom cab making an island of brightness that merely emphasizes the black sea around it. He is a little surprised at how disturbed he feels: he has lived in this city all his life, and has often said he knows it blindfold—now is the chance to test the reality of that claim. He has no more than a few dozen yards to go to his destination, and besides, he is one of the very few people who have been expecting this.

All the same, some primeval instinct made him stop the moment the light went out, and now he has to force himself to begin walking again, feeling at each step that he might drop through the cobbles to fall endlessly through the universe. He cannot help lurching to his left in search of the wall, which turns out to be further than he pictured it, so that he almost loses his balance and his hand thumps painfully against the brick. He wants to cling on with both hands, turn his body to the wall and press himself against it until the lights come back. He is shivering despite his heavy coat and the mild evening, and he feels a curious bristling sensation under the dome of his bowler hat. *Humbug,* he tells himself, *I ain't got enough hair left for it to stand on end.* He has risked his life many times, faced down men with knives, broken bottles, guns. He is not a child, to be scared of the dark.

"Humbug," he says, out loud this time, and feels better, a human being again rather than a formless mass of sensations. "I know who you are now," he says, "and you ain't getting away with it. This is the last time, my friend, the very last time. Got me?" But his boldness only lasts a moment, and he wishes he hadn't ventured on such a dramatic speech. What if someone really is listening? That's the trouble with darkness; you can never tell when you've got company. Embarrassment is another feeling he is unaccustomed to, and it goads him into resuming his walk. Resting the fingertips of his left hand on the wall, he takes a step, then another. The fingers run lightly across the wall as he moves, and he is proud of the way he maintains his balance on the uneven surface.

His progress along the wall is slowed by doorways and junctions between the jumbled buildings, and he clunks his shin against a wooden flower tub he is sure wasn't there when he last passed this way. But his confidence has grown, and the pain only makes him more determined. Already his mind is working on the next problem, that of recognizing his destination when he reaches it. If he can forget a flower tub he must have skirted unthinkingly many times before, can he trust his memory for the door he wants? He should have been counting his steps; too late now.

His fingers touch brick, brick, painted wood, more wood, and then they are holding the cold metal of a doorknob. He turns it, and it opens. Still here, then. What a duffer he would have been to come all this way in the dark, and then find the fellow had packed up and gone home for the night. But no, not on this of all nights, when everything's coming together at last. He takes a deep breath of the musty indoor air, just as dark as the street, but somehow safer, and steps inside. There is the staircase in front of him, so it is the right building after all.

He climbs three flights, noticing that there is no sign of life on the lower floors. Everyone else in the building must have gone home at a normal hour. As he turns the corner after the second landing, he becomes aware of a paleness, not enough to illuminate the steps, but light all the same. By the time he has reached the third-floor landing it has become a clear yellow, a bar of dappled light at the bottom of the door on the left-hand side, stretching out to lap unevenly over the floorboards. He lets out some breath he hadn't realized he was holding and knocks at the door. There is no response, and he knocks again, then a third time. Was that a sound, a clearing of the throat that might have meant "Come in"? He tries the door and it opens.

After the darkness, the candlelight in the room is dazzling. The flames are disturbed by the draught from the door and jump about, creating a flickering effect that feels like rapidly opening and closing one's eyes. Through the optical confusion, he sees the desk at the far side of the room and a dark blur that might be its usual occupant or just the empty space where the occupant would have been. "Sorry," he murmurs. "Excuse me, sir, I just wondered…" He takes a few steps, but, in his disorientated state, he veers off to the right and comes into contact with the wooden back of a piece of furniture. Oh, of course, he'd forgotten that was there. Clumsy great object to have in a place like this.

"What? What?" The man he has come to see rises up almost under his nose. "Oh, it's you."

"Sorry, sir, was you sleeping? I didn't mean to disturb you."

"No, no, I was just thinking. I never sleep. Not even at night."

"The lights have gone out, sir," the visitor says as they shake hands awkwardly across the intervening obstruction. "Good thing you're equipped for it." He indicates the candles.

"Quite." The man is probably smiling. "But let me get you something. And do take a seat."

The visitor skirts the place where his host was recently lying and chooses a plain chair next to an occasional table with one of the candles on it. "Well, sir, thank you, that would be kind on a night like this. A glass of the monstrous fluid would be much appreciated." He chuckles.

"Of course, of course." The host, now coming into focus, as he crosses to the far side of the room, is slightly built and his movements are lithe and fussy at the same time. He stands beside the desk with his back to the visitor.

The latter takes his hat off and puts it on the table beside him. The fire in the hearth is not lit, so he keeps his overcoat on. He is only going to stay for one glass, as there is much to be done tonight. But he has come to talk, and he cannot even wait till he has a drink in his hand. "I shall be glad to take a glass, sir, by way of celebration, for this is a great night for me, dark as it is."

"Indeed?"

"Yes, sir. In fact I think I may safely say that this is the last such night either of us will have to put up with."

The host, still with his back turned, says something muffled that is probably another "Indeed?" He is preoccupied with getting the drink, which must be a more complicated process than one would suppose, or perhaps he has suspended operations until he has heard what his visitor has to say.

"Yes, sir. I know who our man is. I told you I had my sources, didn't I, sir? You pooh-poohed it, as I remember, but there's nothing like the professional touch in these cases, after all. Not that I ain't grateful for your contribution, sir. But I expect you're as keen as I am to see the fellow's antics stopped."

The other has half turned so that the candlelight catches his spectacles and a corner of white forehead. "Of course. And you really believe…?"

"I don't believe, sir; I know it. My chaps are on their way to his residence now, up the hill, as we say round here. Before you know it, it will be my great pleasure to introduce him to you, and then you'll see what's what and who's who. That," he adds pointedly, "is why tonight's celebration is in order."

"Up the hill? You're sure there's no…" His voice dies away.

"Absolutely none, sir. We know the man's name and where he comes from, which is not this country, I'm glad to say, and his position in the world, if that's genuine, which I very much doubt. And most important of all, we know his address, not that

I can pronounce the name of the house. That would be more in your line than mine, sir—it's one of them foreign words, and I ain't had the education you have. Still, education ain't everything, is it? Now, what about that magic potion, sir?"

The host has turned round completely now, and there is a decanter in his left hand. But the object in his right hand is not a glass. It is something stubby and dull-looking in comparison with the glitter of the decanter, though the candlelight just licks the tip, making it look as though there is a small flame at the end. He is trying to talk. His mouth opens and closes, but no words come out.

"I'm sorry, sir. That's just how it is," the visitor says. "No hard f——?" And then he recognizes the object in the man's right hand.

He knows that sound must be the gun going off, but it is not like any gunshot he has ever heard, more like a door slamming in a distant part of the building. There is no pain, just a violent blast of air that pushes him back against his seat. The man in front of him is still trying to speak and looks distressed (are there tears glinting behind the spectacles?) and the visitor feels the urge to help him. He stands up and takes a single pace forward. *It's all right*, he tries to say, *these things happen and I know you didn't mean it, and after all no harm done, so hand that nasty thing over and let's have that drink together*. But now he too cannot speak, and even his intended words are becoming weak and strange-sounding as they pass through his mind, as if someone else is speaking them in a language he cannot understand. He makes one last attempt to assemble his ideas. *I think, perhaps*, he says to himself, *I made a mistake somewhere. After all I may have got this wrong*. It's an annoying thought but it is stuck in his mind now, and no amount of shaking his head will get rid of it.

And then the lights go out, everywhere in the world.

*September 1882*

# Chapter 1

That evening there was a new resident at dinner at Halcyon House, and Cassie was struck by his appearance. He was the only gentleman present without whiskers or beard, which made him look little more than a boy. He had a way of looking round the table for an eye to catch which also struck her as schoolboyish. When Mr. Flewitt, as the oldest gentleman, was saying grace and only Cassie and the newcomer, Mr. Wimbury, had their eyes open, his look was conspiratorial, as if to say he had caught a fellow unbeliever, and Cassie, who was not so much an unbeliever as a person whose beliefs were in a perpetual state of evolution, immediately wanted to argue with him. Her eyes might be open for any number of reasons, and there was nothing to be deduced from the fact.

But Mr. Wimbury's eyes did not dwell on Cassie for long. He was soon examining the contents of his plate as if he had never seen boiled mutton or turnips before, then glancing round at Miss Hartston, Mr. Lyman, Mr. Flewitt, even at Esmé, the maid who served them, mutely asking each in turn what this strange substance was, and was it perhaps dangerous? The only person he did not interrogate in this way was Mrs. Makepeace, who was ultimately responsible, but when his eyes finally reached hers their expression was one of pure delight, as if nothing could give him more joy than boiled mutton and turnips.

His conversation was of a similar character: asking each of them what they did and managing to express joyful surprise to his interlocutor ("A clerk!" "Another clerk, fancy that!") while those mobile eyes, whose colour sometimes seemed blue and sometimes green, conveyed to the others in the room that it was particularly tiresome meeting this clerk, and that *they* were far more interesting. As for Miss Hartston, at least she could say she was not a clerk, since she worked in one of the city's great stores, while Cassie herself caused his only moment of genuine surprise by announcing her own profession.

"A stenographer? What is that?"

"A lady as takes notes in shorthand," Cassie said. "My employer dictates his letters and other writings to me, and afterwards I write them out for him in a fair hand."

"I see. Then you *are* a clerk!"

"Certainly not, sir! I'm a secretary. And a stenographer."

"I see, I see." Mr. Wimbury nodded several times to show his ironic appreciation of the distinction.

"And you, sir, what do you do?"

"Oh, I am a clerk, like everybody else." He nodded again, in a way that suggested to Cassie that he was not to be believed for a moment. She looked forward to interrogating him further about his claims to clerkship later, but when they retired to the parlour for the evening (there was no coffee served at Halcyon House, but there was, so to speak, a coffee-craving interval), she found he had slipped away.

So the evening passed as usual with Mr. Flewitt smoking his pipe and grunting in that cryptic way that made him seem almost about to say something which never materialized, while Mr. Lyman read a sporting newspaper, making circles round his favoured horses with a pencil, and Miss Hartston continued knitting a mud-coloured garment. Normally Cassie enjoyed this time, all the more so as Mrs. Makepeace never joined them for it; it was pleasant to be in the company of others rather than in the chill of her room, and to get on with reading her book instead of feeling obliged to make conversation, but tonight her volume of Madame Blavatsky seemed impenetrable, and she would have welcomed a distraction. What would Dr. Farthing make of Mr. Wimbury? she wondered. He would have observed him closely and drawn many conclusions that were not obvious at first glance. Cassie had worked for Dr. Farthing for eighteen months now, and, though she continued, in his words, to think like a woman, she hoped she had learned something in all that time.

First of all, there was that whiskerless face. She had studied it while his eyes were on the mutton, and seen the embedded flecks of hair that proved he was not one of those men who do not need to shave. The smoothness was an affectation, then; perhaps he thought it made him more attractive to women. But no, Mr. Wimbury did not seem like the sort of man who wished to attract women, at least, not if his behaviour towards her and Miss Hartston was anything to go by. What other purpose could this smoothness have? It made him look younger than he probably was, but he was young enough anyway for that to have no appeal—it was more likely that he would want to look older. Dr. Farthing would grasp the motive at once, but she felt it was still just eluding her. Well, then, what about his profession? She felt—and she heard in her mind Dr. Farthing saying, "Enough of this *feeling*, Miss Pine. What do you *think*?"— that he was not the clerk he claimed to be. There was a thought lurking somewhere at the bottom of the feeling, if she could only unearth it. Of course: it was his contempt for clerks, which he revealed both by his sardonic tone and by his facial expression. ("Observe the eyes, Miss Pine," Dr. Farthing liked to say. "Men may disguise their voices but they can never disguise their eyes!") Not a clerk, then, but why should he wish to hide his true profession? Because it was something he was ashamed of, or which could cause him some trouble or disgrace if it became known. Cassie wished she knew more about professions in general: there were so many a man might do that a woman could scarcely imagine. Dr. Farthing's work brought him into contact with many members of the public, and he seemed always to understand the secrets of their professional lives and how these might affect their *psychic organization*, as he termed it, but he did not always explain his reasoning to Cassie, and she hated to admit she was even more ignorant than he thought her.

Later, as she lay in bed, she went over her thoughts again: smooth face, not a clerk, hiding something. Could Mr. Wimbury be a criminal, one who remained clean-shaven the better to disguise his identity? She did not think criminals were usually so well-spoken, but Dr. Farthing always warned her never to judge a man by his appearance (which struck her as odd since he was always lecturing her on how much could be deduced from it). Cassie had a feeling the process of deduction had taken her further than it was meant to. "And why, Miss Pine?" she murmured to herself. "Because you have not observed adequately. First we observe everything we can, and only then do we begin to think. Because until we have observed, we have nothing to think with!"

She woke with a slight headache and the conviction that she had the beginnings of a fever. She had a shivery feeling all over and a restless sensation in her limbs. Her first thought was for Dr. Farthing, whose reaction to her illnesses was one of his most annoying characteristics: if she went to his office with a cold, he would rebuke her for taking the risk of giving it to him, while if she stayed away because of it, he would ask peevishly where she had been and insist that she should have let him know. If Cassie asked how that would be possible, since a letter would be far too slow, he only replied vaguely that she could always send a messenger, as if there were small boys all over Bayswater just waiting to run errands for her. Even if there were, she could hardly accost them when she was too ill to get out of bed, as she supposed she was. As a man of exceptional intelligence, Dr. Farthing would surely infer that only illness could be keeping her from her work, since her conscientiousness was beyond question. It was perverse of him, for he had never been a demanding employer; sometimes he sent her home an hour or more early, or even gave her the afternoon off, saying he needed to be alone to think. Nevertheless, there was a touch of guilt mixed up with her other symptoms, together with some anxiety, in case she should turn out not to be as ill as she thought.

Every now and then she wondered if she was imagining it, and looked at the travelling clock on her washstand to see if there was still time to change her mind. Each time she did this she concluded that there was, which added to her discomfort. If only the hands would speed up a little! Once they had reached half-past eight, she would know for certain that it was too late to rise, dress and catch the last omnibus that could get her to John Carpenter Street in time to be in the office before him; miss that, and she was definitively late for work, which was, in its way, even worse than being absent, since it was harder to explain. *At eight-thirty*, she said to herself, *I'll have burned my boats*. She shivered at the thought, and looked at the clock again: it was eight-seventeen, and, as she watched, the minute-hand clicked on to eight-eighteen, which immediately made her feel less ill. Perhaps the restlessness in her limbs was only a healthy morning sensation, the desire to get out of bed and resume her daytime activities. But no, there was a weakness at the core of her being that suggested that getting out of bed would be an impossibility. Or was that hunger? It was normal to feel weak in the morning after a whole night without sustenance. Eight-nineteen.

Now a new thought supervened: if she was ill, as she was almost sure was the case, she must have medicine. Cassie was fond of medicines of all kinds, and fixed her gaze on the medicine chest on top of her trunk in the corner of the room, wondering what she should take. A couple of cephalic pills for the headache, perhaps—but no, that seemed better now, as her head had become more used to wakefulness. Only Chlorodyne would do for a condition like this one. That resolution, if anything, was sufficient to nerve her to get out of bed, weak as she was.

The room was shockingly cold, and the carpet scratched the soles of her feet as she crossed the room with undignified haste. She unlocked the medicine chest with the key she wore round her neck (along with that for the trunk), and found the Chlorodyne in its place between the Friar's Balsam and the Epsom Salts. She kept a spoon in there, too; it had the same capacity as a teaspoon but was pleasingly medicinal in form, with a curved handle and rounded bowl, a find in one of the Penge antique shops that she had always treasured. Two spoonfuls were the appropriate dose for a condition like this one. She took them quickly, feeling the dark liquid spread its warmth through her entire being, took the spoon to the washstand to be rinsed later and hurried back to bed.

When she woke, the clock said twenty-five past eleven and there was a knocking on the door. Cassie raised her head from the pillow as if it was unseemly to speak to someone from an altogether recumbent position and said feebly, "Yes, what is it?"

"It's late, miss," Esmé said through the door. "I was wondering if you was all right, or if you'd overslept yourself or something."

"Thank you, Esmé. I've decided I'm not going to work today. I'm feeling indisposed."

"Oh." There was a pause. "Will you be taking breakfast, miss?"

"What, at this time?" Cassie had no idea that breakfast was available so late at Halcyon House. The thought made her unexpectedly hungry.

"Yes, miss. Mr. Wimbury is having his now. Course, it ain't exactly hot, but he don't seem to mind about that. Don't tell Mrs. Makepeace—she's out on chapel business. Thought you might like to have some with him."

"No, thank you. I'm not well," she heard herself say, to her own disappointment. "I'll just stay in bed and try to sleep a little."

"Very good, miss. Is there anything I can get you?"

"Thank you, Esmé. That's very kind, but I've got everything I need."

She heard the footsteps going away. She was now not at all sure she was ill—the Chlorodyne must have had some effect. And curiosity was a tonic, too. Mr. Wimbury having his breakfast at twenty-five past eleven! It was most unlikely that he was a clerk, then, but she had deduced that already. Still, what employer would accept a man who arrived at work so late? There was something devil-may-care about it—the last to rise, sauntering downstairs to a cold breakfast. She was seized with a desire to rise quickly and share that breakfast with him, to cross-question him, casually of course, about his plans for the day. Even just to see him eat it might afford her some clue.

In the course of her work with Dr. Farthing, Cassie had been trained in the observation of human behaviour at countless séances and interviews with clairvoyants, but these, after all, were only a small proportion of the population of London. Anyone might be observed; anyone, to a truly scientific student of the mind, might reveal his or her secrets in a thoughtless gesture. It was not only, Dr. Farthing used to say, the supernatural that was of interest. She rose, washed quickly at the washstand and put on the grey dress she preferred for work. The process seemed to take longer than usual, and by the time she was halfway down the stairs she heard the front door bang. Mr. Wimbury had left the house, and she must hurry after him.

A lady, encumbered with stays, petticoat, bustle and skirts, not to mention the nagging memory of having been recently indisposed, does not walk so rapidly as a gentleman. She lost sight of Mr. Wimbury several times even before reaching Bayswater Road; fortunately, the omnibus had not yet arrived. The subject of her observation was at the front of the queue, and she was able to join the back without being noticed. When the omnibus arrived a few minutes later, she was one of the last to board, and took a seat several rows behind him where she could see without being seen.

He got out at the Strand, and she followed. Here the crowds were greater, and it was harder still to keep up with him, but he did not go far, crossing the road to a large building which turned out to be a theatre. By the time she reached the other side, out of breath and with her skirts wet from the puddles, she had seen him go round the side of the building, so she made her own way there. She found herself in an alley that was both blind and deserted. She remembered the stories of spirit encounters in such places with which Dr. Farthing used to regale her on quiet afternoons at the office, but she remembered, too, that there was usually a scientific explanation for them. ("The impossible happens only rarely, Miss Pine—that is why we think it impossible!") Mr. Wimbury was an unusual gentleman, but he was not a spirit, so he had left the alley by a material exit. And here it was, a side door to the theatre. She tried it and it opened without difficulty. Inside was a dark corridor, leading both left, towards the heart of the building, and right, towards the main entrance. She stepped over the threshold, and was on the point of turning to the left, since that was surely the way he must have gone, when the sight of a mop and bucket abandoned against the wall stopped her. This was a place where she had no business to be, a place for theatre employees. How would she explain her presence if anyone accosted her?

Besides, she had the answer now. Mr. Wimbury was an actor; it explained everything. His face was clean-shaven so that he could change its appearance at will with false beards and whiskers. He rose late because of the nature of the work, which was largely carried out in the afternoon and the evening. He pretended to be a clerk to avoid Mrs. Makepeace's disapproval of what she no doubt regarded as an immoral profession. It was all a little disappointing: she had got up from her sickbed for this!

There was nothing for it now but to make her way back to Halcyon House, so she retreated from the corridor, closed the door gently and left the alley. As she reached the corner of the Strand, intending to find the omnibus stop for the return journey, she found herself face to face with a gentleman, who raised his hat. "Miss Pine! What a coincidence!" It was Hastings Wimbury.

# Chapter 2

"I am really getting to know the West End," Mr. Wimbury told her as she took his arm. "I seem to have been wandering its streets forever. But what brings you here?"

She was too confused to answer him properly. She started to say she was ill, but realized it would explain nothing, so she said something about being on an errand for her employer, but stopped when she noticed he was not really listening, and had indeed started to talk himself.

"—an actor," he was saying. "It is my greatest ambition to play Hamlet."

"Oh. And what part are you playing now?"

"I am playing the part of a young fellow whose dearest wish is to act, which you would think would come naturally to me, but apparently I play it confoundedly badly. No sooner do I get on to the stage, so to speak, than I am sent packing with boos and catcalls. Of course," he continued, "I am using the word *stage* metaphorically. I have not so far ventured onstage. Instead I am interviewed by a series of managers, in offices the size of cupboards. I sit on some Louis XIV chair with the gilt flaking off it amid heaps of wooden swords and shields to be told there is no vacancy for a Second Walking Gentleman at the moment. Often I do no more than wander round the interior of the theatre, watch the rehearsals and explore the areas backstage. It is a queer way to spend one's days, but I must do something if I am not to work. I go to the Adelphi next—though, as it is still rather early for members of the profession, I may have my chop first. Are you hungry, Miss Pine?"

Cassie was very hungry indeed, but shook her head. "I must get back to Dr. Farthing's office. I'll just wait here for the bus, thank you, Mr. Wimbury."

"I could accompany you. To tell you the truth, I have no appointments, only obsessions, and your company would relieve my mind of them. And I always think a lady should not travel alone. Is it far?"

"His office is in the City, in John Carpenter Street, and really, there's no need—"

"Oh, then this is the wrong stop. You want the one on the other side of the road."

"No," Cassie said quickly. "This'll do." He said nothing but looked questioningly at her. "I've been feeling indisposed, so I thought I'd return to Halcyon House." He continued looking, and she was sure he had seen right through her.

"You know, Miss Pine, you are a strange lady. I wonder, what brought you out looking for spirits in the Strand? Oh, I mean it as a compliment, of course—I am a strange man, too."

Cassie was not sure how it happened, but by the time she recovered from her confusion she was sitting opposite Mr. Wimbury in the chop-house and he was recommending a glass of hock and seltzer.

"Of course, porter is the thing for weak nerves, and it is what I prefer to drink. Not that my nerves are weak."

"No, thank you, Mr. Wimbury. My nerves ain't weak either."

"Your lungs then. Have a brandy."

"No, no, the hock and seltzer will be quite all right, thank you." She looked round the room, or rather along it, for it was too narrow to hold tables side by side, and noticed that she was the only woman present; the air was full of pipe- and cigar-smoke. The men looked largely respectable, though—after all, this was the Strand, not Limehouse. When the waiter came, Mr. Wimbury ordered mutton chops and potatoes for both of them, without asking what she wanted, which, on the whole, was a relief.

"Are you really ill, Miss Pine?"

"I feel much better now," she admitted. "And are you really an actor?"

"I wish to be, but no one will take me yet. They say I need my own costumes and make-up."

"Then you must get them."

"I suppose so. But what if I get them and still no one will take me? I have little money to spare. I am devoting most of my savings to the rent at Halcyon House and the expenses of travel and"—he nodded towards the plates which had been set before them—"sustenance. These men who interview me are, to tell you the truth, somewhat discouraging. I get the impression they believe there are too many actors in the world."

She touched him lightly on the sleeve. It was the part of him where her hand had rested when she took his arm in the street, so there did not seem to be any impropriety in the gesture; it felt more like returning to a room a few minutes after she had left it. "Mr. Wimbury, you mustn't anticipate failure. I have the advantage of you now. I'm already a woman of business. But do you think it was easy for me to become such a thing? If I'd of stayed where I was, I would of spent my life behind the counter in my pa's tobacconist's shop in Penge. Perhaps, if I was specially lucky, I might of got married to one of the travelling tobacco salesmen. Instead, I am what you see."

"A woman of the world." Hastings smiled. "And what is it you do in the world?"

And Cassie, who never talked about such things, found herself explaining about Dr. Farthing, and the work she did for him in the City. "I've been present at a good few séances. I've seen tables rise from the floor and I've heard the spirits rapping on them. I've seen ectoplasm coming out of the medium's mouth."

"It sounds rather disgusting. But aren't these séances mostly a sham, a trick by the mediums to defraud the people who come to them?"

"Yes, Mr. Wimbury, most of them. They make the ectoplasm out of silk or cotton waste dyed with luminous paint. Some of these mediums put something in their mouths to disguise their voices, like the things that Punch-and-Judy men have. Some of them have got accomplices hidden in the room who do the voices of dead children or Red Indian spirit guides. Dr. Farthing is very good at detecting tricks like that."

"And yet you still believe—?"

"The two of us must of been to dozens of séances, and there was maybe three of them where he couldn't see how the trick was done. Of those three, he's almost sure that one was a fraud, the second one he hasn't made up his mind about yet, and as for the third, it just might be genuine."

"But only very nearly?"

"Oh, Dr. Farthing don't hold with believing in anything for certain. He says certainty locks the mind, a bit like rigor mortis in a corpse. *Very nearly* is as certain as he ever gets. I dare say he only very nearly believes that I'm in the room with him, taking down notes in shorthand."

"But you don't share his scepticism, Miss Pine?"

"No, Mr. Wimbury. He says it's one of the limitations of my sex, and for all I know he could be right. But to be quite honest, I've never met anyone who practises scepticism quite the way he does. It's as good as a religion with him."

"You seem very devoted to this Dr. Farthing."

"I've learnt an awful lot from him. He's a very remarkable man."

"And like a father to you, I dare say?"

"Good heavens, no!" Cassie said, laughing.

He shrugged. "You are indeed a woman of the world, Miss Pine. A woman of several worlds, come to think of it."

"And all because I wouldn't stand for being a failure."

"You must be very brave."

She did not think he was being ironic; if he remembered her earlier talk of indisposition, he gave no sign of it.

"Promise me something, Mr. Wimbury. You won't stand for being a failure either. You will do whatever's needful to get to wherever it is you're going. You may find you've got to take a funny sort of path, like I did." She raised her glass to him. "To your success. I shall watch your career with the greatest interest."

# Chapter 3

Backstage at the Villiers Theatre they were rehearsing a night scene. First, the sun had to set, which was achieved with a row of gas battens stage left, with a red medium tingeing the light. Then, on the other side, the moon began to rise by means of a contraption called a moon box, which was mounted on a trolley and wheeled slowly up a ramp till it was just below the level of the flies; the moon was a light inside the box, shining through a crescent-shaped aperture. As Hastings stood watching it, a red-bearded man rushed up to him, spluttering. At first he was inarticulate with rage, and Hastings assumed he was about to be thrown out. "Where is the moonlight?" the man said eventually. "Why is the moonlight not lit?"

Hastings was too perplexed by the situation to explain himself properly.

"Call yourself a gas-boy? What the blazes d'ye think we're paying you for, eh?"

Still making up his mind whether to be insulted at being called a boy or flattered by being made responsible for moonlight, Hastings was struck by the reference to payment. Throughout the tedious time he had been going from theatre to theatre, no one had mentioned the possibility of paying him—indeed the implication had all been the other way round, that he should himself pay out the remains of his savings for a few weeks' apprenticeship in the art. For once, too, someone was suggesting he *do* something, other than go away. He was an actor, was he not? He would play the part of a gas-boy.

"Sorry, sir," he said, putting the subtlest touch of cockney into his voice, "I wasn't thinking. Moonlight, did you say?" He ran his fingers through his hair.

"Yes, boy, moonlight! The gas battens, stage right. Get up in the flies and light them."

He knew the way to the fly galleries, having wandered in those regions before, but had no idea how to light the battens. He nodded, however, and bustled off, still in character. Just as he was making his exit, a wiry grey-haired man appeared at his side.

"Here, boy," the man said. "You'll need this, won't you? And come and see me afterwards, all right?"

At first he thought he was being handed a spear, and instinctively straightened himself in military fashion. But this was more like a pike, so that he could hardly hold it without overbalancing.

"Got matches?" the man said, and Hastings must have nodded, for he continued. "Good. The mediums is already in place. So you just got to switch on the tap and light the jets with the spirit burner. Think you can manage it? I'd do it myself, only I got my hands full with the footlights. All right?"

"Yes, sir."

"Don't forget, come and see me. You'll find me down the float."

Hastings climbed the narrow staircase to the lower stage-right fly, which was illuminated only by the lights from the stage, and picked his way among coiled ropes, hulking iron windlasses, cables, chains and pulleys. Here was the great fan they used for making wind, here the counterweights and lines that worked the curtain and act-drop. He looked out over the stage and saw that the moon had stopped its upward progress to wait for him. The length of gas battens he had to light was still twenty feet above his head. Groping his way back through the machinery he came to an iron ladder leading up through a trapdoor in the ceiling. It was not easy to climb a ladder with a long pole in his hand, but he managed it somehow and emerged into the upper fly with it unbroken.

There were two rows of battens to be lighted, one for each colour, so close he could almost reach out and touch them. Each batten was little more than a gas pipe, hung from the roof and enclosed in a wire cage, round which the gauze medium was wrapped to give the coloured light. He struck a match and lit the spirit-soaked pad on the end of his torch, which lapped up into an iris-blue flame, and found and turned the gas taps without difficulty. There was a moment of fear, as he heard the gas hissing into the theatre and knew it was up to him to light it before it spread out into a combustible cloud. But it was easy. He paid out his long fishing pole, first into one burner then into the other, and the gas jets lit in succession, petals of blue that brightened to white inside their tube as they grew hotter. He watched the beams stretch out from them, Prussian blue and burnt umber, and marvelled that he had made something out of fire that looked so chilly. He nearly forgot to put out his torch as he made to descend the ladder.

By the time he returned to the stage, a group of hands was busy sticking stars on a backdrop, each one consisting of a sequin hung on a bent pin. As he passed by, the disturbance made them all shake and twinkle. The moon was moving slowly up its ramp again, and the light he had made for it turned his skin and those of the stage-hands blue.

He found the grey-haired man among the sunken shoal of footlights in front of the stage, changing the chimneys to coloured ones. "Fiddly business," the man said, "and you ought to wear gloves, really. Even I use this handkerchief, and my hands is like leather. Want to change one?"

Hastings had changed the chimney on an Argand oil lamp at home, so he knew what he was doing, though it scorched his hands through his folded handkerchief. Again the light changed colour, a shaft of aquamarine that was previously white.

"These here gas Argands," the man said, "is a fag to light and a fag to change. What we ought to have is a Defries float with fish-tails instead of all them chimneys. And pilot lights, and all. But the management ain't going to give me that, not they. Too stingy."

Hastings agreed politely.

"Now young Samuel," the man continued, lying full length on a wooden support to reach the next chimney, "took his pay last Friday, and ain't been seen since. I been doing his work since then. If you ask me, he's off down the Adelphi where they got one of them Strode floats, what burns upside-down. Ever see one of them?"

"No, sir."

"Don't call me sir—sounds funny when you're in among the burners. My name's Eweson. Young Samuel, you see, has an eye for a good float, and I think he wanted to try his hand at one of them things. Not sure about them myself. Breaks down more often than not, so I've heard. But Samuel wants to get on in the world."

At last he returned to an upright position, and sat on his beam examining the ends of his fingers. "Gentleman, ain't you?"

"I'm glad someone has noticed," Hastings said, laughing in what he hoped was a self-deprecating way.

"Worst cockney accent I ever heard," Mr. Eweson said, "and I've heard a few frightful ones in this place." He smiled. "See, governor, the thing is, I'm in a bit of a fix now Samuel's gone. A gas-boy ain't nobody much—lowest of the low, really—but the lowest of the low can be the most useful in their way. I need someone I can ask to go anywhere and do anything. Dangerous work, sometimes. Helps to be young and nimble. Course, it ain't something I could ask of a gentleman, governor."

"I'm not a gentleman, really," Hastings said quickly. "I am an actor, and an actor knows no class. No need to call me governor, either. My name is Wimbury, um, Hastings."

"And you want to do stuff like this? Turning taps and changing mediums and lighting nibs and clambering up in the flies and on the gridiron?"

"No," Hastings said, "of course not, but…"

"But you want to be in the theatre."

"Yes, as an actor. When I get a role…"

"You'll leave me in the lurch, like young Samuel did. All right then, don't suppose it'll be soon, and in the meantime you can do the job."

"Thank you. Er, Mr. Eweson, I don't like to ask—"

"Pays ten bob a week."

"Ten shillings! But I can't live on that!"

Sitting there on the wooden beam with the shafts of blue light behind him, Eweson looked like an elf on a toadstool on a midsummer evening. "What you living on now?" he said.

# Chapter 4

One lunchtime after the new production had begun, Hastings brought Mr. Fritham, the head limelight man, his pie in the upper right fly gallery. Between the limelight men and the gas-men there was a certain coolness and mutual distrust, and, though Mr. Eweson, as chief gas-man, was Mr. Fritham's superior, yet Fritham, taller and statelier with his white whiskers, was the more imposing figure, and the two seemed to be each at the head of a rival court. As the gas-boy, Hastings was naturally expected to be loyal to Mr. Eweson, who sensed his fascination with the limelight, and, though too good-natured to reprove him for it, snorted and changed the subject whenever Fritham or limelight was mentioned.

"Lime, my boy," Fritham said, not for the first time since Hastings had known him, "is the most powerful light on earth. Set up a limelight on the white cliffs of Dover and you'll see it in Calais, easy. Further still, I shouldn't wonder. Lime'll throw the shadow of your hand on a wall ten miles away. It'll turn night into day if you have enough of it." He took a bite of pie, as a man arrived with a gasbag and wanted to know where to put it. Fritham gestured with the pie towards a stack of them in a far corner, higher than Hastings's head.

Hastings had seen these fellows walking up and down the Strand in the days of his unemployment, and never guessed what they were; the gasbags were almost as big as they were, but lighter than they looked because of the insubstantial contents, and the men carried them hoisted on one shoulder. The bags were stacked in the flies until needed, then the limelight men connected them to the burners and placed weights on the bellows so that the gas was pumped slowly out.

"What did you think of *The Black Sheep*?" Fritham asked.

The current production at the Villiers, a melodrama called *The Black Sheep of Poulter's Meadow*, was creating a sensation with its nightmare scene, and the auditorium was packed every evening, watching in fascinated repulsion as the young murderer Poulter, played by the Juvenile Lead, Mr. Rowlands, in nightgown and nightcap, prepared to get into his bed downstage right. He put down his candle on the bedside table, said his prayers, his voice shaking, then climbed into the bed and drew the curtains behind him, providing a screen to allow Rowlands to slip out the other side into the wings.

The rest of the stage was used for his guilty dream: the cottage where the murder had been committed rose out of the stage floor, hidden at first by a screen of gauze. When the limelight, coloured pink and yellow to indicate the lost happiness of the place, fell on the screen, the gauze seemed to dissolve, and the cottage swam into being. Upstage, a green limelight fell on young Poulter, the knife in his hand made visible behind the gauze. The cottage sank away and the green limelight picked out the old woman he had murdered sitting at a table, counting her money. Individual rays of limelight, white this time, and with an intensity that no other source could provide, struck the knife and the basket of money. As Poulter moved, ever so slowly, his knife raised, towards the old woman, the limelight moved, too, gleaming on the blade. She saw him, and rose, striking the table and money, which fell away, lowered beneath the floor. The old woman raised her hands in supplication, but Poulter, remorseless, continued to advance towards her. He struck, and a single beam of red limelight pierced her chest as she fell to the floor. Poulter now advanced downstage, and squatted there, his head in his hands, while the old woman disappeared from view. (She, too, had gone the way of the cottage and the table, lowered beneath the stage on a mechanical platform.)

Now came the *coup de théâtre*: a phantom of the old woman appeared upstage. It was ten feet high at least, and shimmering with blue and green and umber light. The face and dress were hers, but the eyes were hollow, and there was a gaping red wound in her chest. This was done by means of a magic lantern, a box with a limelight inside it focused through a glass slide imprinted with a colourized photographic image. Poulter, still clutching his brow, rose to his feet, as if he had heard or intuited the terrible presence behind him. He lifted his hands in horror, and the phantom lifted hers in an echo of his gesture. Her mouth opened and closed (by means of a second slide alternating with the first), and blood was seen running from her wound (though it appeared to pulse in and out rather than running exactly— but the effect was still terrifying). Poulter screamed. The stage was flooded with the light of red fire, which fizzled and gave off chemical smoke in the wings, causing the front row of the stalls to cough. General hysteria of the audience. Curtain.

"Tell you what," Fritham continued. "If you ain't got nothing better to do, you can come up here tonight and help me weight the gasbags. Could do with a hand."

On a quiet afternoon in December, Hastings was hiding in one of the fly galleries writing a letter to Flora—he was too tired when he got back to Halcyon House late at night to do anything other than sleep. "Darling, I cannot!" he wrote. "The thing is impossible! No one regrets it more than myself, believe me." He was still learning the lore of the theatre, and had only just become aware of the very different way they had of regarding the holiday season. It was true that *The Black Sheep of Poulter's Meadow* would be closing in a few days' time, and the next production, *The Amethyst Princess*, would not open till the day after Boxing Day. But he must work the two days before it opened, yes, on Christmas Day and Boxing Day themselves. There were rehearsals to light, and he could not take leave of absence when he was so new to the work, and Mr. Eweson much occupied. Yes, it really was work, even if his letters sometimes gave the impression he did nothing but sit around watching limelight men turning their spindles and actors disappearing in a puff of smoke. Even if he could get away on Christmas Eve, it could be for one day only. He would be expected to see his aunt first, and he doubted if Flora's family would welcome him afterwards for tea.

Perhaps when *The Amethyst Princess* was running well he could ask Mr. Eweson for a couple of days off. He could then come down to Reigate at his leisure, when her father was safely back in his office. They could walk in the woods and have tea at Murcheson's in Reigate, and he could give her her present then.

*The Amethyst Princess* would be a sensation. She should try to persuade her father to let her come to see it. It was not so much a pantomime as a fairy entertainment for the holiday season. There was a chorus of sixteen fairies who danced and sang in a most heartbreaking manner, and a princess for each of the gemstones, with the appropriate coloured fire associated with her. The amethyst fire for the princess of the title was made to a formula never before tried. Also much use was made of the fly lines—there were fairies up among the battens for whole stretches of the performance, and very fetching they looked with the coloured light glinting off their wings.

Yesterday, he wrote, he had taken advantage of his proximity to Mr. Roderick, the manager who first (unwittingly) assigned him to his present duties, to ask him if there might be a role for him on stage in the new production. He was supervising the harnessing of a sapphire fairy at the time, and it was some minutes before Hastings could attract his attention. "Yes, yes, what is it?" Roderick said finally.

"About a role," Hastings told him, "you promised me a role in the play." This was untrue, but perhaps Roderick was distracted enough to believe it.

"What?"

"I could be one of the Diamond King's retinue. It does not have to be a speaking part at this stage of my career."

Instead of replying he called Mr. Eweson over and asked what the gas-boy was doing on the stage.

"Changing the chimneys in the float," Eweson said.

"Well, get him down there," Mr. Roderick said. "He keeps getting in the way."

Hastings noted, however, that Roderick did not actually refuse his request, and he resolved to renew it when the opportunity arose.

# Chapter 5

Flora came down to tea with her mind running on a letter she had received from Hastings that morning, intending to take no more than a cup of tea and a slice of bread and butter to fortify herself before writing to him in reply. There was the curate sitting in one of the Hepplewhite chairs, with Mabel beside him, gazing in girlish admiration, and Mama on the other side, gazing with the matronly equivalent. He rose as she entered, and bowed carefully so as not to spill his tea. She was relieved that he did not give her one of those long, intense looks he had applied at the skating party the other night, but merely a courteous regard, and then, after she had taken her seat, resumed his own, and turned back to Mama to continue their conversation.

"The Archdeacon, I am afraid," Mr. Pilkins said with a sigh, "is showing signs of going over to Oxford."

"I'm sorry to hear it," Mama said, "but at least Oxford is not Rome, is it?"

"No, it is not, at any rate, that." Both of them nodded gravely. As if Mama knew the difference between Oxford, Rome and anywhere else! Flora took a sip of tea and picked up her slice of bread and butter, trying to give the impression that eating it was a demanding responsibility that left no room in her mind for other matters. But all the while she was brooding on the letter:

*If it were not for Mr. D'Oyly Carte's electric fairies in the production of Iolanthe at the Savoy, I believe our amethyst fire would make us the sensation of the season. It burns almost too vigorously, throwing off sparks of yellow among the purple flames. Mr. Eweson says electricity may be all right, but who can tell? We have had some sixty years of gas and you know where you are with it, but this other stuff that you can't even smell—who knows what the dangers are? One day we will hear that the whole of the Savoy has been fried overnight. And Mr. Fritham says that electricity will never produce a flame to outshine limelight: can it throw the shadow of a man's hand on the wall at ten miles' distance, &c? No, he says, before I can even answer him, I thought not.*

What troubled her most, though she hardly liked to admit it to herself, was the bold and affectionate way he wrote about the women his new profession led him to associate with. All those cockney dancers playing the fairies, not to mention the famous Mrs. Beveridge, who was said to have consorted with a succession of marquesses and viscounts, even, so it was whispered, with one more eminent still. Hastings, of course, was too noble to be sullied by such company, and indeed wrote lightly of its follies in a way that a gentleman might permit himself, though it would never do for a lady:

*Not every woman here behaves quite respectably, but, as I told you before, it is all make-believe. The fairy fire is made of chemicals, the coloured lights are gas and quicklime, the people anoint themselves with make-up and their emotions are as false as the other illusions. Many men have been lured by these will-o'-the-wisps: lines of them wait at the stage door every night with bouquets in their hands, most of them for Mrs. B, but a considerable number for the lesser fairies also. You need not worry that I shall ever be one of them. I am an initiate of the theatre now, not a distant and adoring votary.*

"I understand they do a great deal of good, though," Mama said. "The Oxford clergy, I mean."

"Oh yes, indeed," Mr. Pilkins said, "if you call that sort of thing good."

"Have you finished your tea, Mr. Pilkins?" Mama asked. "No doubt you are longing to take a walk with Flora in the garden."

"A delightful afternoon, Miss Burlap, is it not?"

Flora agreed that it was, though, as the sun was just setting, *evening* would have been a better word. There had been no more snow since the New Year, but the covering on the lawn had shrunk only slowly. Footsteps had come and gone over it so many times that in places it had been worn away altogether, though the snow still held out under the tulip tree, and in the vicinity of the rhododendrons. The paths had been long ago shovelled and swept, and there were old heaps of dirty snow beside them.

"Do you know," he said, "I have thought much about our skating on the pond the other evening, and how much I enjoyed it. I do hope you are recovered from your injuries?"

Flora had spent a joyous hour sliding from one gentleman to another in the lantern-light, listening to the music of the band playing quadrilles by the side of the pond, feeling the cold rising from the ice, the wind scouring her cheeks, the delicious panic each time she was launched from an arm into the few feet of precarious gliding before the next one. It was not her fault that at one such moment she sailed into a branch projecting from the ice. Mr. Pilkins, who had been next in line to receive her, was most gracious in helping her to her feet again and leading her to the bank, and still more solicitous in plying her with punch. She had not thought him a man of much interest till now; there always seemed to be a new curate at St. Bridget's, and he was quieter and more distant than most, but noticing this time how much taller he was than herself, which was not true of many gentlemen, and how the arm with which he supported her on their journey to safety trembled a little as if he was excited by such close contact with her person, she decided that he was, after all, someone worth talking to. Not that she had much choice, for, even though she was not in pain, she could hardly accept the role of invalid and the cosseting that went with it and then get up again as though nothing had happened. So she sat back and conversed, as was expected of her, and found him a pleasant conversationalist.

Who would have thought there were such entertaining stories in the Apocrypha? She made him tell her some of them twice, not always grasping the difficult names at first hearing. When a man was really enthused by a subject, he became much more personable. There was a slight flush in his cheeks, no doubt partly from the skating, and a hint of fire in that deep voice that she would never have suspected earlier, though he seemed shyer than ever. He did not know what to do with his eyes. Either he was gazing at her more intently than was courteous, or he would stare at the trampled ground as if addressing his remarks to that. The eyes were a deep glossy brown, like a well-polished mahogany table.

Now he seemed to think that this insignificant accident had forged a bond between them. "Yes, quite, sir, thank you," Flora said. "I was hardly injured at all."

"Oh," he said, rather disappointedly, as if it would have been more to his credit had she broken a leg. "It was a great pleasure for me, in any case, to have been able to assist you."

It is impossible to curtsey successfully when the gentleman one is trying to curtsey to is walking beside one. Flora contented herself with a sort of nod, but even that was less impressive than it might be since her face was turned down towards the path anyway. She probably looked like a horse refusing a fence. The arm she was holding trembled, and a feeling of dread was rising in Flora, too. They had only spoken seriously for the first time a few days ago—surely he could not be thinking…? But some feminine instinct, of the kind she had read about in novels, took over at this point, and she found she knew his thoughts. If only she could stop him putting them into words! Already, he had stopped walking and turned towards her. He glanced down, and she could see him weighing up in his mind the case for and against kneeling on that cold and muddy surface: on the one hand it would be a proper display of his earnestness and devotion, while on the other it would be a great sacrifice of comfort and dignity. He had begun to lurch in that direction when she forced herself to speak.

"I was most interested, sir, in what you had to say that evening about the Apocrypha."

They were facing each other now, an east wind having blown up suddenly, which set all their clothing in motion and rasped at Flora's face and hands. He stopped midway through his descent, but did not straighten up again, so that he was half crouched, his face almost level with hers, and, even in the twilight, she saw a brief expression of agony contort his features. She could tell where he wished the Apocrypha at that moment.

"I have never read the Apocrypha," Flora said, "though I hope I am a faithful student of the Old and New Testament. Where would you advise me to start?"

"It is not," he said, "it is not a volume for, er, ladies. I mean, not for lay persons. I mean, I should not advise… Please, Miss Burlap, stick to your Old and New Testaments. They are all a Christian needs. Indeed, the very meaning of the word Apocrypha—" Catching himself about to deliver a sermon, he subsided with a gulp into silence.

"I have heard," she said cruelly, "that Maccabees is a very improving text. And also Esdras."

Seizing both her hands, he gazed into her face with as much ferocity as passion, an impression only enhanced by his wind-reddened cheeks. "Miss Burlap," he said, "I am not in a position to marry—"

She thought for a moment he was referring to his half crouch, and was about to reassure him. She stammered something, and he saw that he had begun what he had to say at the wrong end.

"I am not, but I hope some day to be in such a position, and when that day comes… I wish you to know, Miss Burlap, that I greatly esteem your person, and that your respectability and your honour, and your qualities of mind…"

"Oh no, sir," she said, not entirely sure what she was contradicting, but feeling that modesty required so much of her.

"Oh yes, I assure you." He stopped again, and they stood facing each other, panting slightly.

"I have spoken," he went on, "to your mother, and intend to do so to your father also, when he does me the——, when he is at home. Meanwhile, I thought it incumbent upon me to declare myself at once to you."

Were a declaration and a proposal the same thing? The tense he had used seemed to put the question in some curious hypothetical region where she could not get at it to refuse him. Had he proposed already, leaving her no choice in the matter?

"Please, sir, I beg you——"

"I know this must come as a shock to you. But may I dare——?"

"No, sir. I understand what you mean, and I am most flattered, honoured, but let me assure you now that the thing is impossible. I greatly admire you, sir, but I——" She stopped, horrified. So desperate had she been to cut him off at any cost that she had arrived at the brink of doing so with her one unanswerable argument: *I cannot marry you because I am betrothed to another*. The secret would have been out then, no doubt to be blurted by her suitor to her family in explanation of her refusal, and they would know at once who her fiancé must be, that young gadabout with his mad dreams of the theatre. Perhaps she could swear Mr. Pilkins to silence, but could she be sure he would keep such a promise, having no reason to feel himself obliged to her? Besides, even if he did, she would remain haunted by the fact that there was another person in the world who knew her secret.

"Say no more, Miss Burlap," he said, "I understand you entirely. You are young and had not looked for such a declaration so soon, and from such an unexpected quarter. But I am heartened that you do not dismiss me."

"Oh, but, sir!"

He squeezed her hand. "Let it be understood between us," he said. "Of course, I shall say nothing to anybody."

His fear seemed to have left him, and they resumed their walk, Flora thinking all the time about what each of them had said and what it might possibly mean. He left her at the French windows, and went out through the garden gate, no doubt to avoid speaking any further with Mama. And she walked back around the garden in the dark, circumambulating three times, until it was nearly time to dress for dinner.

She did not think she could be engaged to him. He had not asked the question—indeed, the vanishing of his nervousness must have been due to the fact that he had put the question off, finding them both unsuitable at present for such a commitment. But he seemed to think them in some way provisionally engaged: *let it be understood*! It was not understood by Flora! She repeated his words and hers in her mind, and was sure she had not promised him anything. But somehow the fact that he did not actually ask the question had allowed him to go on believing that she had done so. Was she really betrothed to two men at once?

# Chapter 6

One evening, about an hour before the curtain was due to rise, Hastings found himself lying face-down on a narrow strip of iron a hundred feet above the auditorium. He was on one of the branches of a gigantic gas-fuelled chandelier, which was roaring all round him. Already both the air and the metal pressing against his chest and groin were unpleasantly hot; soon they would be unbearable. The only way to avoid being baked alive was to crawl back to the safety of the gridiron, but the path of retreat was closed to him. A few yards in front of him, burning so fiercely he could hardly bear to look at it, was a furnace higher than a standing man. It was the heart of the gasalier, the sunburner.

The gasalier was so huge and fierce it created its own weather, a scorching heat in the upper regions that caused the common people in the gallery to sweat, gales of colder air that took the place of the hot rising air and roared through pit and stalls making eyes water and noses run, and rendering the lower audience vulnerable to influenza and rheumatism.

It was Hastings's responsibility to light the gasalier every evening, lowering himself through a trapdoor from the gridiron to a ladder, which took him down through a flue about six feet in diameter, with the main gas-pipe to the gasalier running down the centre of it. At the bottom was a cage, where he stood and assembled his torch, fixing the lighted spirit burner to the end.

The two parts of the contraption were controlled from separate gas supplies, each with its own stopcock. On the perimeter was a ring of fourteen baskets of gas burners, or nibs as Eweson called them, extending from the centre on brass arms and hung with swags of crystal drops. These he must light with his pole, a process like fishing for trout, though with a cumbersome rod some twenty feet long. He would light one nib after another, then shorten the pole to engage with the sunburner at the centre of the structure, which was like a great bronze vase of the kind used for tulips in grand country houses, except that its blooms would be the flames of several hundred individual burners. He had to reach down and light them from the bottom up.

That evening an outer nib failed to light. He passed on to the others, which flared up successfully, then angled back to the reluctant basket with his rod. Still it would not light, and he guessed he must have knocked the delicate valve that governed the cluster of burners with the torch, obstructing the flow of gas. This was a challenge to his fishing skills; with the right cast he might perhaps flip the valve back into place and light it at the same time. He tried this for a minute or two, and, just as he was about to give up, his rod became entangled with one of the longest swags of glass drops on the gasalier. Several shakes of the rod failed to disengage it, and at last he tugged too hard and heard something snap. The rod swung free, and he had to fight to keep his balance.

Peering out, he saw a long line of gleaming drops stretching down into the darkness. The swag he had been struggling with was broken and hanging down above the pit, where it could fall and injure someone in the audience later in the evening. Mr. Eweson had warned him that such things could happen, and so he carried with him a pair of nippers. He would have to climb out along the gasalier, cut the wire, and let it drop down into the stalls, and he could light the reluctant basket at the same time.

He pulled in the torch, dismantled it, and climbed through the bars of the cage. Wrapping his left arm for support round the sunburner, he reached back up through the bars with his right and took down the spirit burner from his torch. With this in his hand, and the nippers in his pocket, he inched along the iron branch, which swayed with every movement, till he reached the hanging swag. He rested the spirit torch on the surface, took out the nippers, and cut the wire, letting the swag drop silently on to the seats below. Still prone, he manoeuvred the nippers back into his pocket, and regained the torch. He had to fumble with the valve on the basket of burners till he felt it fall into place, and managed to light the burners.

Scrambling round to make his way back left him winded, and he lay for a while face down on the branch to recover, aware of a slight hissing in his ears, a sulphurous and suffocating smell, a sensation of heat on the top of his head, a yellow glare inside his closed eyelids. Then he opened his eyes and raised his head. Before him was a roaring brilliance: the central vase of the sunburner was alight.

In climbing through the grating, he must have nudged the stopcock that governed the jets of the vase, then, as he lowered himself onto the arms of the gasalier, spirit torch in hand, he must have lit one jet after another, leaving a trail of flames. With the gas full on, it could not have taken long before the remaining jets were ignited, cutting off his only route back to the gridiron.

Before and all round him, the flames were guzzling the last of his air so that he could not breathe properly and began to feel dizzy. He called out for help, but his voice sounded so faint against the roaring of the burners and of his own blood in his ears that he hardly knew he was shouting at all. Mr. Eweson and the other gas-men must be busy about their tasks in other parts of the theatre, while the actors and stage-hands would all be readying themselves for the performance. Who would notice a missing gas-boy? The iron was beginning to scorch his thighs through his trousers, and he shifted his position as much as he dared, pointlessly, for it only made the discomfort return in another part.

He had to make a choice, whether to burn and suffocate here or cast himself over the side to be smashed to pieces below. It seemed a curious end to all his ambitions.

When the burners in front of him went out, he thought for a moment he had died. Then he realized that something or someone had saved him, interrupting the gas supply. He tried to rise. "No," a voice called from somewhere up above the burner. "It is not safe. Wait there."

He lay on his stomach with his eyes closed. When he opened them again, it was cooler and quieter, and almost dark. His rescuer, whoever he was, must have turned off the outer gasalier baskets as well as the sunburner, and Hastings felt irrationally annoyed about it, after he had gone to all that trouble to light them.

"It is not so hot now," the voice said. "I think you may return, if you please, sir." He wondered who had saved him. It was not Mr. Eweson, or any of the gas-men: there was no cockney in that voice. There was an accent of some sort, but he was not sure what. He began to crawl, keeping his head down, reluctant to look at the sunburner again, as if it might reignite at any moment. He only realized he had reached it when his head bumped up against one of the burners. Then he lay and rested a little more. "Please to climb," said the voice.

There was a man standing in the cage and reaching down as though to help him up, though he was too far away to do so. He gave an impression of startling whiteness.

The sunburner was cool enough to climb. Hastings slipped on its nibs and projections a dozen times on his way. When he was near enough, the man in the cage took his hand and heaved at it with unexpected strength, nearly wrenching him from his footing; Hastings called out to him to stop, and the man asked his pardon, in that curious voice.

There was not enough room for both men in the cage. Hastings tried to explain this, and finally the stranger understood, and left nimbly, seeming to leap up the flue. Hastings could now see what was peculiar about the man's appearance as his coat tails vanished up the flue. He was in evening dress, and the impression of brilliance Hastings had received previously was a dress shirt front and white tie gleaming from the cage.

The visitor was sitting on a winch in the gridiron, a slim man, probably in his forties. His hair was black and worn long; he had whiskers rather than a beard, and an unusually long moustache which descended to below the level of his jaw.

Hastings tried to thank him, but the man raised a hand to stop him, smiling. "At least your engine is lit. Perhaps you are not too busy now? I am a great lover of the theatre, and would be glad of an opportunity to talk." His accent was neither French nor German, indeed, it was hardly an accent at all, more the verbal echo of a subtly different relationship to reality.

Hastings found a heap of ropes and old bits of stage machinery and sat on that. His visitor was curious about everything, asking questions about gas lighting and the difference between that and limelight, and Hastings answered him as best he could.

"But you must be a great scientist," the stranger said, "to harness such infernal powers in the interests of amusement. You studied them for many years, I suppose?"

Hastings muttered something in response.

"We have no such wonders in my country yet, so it is all a great excitement to me. I like best your present production, *The Amethyst Princess*. All those beautiful ladies with their wings and sparkles, and the fires of many colours, and all the varieties of light. Can you blame me that I attend every evening?"

"What country do you come from, sir?"

"You will not have heard of it. It is a very small one, and quite old." He said *old* apologetically, as a thing to be ashamed of. "That is why I admire Great Britain with all her sciences and cleverness."

"Is this your first visit?"

"Yes, the first, and I came straight away to the theatre. Even in my country, we have heard of the celebrated Villiers Theatre."

"Do you have theatres in your land?"

"We have some old traditions of singing and dancing with telling of legends, yes. The peasants do it on days of festival, and I have sometimes watched them when I had nothing better to do. But it is not theatre as you have it here, with all your scientific wonders. That is why I am so delighted to make the acquaintance of one so expert in these matters. I am Count Nollo."

Hastings introduced himself. "You are perhaps a diplomat, sir? An ambassador?"

"Not officially, no. My country is so little known in the great world that as yet we do not even have an embassy here. My interests are very various, and the theatre is one of them, as you have seen. And like many of the more advanced of my countrymen, I am concerned with bringing the light of the modern world into our dark land. It will perhaps surprise you that I have started with the theatre, rather than, shall we say, the cotton industry, but I am not a merchant. We weave very good clothing where I come from; it is something we take pride in, but that is work for the peasants. I respect their skill, and no English mill could make finer produce. No, for me, England will always be the land of Shakespeare, 'This precious stone set in the silver sea.' Tell me, how long have you been in gas?"

Hastings could not hold back; he had no one to confide in except Flora, and his letters to her were beginning to seem like messages sent to another world—how could she understand them in her comfortable house in Reigate with nothing to think of but ice-skating and tea-parties? He had told Eweson of his ambitions at the outset, but he too was in no position to understand the dreams of an artist. From the moment Hastings took the job, he was just the gas-boy to those he worked with. And here was a man with a feeling for Shakespeare, one who understood the poetry of the theatre. Hastings explained that he hoped, in time, to be a Walking Gentleman, and from there, little by little, to work his way up to Juvenile Lead, and in due course to be an Actor–Manager. He would have a company dedicated entirely to Shakespeare, putting on every play in the most daring of productions, with limelight and amethyst fire in abundance, and himself in the leading roles. He gabbled in his eagerness, and when he had finished he looked at the Count in consternation, expecting to see an expression of scepticism. But he was perfectly grave—indeed, his face did not show much expression at any time, in contrast to his body, which, even at rest, seemed to pulse with energy as if he had discovered a new and potent way of sitting.

"And, which," the Count said softly, "is your favourite of Shakespeare's plays?"

"*Hamlet*, unquestionably."

"A young man's choice, but a good one. And the part should only be played by a young man, I think. Irving is already too old. I believe you would make a fine Hamlet, perhaps one of the best."

"You flatter me, sir."

"No, no, I am serious. It is sad to observe such talent cooped up here where no one can appreciate it. And yet, I suppose, your time as a gas-boy—forgive the undignified term, which I cannot apply to your distinguished person without wincing—your time in this role will not be wasted. When you are an Actor–Manager, you will need to understand these scientific aspects of the craft."

He rose to go. Hastings stood up, too, and they shook hands. It was not nothing to shake hands with a Count! He must be the only gas-boy in the West End who could say as much.

"I love this place," Nollo said, gesturing around the dim space they stood in. "It reminds me of my country." And then he was gone.

# Chapter 7

The first Hastings heard of the new production was when Mr. Eweson sent him to the trade door to take delivery of some boxes of green fire. "Only green?" he said. "I prefer the amethyst myself."

Eweson was changing the mediums on the battens as he had been when Hastings first met him. "See, this is what's wrong with you, Hastings," he said. "You're always inquiring into the wherefores of matters what don't concern you. It ain't for such as us to criticize the colour of the fire in a play. That's a matter for the *artistes*, as they call themselves."

"For such as us, Mr. Eweson?"

"Well, for such as me, then. Though I'd thank you to remember, Hastings, that you *are* such as me in the present circumstances, even if you was such as them before."

"And will be again, I assure you. Why green, anyway—isn't that the usual colour for ghostly manifestations? Are we to stage a ghost play? I think I should enjoy that."

"Not *a* ghost play," Eweson said. "It's *the* ghost play if you insist on knowing. Think you can light *Hamlet*, do you?" He chuckled.

"Light it, Mr. Eweson? I can do more than that! I can play every part, right down to the gravedigger, including Gertrude and Ophelia."

"You ain't called on to do any of that for the time being, Mr. Wimbury. Just go and fetch the bleeding fire."

"Very well, of course, of course." Hastings didn't move, though, but stood there beneath the float, shifting his weight from one leg to the other and clapping his hands against his shirtsleeves as if he were cold. "There's a lot to be said for starting one's career with the Ghost:

I am thy father's spirit,
Doom'd for a certain term to walk the night,
And for the day confined to fast in fires.

Green fires, obviously, some of which still clings to him as he walks the battlements. It isn't a big part—I should call it a modest one, really—but it sets the tone for the whole play:

> I could a tale unfold whose lightest word
> Would harrow up thy soul, freeze thy young blood,
> Make thy two eyes, like stars, start from their spheres,
> Thy knotted and combinèd locks to part,
> And each particular hair to stand on end
> Like quills upon the fretful porpentine.

If you can't make the audience shudder with those lines, then what kind of an actor are you?"

"It ain't the actor as does that," Eweson said. "It's us, and our green fire, and our battens and limelight. The actors just stand in front of it and put a few words to it. Not even their own words, neither."

"Yes," Hastings continued, "quite a modest ambition, but a good starting point. And look at it this way, Mr. Eweson. I would, in a sense, be playing Hamlet already. The Ghost is Hamlet, too, the real Hamlet, the one who trod the earth before the poor portly prince was thought of. Anyway, I should call it a good compromise, wouldn't you?"

There was no reason why Hastings should not have been added to the supers, perhaps to sit in the court applauding the fencing match and crying out in dismay at the end when everybody dies. It was not as if he was busy with his gas duties every moment of the performance. At least then he would have fulfilled the least of his ambitions, to stand on a stage before a West End audience. Perhaps if he had asked to do that instead of asking to play the Ghost, his request would have been granted. Or perhaps not—Mr. Roderick had finally grasped who Hastings was, both the gas-boy reality and the Hamlet pretensions, and clearly did not care for this menial whose cockney accent came and went so disconcertingly. He told Hastings to get back to his gas work; there was a line between the tradesmen and the

artistes that could not be crossed. Hastings poured out his grief
in a letter to Flora:

One day, my darling, I will stand on that stage with that
green fire burning all round me. I will be young Hamlet,
not the Ghost, and yet they will see the Ghost in me too, in
my terrified eyes, in the determined set of my shoulders, and
they will hear it in the quaver of my voice, thrilling with
horror, yet charged with love and respect. It is a daunting
challenge! Hamlet has scarcely a complete paragraph in
the entire scene, and most of his utterances are interjections:
"Alas, poor ghost!", "What?", "O God!", "Murder!" Any
ordinary actor would cede the stage to the Ghost at this
moment, keeping his powder dry for the later scenes. It is
how even Irving plays it, and I have no doubt at all that
Mr. Rowlands, in his turn, will be only too glad to vanish
into the shadows at such a moment. But that is not my
way, dearest. Believe me, you have not heard Hamlet at
all till you have heard the tone in which I say "What?" (I
practise this and other such abbreviated lines as I lie in my
bed at night, for I have realized that it is in these, not in the
great speeches, that the test of the true actor lies—can he
say "What?" so that the whole auditorium trembles?)

I told Mr. Eweson, and repeated it to Mr. Roderick,
that the Ghost is the real Hamlet, the one whose tragedy
underlies the whole play, and that only I could play it
with the sublimity it merits. All true enough, and it takes
a considerable actor to speak great lines—but it takes a
still greater one to reflect those lines in his own almost
mute person. Well, Roderick has rejected me as the Ghost,
fool that he is! He will, I trust, live to see me triumph as
Hamlet. But it will all be for naught, my darling, unless
you are there to see it, too. Dare I hope...?

Flora's letters had become more infrequent of late. They also
seemed reserved, as if there were some topic she did not like to

touch on. He knew that it was rash to be away from her so long; a young lady of her stately looks was never without admirers, all of whom, no doubt, were more likely than himself to win her parents' approval. He had not been able to afford to give her anything for Christmas in return for the pearl cufflinks she had given him—what kind of fiancé behaved in such a manner? He did not know how to finish this letter; it was bad enough confessing his failure, but to do so to one who was, perhaps, another of his failures was just too much.

He had been writing in the gridiron, sitting on a coil of rope and balancing the paper on his knee. The dim light that came up through the gaps between the beams from the stage below was supplemented by his own dismantled spirit torch, which rested on the beams beside him along with an épée he had purloined from the props room, which he took everywhere with him now.

"I see you have a sword," a voice said.

Hastings turned. He was sitting further from the hatch than he had been on their previous encounter, and the Count had contrived to climb the ladder and emerge through the hatch without being noticed. In the dimness, it was surprising that he was able to see the sword at all, and Hastings felt almost as if he were being spied on. Nevertheless, he must remember his manners; the man had a title after all, even if not an English one.

"Good afternoon, Your Excellency," he said. "Pray, come in."

"Thank you," the Count replied, a smile evident in his voice if not quite discernible yet on his features. "I find that I am in already. I hope you will excuse the intrusion, Mr. Hastings."

Hastings did not have the heart to correct the error. "Of course, Count. Take a seat if you can find one. I am sorry that—" He had been going to make some apology for the poor accommodation. Halfway through, however, he found himself thinking of all the other things he was sorry for, or about, and was unable to finish the sentence.

The Count picked his way towards him till he was standing at his side. He did not look for a seat but, stooping slightly, put a hand on Hastings's shoulder. "You are troubled, young man."

Hastings nodded.

"Ah," said the Count. "I remember well the distresses of your age. Some of them are no more than chimeras, others, they are the woes of life itself, glimpsed from the entrance to it, so to speak. Which are yours?"

Hastings said nothing.

The Count gave an affirmative grunt, as if agreeing with the reply he had not received. He took the hand from Hastings's shoulder and began to pace up and down, a delicate process on the beams of the gridiron. He would walk ten paces along the length of a single beam, his back to Hastings, then pivot on one leg, turn and walk back again. He continued talking throughout, the steadiness of his voice giving no suggestion of the concentration necessary for his movements.

"Of course, you must realize that my youth was very different from yours. I did not live in a great city surrounded by shops and theatres. There was no gaslight where I come from, no omnibuses and hansom cabs, no horses even. Can you imagine modern life without horses? It is unthinkable! But then the life that surrounded me was not modern; it had not changed for many hundreds of years. But this should have been enough for me, should it not? It was my country, and my status in it was not inconsiderable. And yet, and yet!"

"You were not happy, sir?" Hastings was becoming interested despite himself.

"It was my country and yet it was not. I had never lived anywhere else, and yet I felt, obscurely, that it was not my home. This cannot be comprehensible to you?"

"On the contrary," Hastings said, "I have felt something similar myself, though I could not have expressed it as you do."

The Count gave a brief snort of laughter or self-disgust. "If I say it was a dark land, you will think I am speaking metaphorically, will you not?"

"Well, yes, what else?"

"Ah, Mr. Hastings, I wonder if you will believe me! Where I am from, light—the light you take for granted, which wakes you every morning—is a precious thing. We have fires, to cook our food and warm our sleeping quarters, but fuel is scarce so we use as little as possible. We spend much of our lives in a darkness so complete that you have probably never experienced the like, the kind of darkness that is solid. It is as if the whole world were a blindfold, as if one lived in the heart of the earth with no space around one, no possibility of movement. One may go years without seeing sunlight, and plenty of my people never make the effort to do so; it means nothing to them. But I was different. There was a place I used to go, a room"—he had stopped walking at the turning point of his beat, and was now squatting with his face towards Hastings—"a room I knew of that could only be reached by a journey of several leagues. I would start off for it very early in the morning, timing my arrival for noon, because I knew that at that hour, and for a matter of minutes only, a ray of sun would strike down into it, all the way to the floor. It was a little like your limelight, Mr. Hastings, with what I believe you call a colour medium attached to it, a yellow medium in this case. It is ironic, is it not, that the light I travelled so far to see was yellow—that was, after all, a colour I could see at home, in the light of the cooking fires. Oh, but this was a very different yellow, paler, for one thing, and steadier. Besides that, it had the quality of waking up what colour there was in the walls around me in a way that firelight never did. I saw bluish white in the limestone walls, a rusty tinge in the trickles of water that ran down them, veins of sparkling minerals in their hardness, green and purple and colours whose names I did not even know. And I swore, in the few minutes of looking that were vouchsafed me, that one day I would go to the place where everything was colour, the place I have since learned to call the modern world. Do you understand that, Mr. Hastings?"

"Forgive me, Count," Hastings said. "I don't doubt you for a moment; what you say carries the greatest conviction. But I have honestly never heard anything like it. What can you possibly be talking about? Where on earth is this country of yours?"

"You have heard, perhaps, of the Land of Darkness? The chronicles tell us that the armies of the Emperor of Persia were about to slaughter hundreds of Christian people when the Christians fell on their knees and prayed to God to save them. A black cloud descended and the Christians escaped, but the Emperor's armies were trapped by the darkness, and their descendants remain there to this day. Those in the neighbouring lands know that there are people living there, because they can hear their voices, and the neighing of horses and crowing of cocks. Alexander the Great is said to have ventured there, and to have drunk of the water of the Spring of Life that could only be reached by crossing it. That land is my home, though I have, alas, so far failed to find Alexander's spring. But now, perhaps, you see why dark places, such as the one where we are at present, remind me of my country."

"It is fantastic," Hastings said. "I can hardly believe…"

"Of course not. I could hardly expect it. But it is the lot of us inhabitants of the smaller and older countries to have lives that are unimaginable to dwellers in the great cities of Europe and America. We Cimmerians are perhaps not even the strangest."

"You call yourselves Cimmerians?"

"Cimmeria is the oldest name for our country and the one that I prefer, but we have other names: Hanyson, Hamson, and so on."

"I am not a scientist, Count, and I am, I suppose, a Christian—at least, I was brought up in the Church of England—but what you tell me is an impossibility. God would not, does not, intervene in human affairs in the manner you describe. And what kind of cloud would it be that would extinguish all light and remain unmoved for centuries? Besides, how do you live?" When the Count did not answer, Hastings grew apologetic again. "I do not mean to offend you. It is just that I cannot understand."

The Count smiled. "What I have told you are the legends of my country. England has its legends, too, does it not? The land that was founded by Brutus, who fled there after the fall of Troy, where Joseph of Arimathea planted the Holy Thorn, where King Arthur sleeps under a hill waiting to rise again to defeat your enemies in your hour of greatest need. Our legends are no more true than those. But the darkness is real enough."

"How could it be?"

"Think of what I have told you, Mr. Hastings, how I travelled leagues to see a room with a sunbeam in it. Does that not tell you? What do you need in order to keep out the light?"

Hastings shook his head.

"A roof, my dear sir, a roof is sufficient! And walls, of course."

"But I still don't... Cimmeria is indoors?"

"If you like to call it that. Oh, there is some truth, I think, in the legend of our foundation. Not about the Emperor of Persia and the black cloud, but that at some point in our long history (which goes back a great deal further than either Christianity or the Persian Empire, by the way) my ancestors needed to shelter from their enemies. So they took refuge—where do you think?"

"In a cave?"

"Inside a mountain. The caves in limestone country are, as I am sure you know, caused by the gradual eating away of the rock by water. Over the millennia they develop into complex systems of tunnels, great halls, underground lakes and rivers, and so on. Animals often shelter in such places, and so do human beings. I am told that some paintings were recently discovered in a cave in Spain, the work, apparently, of primitive man. And there are still people who live in houses hewn into the rock in many parts of the world. But I think Cimmeria may justly claim to be the world's only subterranean empire."

"And you can survive in that way, in the dark?"

"As I told you, it is not totally dark, but we have, over the centuries, become adapted to the conditions we live in. Our eyes are not blind, but, on the contrary, abnormally sensitive. For two years after I first began to live in the outer world I was obliged to wear spectacles of smoked glass to protect them from the sunlight. I still prefer to move about mostly at night."

"But what do you eat? Surely you need sunlight to grow crops?"

"Mushrooms." The Count laughed. "And bats. There is a surprising amount of meat on a bat."

# Chapter 8

Cassie had never been a good sleeper; no matter how tired she was when she went up to her room, no sooner had she lit her oil lamp than the events of the day just concluded and those she projected for tomorrow would rise up before her eyes, darkened and magnified like the shadows which looked down at her from the walls. They loomed larger still when she put out the light and lay back on her pillow. Her nights were a patchwork of dreams and obsessive thoughts, the latter so muddled that they were easily confused with the former, so that by the time morning did arrive she had no idea how much she had slept, though she knew from the sheer unlikeliness of some of her memories of the night that she must have done so.

The evenings reading Madame Blavatsky in the parlour were not a good inducement to peaceful repose, nor were her daytime conversations with Dr. Farthing, who was investigating a poltergeist at the moment. "It is the most economical of ghosts. It is as if the spirit had decided to reduce its manifestations to their simplest and most efficient form. Consider: we know that a ghost *is* a ghost and not one of our fellow mortals by something missing from its material form. It may, for example, lack a head. Or it may have an entire body but no substance, so that it can walk through walls or vanish at will. The poltergeist, or racketing spectre, is more insubstantial still; the only aspect of life remaining to it is sound: footsteps, for example, or a sharp rapping on the wall, or, very occasionally, a human voice, laughing demonically, perhaps."

Since she had returned to Halcyon House after a troubled Christmas in Penge, her nocturnal experiences had changed their nature. Her room seemed intimidating, with its wardrobe door that would never shut properly and its floorboards that creaked not only when she walked on them, but even when she was in bed, as if in retrospective protest at the walking she had done previously. It was chilly, even though she slept with her window closed to keep out the sounds of the urban night. And she was distressingly aware that her room was in a large house whose other inhabitants were more or less strangers to her. She heard their footsteps at odd times during the night, sometimes distant, sometimes crossing the landing of the floor outside her door. Occasionally she would hear a voice, crying out, as if in sleep. Once she woke with a start to hear a cry of "What?", and again, "O God!" Then there was a pause, and then—she would have got out of bed to investigate had she not been certain this was a supernatural manifestation and there was nothing she could do to help the speaker—"Murder!"

She would sit up as long as possible in her room, putting off the moment when she would have to take to her bed and lie helpless in the dark. She extinguished the oil lamp while fully dressed and read by candlelight in her chair. The disadvantage of this was that she tended to doze off where she sat, to wake with a start an hour or two later. And one night she woke in this position convinced that she had just heard a door bang downstairs. She looked at her travelling clock and saw that it was ten past midnight.

Yes, it must have been the front door. She heard a stair creak somewhere quite close, and then the footsteps of someone walking very slowly, putting down each foot as stealthily as possible, and somehow in the process making the sound more intrusive than it would otherwise have been. Cassie told herself it was only one of the residents returning late to his room after visiting some hostelry. But what if it wasn't? A truly scientific investigator must ascertain the facts. The steps had reached the landing outside and stopped abruptly.

Cassie took a deep breath, then took the candle in one hand and opened the door. A gentleman, still wearing his hat and coat, was standing with his back to her. She saw his shadow rise up on the door in front of him. "Mr. Wimbury!"

The key he had been fishing for in his pocket dropped from his hand.

"Oh, I'm sorry to startle you."

"Miss Pine! Excuse me." He bent down to pick up the key. In doing so he stepped back, almost bumping into her, and she stepped back in her turn to make room for him, which brought her into sharp contact with the door jamb and caused her to drop the candle. It went out, leaving them both in darkness. There was a glimmer of moonlight through the window at the end of the passage, but Cassie, accustomed to the light of her candle, could see nothing at first.

"Allow me," Mr. Wimbury said, groping at her feet. She felt his hand crawling over her slippers and cried out. "Oh, I do beg your pardon, Miss Pine. I think I have your candle."

"Oh, sir!"

"There is no need to be alarmed, I assure you. We will have light again in a moment, if I can find my matches. I am so sorry for the accident." There was a pause. "Er, do you happen to have any matches of your own?"

"In my room, certainly."

"I wonder if you would be so good as to get them? My box seems to be empty. I use a lot in the course of my daily work, and I must have neglected…"

Cassie's eyes had just been adjusting to the moonlight. No sooner had she re-entered her room than she found herself in darkness again, all the more complete as she had pulled the door almost closed behind her from an instinct of modesty. She blundered at once into her chair and a protruding point of the cane jabbed her in the thigh, causing her to cry out.

"Are you all right, Miss Pine?" Mr. Wimbury had entered the room behind her and she felt his hands on her upper arms.

Cassie gasped.

"Oh, I'm sorry, I don't mean to… I thought you might have fallen."

"No, no," Cassie said, "I'm quite all right, thank you, sir." The hands released her. "There's a cane chair in my way. Wait a moment, please. I can't see anything."

"Ah, I know it well. Not this particular one, of course. I have one in my own room and it is more like a thorn bush than a piece of furniture. Here, let me move it for you." She was aware of his body brushing past hers, and did her best to squeeze out of the way, but there was something obstructing her which she supposed must be her wardrobe, though she was not sure that she had last seen it in that position. After all, there was nothing indecorous about the contact—it was not really a body touching her, only a coat, and the her that it touched was only clothing also. More decent than dancing, she told herself, and then remembered that it could not be called decent to dance with a gentleman in a dark bedroom.

"A mere inconvenience," Mr. Wimbury was saying. "We will have everything to rights in an instant. D—!" Cassie felt a sudden pain in her ankle and cried out. Mr. Wimbury cried out at the same time, and their mingled shouts were followed by a double noise, the delicate crash of the chair falling to the floor and a heavier, more muffled sound that must have been Mr. Wimbury following suit. "I'm sorry for the unsuitable language," his voice said from somewhere below. "Forgot where I was for the moment."

"You tripped over my foot," Cassie said. "My ankle is bruised."

"I'm sorry about that, too. I say, Miss Pine, it is rather dark in here. Would you mind opening the door? There is a little moonlight in the passage, and it might help us to get our bearings."

When they had lighted the lamp, Mr. Wimbury sat without ceremony on Cassie's bed, and she was still too dazed and breathless to make a fuss about it. He was pale and hatless. (The hat must still be on the floor somewhere.) "Do you, by any chance, have a drop of brandy in the room?" he asked.

She shook her head. "I've got some Chlorodyne, if that would do?"

"Is it good for bruises? I have hurt my knee, and I think my right wrist may be sprained."

"Dr. Collis Browne's Chlorodyne," said Cassie evangelically, "is a specific against all kinds of minor ailments and injuries. I've never known it to fail me."

"Well, then, some of that would be most welcome, thank you."

Cassie went to the medicine chest and poured some Chlorodyne into a small glass. He drank it in one gulp.

"This is queer stuff, but I think it's doing me good. Are you having some yourself? I'm sorry to have injured you."

Cassie shrugged and splashed some into the glass on her washstand. The liquid performed its usual miracle, as if another lamp had been lit, this time inside her. There was still a pain in her ankle, but it was somehow a holy thing, to be treasured rather than shrunk from. The same applied to the presence of a gentleman in her bedroom. As the warmth spread through her body, it acquired a significance that no one but herself could possibly understand. She was ministering to him, was she not? And that was a vocation of the utmost importance—any suggestion of indecorum was a petty misunderstanding, beneath her dignity.

"I am afraid we made rather a noise," he said.

"Oh, it was nothing. Nobody will take any notice. Old houses are noisy by nature."

"They don't usually cry out, or say improper words."

"Are you feeling better?"

"Very much better, thank you. That stuff of yours is quite the thing. Perhaps if we had some more, just in case?"

Cassie poured them second doses, and Hastings, after swallowing his, handed his glass back to her regretfully. "I suppose I'd better be going." Instead he returned to the bed and sat down again, as if he had not even noticed his stated intention. "What was it you wanted with me, Miss Pine?"

"What was it I wanted?"

"Yes. You called to me as I was unlocking the door to my room. I suppose you must have wanted something?"

"Oh, yes. I wanted to ask if you had the correct time. It's just that my clock has stopped."

"This one? It seems to be ticking, and it says twenty past midnight, which I should think—" He took a pocket watch from the depths of his coat. "Yes, it is the right time."

"It must of started again when you fell over."

He raised his right leg and crossed it over his left knee, a posture only men used. She did not think it could be comfortable. "What do you want from me, Miss Pine?" he said. They were almost the same words he had used a moment ago, but his tone suggested he meant something different this time.

"Me, sir? You are mistaken—I don't want anything."

He said nothing, but continued to look at her in a way that insisted on another response.

"Well, then, if you must know… You are a puzzle to me, Mr. Wimbury. I cannot make out your behaviour. A few months ago, you was so good as to give me lunch, and we talked about your theatrical ambitions. I offered you some advice, then, sir, which I hope you profited by. Since then, you are hardly ever at supper, and otherwise I've heard nothing of you, except those footsteps of yours. It was almost like you'd disappeared from the house, and left only your footsteps which for all I knew might of been somebody else's altogether!" Cassie was aware she was making very little sense. "And as for you, you could of been anywhere!"

"But, Miss Pine, I have been here all along. That stuff of yours is terribly good, by the way." He laughed. "I am tired after a long day's work. I don't say it has revived me, but it somehow makes me enjoy being tired, if you know what I mean."

"Well," she said, "I told you I was following your career with interest. Was it decent, was it cordial, to keep me guessing like that about what you were up to?"

"Excuse me, I don't wish to offend you, but I really have no idea what you are talking about."

Cassie was appalled to hear herself giggle. She should have used her medicine spoon for the Chlorodyne. "I suppose I just missed you, that's all. We had a nice talk, didn't we, Mr. Wimbury? About the spirits? And then you vanished, just like one of them."

"I didn't vanish, Miss Pine. I took your advice and found myself some employment."

"So you're an actor now?"

He smiled slyly. "No, Miss Pine. That's where I took your advice. Do what's needful, you said. I am not an actor yet, but I can honestly say I am a gas-boy. Do you mind if I take my shoes off? I think I could sleep a little."

"A gas-boy, what's that?"

But Hastings didn't answer. He had stretched out on her bed and closed his eyes, and was now breathing gently in a regular rhythm. *I must get him to move in a minute*, Cassie thought. In her present state of mind, it did not seem all that urgent.

# Chapter 9

The first rehearsals for *Hamlet* used no green fire or limelight. Not even the battens were lit, as all that was necessary was a tee-piece, a simple arrangement of piping and burners that produced a long line of flame to light up the back of the stage. Hastings was required to light the tee-piece at the beginning of each rehearsal, and return later to extinguish it, but he took every opportunity to hang around in the wings watching the performance. He had a particular interest in the Ghost, feeling that Mr. Roderick had cheated him of the part. The actor playing it was the company's First Old Man, Mr. Barnes, who doubled as Polonius, which only increased Hastings's resentment. Why should he have two parts, and would not the audience recognize that it was the same actor playing both? Besides, the Ghost, it seemed to him, was not truly an Old Man role. He appeared in his armour, a man of war, not a doddering old counsellor like Polonius. Barnes was clearly too old for the part. He was still reading it from the book, which Hastings found strange. What actor did not know *Hamlet* by heart? Barnes, fat and in shirt sleeves, pacing up and down beneath the tee-piece in a way that was supposed to look portentous but was more like the lecturing of an aged professor, was hardly a menacing figure.

"It will be different," a voice said, "when he is in full armour, and has the benefit of your green fire."

Hastings turned. It was the Count, smiling up at him, and looking, somehow, less imposing than he had in the gridiron.

"I had hoped for the part myself, Count," he said shortly.

"Tchah. It would not do for you, you are too young. I have you earmarked for the Prince himself. That is the word, 'earmarked'?"

Hastings nodded.

"Your language is full of surprises. One expects it from Shakespeare, but… You know, Mr. Hastings—"

"My name is not Hastings, Count. Or rather, that is my Christian name. My surname is Wimbury."

"Wimbury, Wimbury. Excuse me, I beg your pardon. Where I come from people have only one name and it is quite sufficient for us. I shall remember in future. I was about to say, I am a little uncomfortable standing around behind the scenes here. It has been borne in upon me by some of your colleagues—not your respected self, of course—that I am not welcome in this theatre."

"Oh come, sir, you must be mistaken!"

"No, no, it is no matter. Do you have a few minutes to spare, Mr. Wimbury? Or perhaps a little longer? I wonder if we might go somewhere that is more convenient for conversation."

"Well, um—" Hastings looked round, as if expecting to see Mr. Eweson appear behind the Count.

"It will be to your advantage, I assure you."

"Well, I dare say the theatre could spare me for a short time. There is a public house nearby that I have sometimes visited."

The Count suppressed a shudder with almost complete success. "If you think it is private enough for our purposes? I have some things to say to you which are best kept confidential."

"Oh, no one will be listening," Hastings said. "Nowhere is more private than an English public house, in its own way."

At the Duke of Buckingham, Hastings was surprised by the confidence with which the Count, despite his apparent reservations, strode into the saloon bar first, and stared round the crowded premises. "This will never do," he said.

"No one will take any notice of us, I promise you," Hastings told him. "Look, there are tables in little compartments, with stained-glass screens."

"We can still be heard," the Count muttered, "and glass is transparent. Wait here a moment."

He went to the bar and, ignoring the other customers there, addressed the barman, employing a certain amount of foreign-looking hand-waving. *I must remember this when next I am called upon to play a foreigner,* Hastings thought.

"This is good," the Count said, returning. "I have been able to engage a small room upstairs where we can talk in private. And I have taken the liberty of ordering us a bottle of wine. I am not fond of beer."

The room proved to be very small indeed, with a plain trestle table and a lot of chairs stacked around the walls. The servant who escorted them there took down a couple of chairs from the pile for them, with a grumpy air which was dispelled when the Count presented him with what must have been a handsome tip. He was back quickly with the wine and glasses and received a second tip which pleased him still more.

"Would you like me to pour, sir?"

"No, I thank you. We wish to be private. Draw the cork, if you please, and leave us."

When the boy had gone, the Count poured glasses for them both. The wine was thick and inky black and the flavour matched its appearance, having something of tar about it.

"What is the wine, sir?" Hastings asked. He had already made up his mind that he would drink as little of it as was consistent with politeness.

"You would not know it. It is from a country not all that far from my own." Hastings was trying to read the label, but it was stained and faded, and the few letters he could read meant nothing to him. The Count took a sip and sighed. "This is the nearest I can get to the wine of my own country, and it makes me feel a deep nostalgia. Cimmerian wine is darker even than this and has a fuller flavour. But I congratulate you, Mr. Wimbury, on leading me to a public house that stocks this one. It is a rare treat."

"Wait," Hastings said. "You grow grapes in your country?"

"Certainly."

"But I thought—forgive me, sir—I understood you to say that it was dark all the time and that your countrymen subsisted on a diet of mushrooms and bats."

The Count laughed. "Mushrooms and bats are our staples, indeed. But one cannot live by bread alone, and the same is true of those beloved nocturnal staples of ours. You see, Mr. Wimbury, our country is not entirely dark." He leaned across the table as if intending to whisper a secret.

"No?"

"No, indeed. The cave system where my people first took shelter thousands of years ago has been a hospitable home to us, and we have grown to love the dark, and to feel safe there. It is the heart of our culture, the true Cimmeria. But caves have entrances and exits, after all."

"I suppose so."

"We are not entirely cut off from the world outside. We have always ventured out to hunt, when the bats became too monotonous, and over the years some Cimmerians have learned to like the outside even more than our original home. These people now live there permanently, in their mud-and-straw huts on the flank of the mountain which accommodates their fellow countrymen. There they are able to grow cereal crops, fruit and vegetables, and to pasture sheep and goats. And they grow vines on the lower slopes where it is warmer and more sheltered. To the other peoples of the area, these mountain-dwelling Cimmerians are the only ones they know; if they have heard of the dwellers in the dark, they think of us only as a legend, which is as we wish it. We have been hiding for centuries, and it suits our temperament to remain so. To tell the truth we rather despise our outer brethren, who are simple folk of no breeding or culture. We are not, I am afraid, a democratic people." He sighed. "Still, it suits us to do business with them. They give us their produce and, in return, we give them certain of our treasures, which they can trade with their neighbours in the great world, and everyone is happy."

"What treasures do you give them, sir?" Hastings asked.

The Count felt in his waistcoat pocket. "Oh, things like this!" He threw an object on the table.

Hastings gasped. "Is it real?"

"As real as I am."

"And you just carry it around in your pocket like that?"

"I told you, these minerals mean little to us, though we are glad that others value them. Take it! I brought it as a present for you, and a token of the seriousness of my intentions."

"I could not possibly, sir!"

"No, take it. I am sure there is someone you could give it to as a present, a lady perhaps? I am sorry it is not set."

"Well, if you are sure…" Hastings reached for the stone and put it quickly in his own pocket.

"There! Now you have a small part of my country on your own person. I was talking of the outer Cimmerians, with whom we usually trade such substances. Perhaps you were amused when I referred to them as a people without culture? After all, what kind of culture can exist for my inner brethren, in the dark? We cannot read books."

"I hadn't thought of that." Hastings took another sip of wine. There was some kind of spice in the flavour he thought, cloves, perhaps. It was not so bad if you did not think of it as wine.

"Instead our culture is entirely oral. We sing or speak our poems and stories and scriptures, though I suppose scriptures is not strictly the accurate word."

"So you have a religion? Are you Christian?"

"We are more what is known as Manichean. We believe in two gods, or it might be more appropriate to call them principles, a principle of Light and a principle of Darkness. The Dark was the first of these to appear on earth, and then the Light came and disrupted it. Until there was light there was no distance in the world."

"What do you mean?"

"It is only when there is light that people can see they are separate from each other. In pure darkness, such as you have perhaps hardly known, there may be voices, feelings, smells, all the constituents of humanity without any sense of alienation. One is a people, not a person. That is our Garden of Eden, the world as it was before "Let there be Light!" ruined everything. And one day we believe that Darkness will return. That is no doubt another reason to despise our weaker brethren who have, as we see it, capitulated to light."

"You speak very movingly, sir."

"For one who has himself capitulated? Yes, Mr. Hastings, Wimbury I should say, I acknowledge my sin, as the Cimmerians would call it, my betrayal of the Great Dark I was born in. I am a heretic, a lover of Light. Here in London"—he leaned forward again—"you have so conquered the dark that it is being driven even from its natural abode of night. One day you will succeed in abolishing the night altogether, and then there will be no need for sleep! Think of it, Mr. Wimbury, a world lit entirely by gas, where every man has all the time he needs for work, for study, and for enjoyment. It would be like having two lives. And this is why I so respect your calling, as an Engineer of Luminosity."

"It is not my calling, sir." Hastings raised his glass to take another sip, thought better of it, and merely studied the tarry liquid.

"Forgive me, I know it is not. And yet it can do no harm, as I told you before, to understand the mechanics of the light that will illuminate your eminent person when you are playing the Dane."

"But I am not to play Hamlet, sir. That honour is to go to Mr. Rowlands. He is an actor; I am merely what you are kind enough to call an engineer, though my colleagues' term of gas-boy is more accurate. And I shall probably remain a gas-boy until I tire of the theatre and go back to Reigate, where I come from."

The Count drained his glass and topped up that of Hastings, though very little had gone from it, before refilling his own. "You will find it is an acquired taste," he said. "Take a big sip. It will give you confidence, which is sorely lacking in you at present."

Hastings did as he was told. "I was wondering what it reminded me of. There is a medicine called Chlorodyne, which I tasted recently." He stopped and glanced quickly across the table, wondering if the Count's accomplishments included mind-reading, but the other showed no interest in his comparison.

"Now then, we come to it. Mr. Hastings Wimbury, my proposition is this. You shall play the Dane, and what is more, you will do so while you are still young enough for the casting to be appropriate."

"How can that be, sir?"

"I shall arrange the production. I am not without means. When I say arrange, I do not mean produce the play. That shall be your own responsibility, for I know that you have brooded long on the subject and have many ingenious and original ideas of your own."

Hastings sighed. "But, Count, forgive me, I have played Hamlet before, in the Reigate Playhouse. It was an amateur production and was, if I may say so, very well received. But I have no wish to take part in another amateur production. My dream is to play the role here, on the West End stage, and, for all your distinguished generosity, I am afraid that is not something you can arrange for me. I am, of course, exceedingly grateful for the offer."

"I am not proposing an amateur production, but one of national significance."

"I have no doubt, Count, that you are a man of great distinction, and, if you will excuse my mentioning it, of great means, too, but I doubt very much if you have any understanding of what it would take to mount a production in the West End."

"I am not referring," the Count said, "to the West End."

"Then how can it be of national—? Oh." Hastings downed his glass quickly in the hope that it would steady his nerves. Instead it gave him the momentary impression that his brain was being assaulted on two fronts simultaneously.

"I see you are beginning to understand me." The Count smiled.

"I'm sorry, sir, it really is out of the question. It is, I suppose, a great honour you are doing me, but the idea is—I'm sorry, I cannot think of any other way to put it—absurd. And when all is said and done, I am an Englishman."

"A countryman of Shakespeare! Whose plays are loved and admired not only in England but in every nation on earth, every nation where culture is valued. Well, perhaps every nation but one. Mr. Wimbury, what I am proposing is unique. It would not even have been possible before our present age. Any Irving, any Rowlands can play Hamlet to an audience who know 'To be or not to be' so well they do not even hear the words any more. Do you think the London theatregoers are terrified of the Ghost, smitten with the beauty of Ophelia (that is the word, *smitten*?)? Do they weep at the end for the poor heroic Prince gasping out his dying wish for the succession to fall to Fortinbras? No, they are thinking of the late supper they will enjoy afterwards, the cold chicken and champagne. But in Cimmeria, they will be hearing the words for the first time, they will be stirred by the story as nothing has stirred them in their whole lives. A virgin audience, Mr. Wimbury! Does Irving have that?"

"But it will be dark!"

"Yes," said the Count, refilling Hastings's glass. "I have thought of that, too."

# Chapter 10

Hastings unlocked the door of Halcyon House and stepped into the hall. The light of the full moon glimmered through the stained-glass panes of the fanlight and cast complicated patterns on the tiles and walls. Nevertheless, remembering the confusion of last night, he took a candle from the box on the shelf and lit it before making his way upstairs. As he reached the turning, he became aware of a fainter light reaching out to meet the candle's glow; she was awake.

He had been woken at dawn by a violent commotion which turned out to be Miss Pine tugging at and shaking him to rouse him and send him back to his own room. She was still fully dressed, so she had either slept like that, or stayed up for several hours hoping he would come to of his own accord. Their subsequent conversation had taken place in whispers. He must not tell anyone of this, he must keep his voice down, and not clatter on the landing. And then, just as she pushed him out the door, she had said something ominous: "We've got matters to discuss, sir. I'll see you tonight."

He could not imagine what she had meant. They had talked of nothing that evening except his job as a gas-boy and the fact that they had not spoken recently. It had been scarcely more than passing the time of night. The most significant thing about the encounter was that she had given him that peculiar medicine, which had not only sent him to sleep but induced the most colourful dreams. He did not relish the thought of a discussion with Miss Pine at this hour, still less if she was proposing to dose him again. There was a stair that creaked, the third from the top, and he took special pains to avoid it this time. With any luck she would not hear him.

No sooner had he set foot on the landing, however, than Miss Pine's door opened and she appeared, candle in hand. She pressed the forefinger of her free hand to her lips, which gave her something of the look of an allegorical figure. He smiled in what he hoped was an agreeable manner and made for his own door. As allegorically as before, she beckoned with the forefinger. Hastings replaced the smile with a more apologetic one, but she darted from the doorway and took him by the wrist. He had no choice unless he wanted to wake the whole house with an unseemly scuffle, so he sighed and followed her.

Once inside the room, they took up their positions of the night before: there was no other way to accommodate the two of them. Hastings had the uncanny impression that no time at all had passed and that all the events of the last twenty-four hours were about to happen again. It was a relief when Miss Pine opened the conversation with different words from those she had used last night.

"I do hope you've had a pleasant day, Mr. Wimbury." She kept her voice low.

"Yes, thank you, very pleasant," he said, thinking how astonished she would be if he told her anything of the conversation he had had with the Count.

"Good. I'm sorry to ask you into my room again, especially seeing as it's so late, but it is the only place we can talk quietly without disturbing them in the other rooms. I'm sure you understand my reasons."

"To be quite honest—"

"Oh, it was at least as much my fault as yours, I realize that. Maybe even more, since I am a woman," Cassie said, twisting her fingers painfully round each other. That must be the gesture known as wringing one's hands. He had never seen it before, and wondered if he should remember it for the stage, but he wasn't sure if it was appropriate for male roles.

"What was?" he asked, noticing belatedly that she expected him to say something.

"Oh," she said, "so that's the line you're taking, is it? I must say I expected more from a gentleman like you, Mr. Wimbury, even though, no, particularly *because* we come from different backgrounds."

"Do we? I mean, yes, I suppose we do. What was it you expected from me, Miss Pine?"

"That you would take some of the blame on yourself, more of it than me, that is. After all, I didn't invite you into my room."

"You most certainly did!" Hastings said. "You stood at the door beckoning. That may not be an invitation in your book but it is so in mine. I am an actor, you see, and gestures are important to us."

"I am not talking about tonight," Cassie said. "Tonight is different—we aren't what we was to each other before. Now you've got the right to be here, almost; some people might even say it was a duty. But last night is what I'm talking about, and I never asked you then. Drop a candle is all I did, which anybody might of done under the circumstances."

"As I recall, I came into your room to get some matches. And you tripped me." It seemed important to make his own account as combative as possible.

"You fell over my foot, Mr. Wimbury, and injured it severely. It still hurts in point of fact."

"Well, I was quite shaken up myself."

"I know you were, sir, and I'm not saying it was anybody's fault," Cassie said, contradicting her earlier statement. "So I felt called on to minister to you a bit before asking you to leave. That seemed to me the womanly thing to do. Maybe I was wrong."

"No, no, I'm sure you weren't."

"And the thing is, Dr. Collis Browne's Chlorodyne is strong stuff, and apparently you aren't used to it. I make allowances for that, sir. But—" Cassie was very pale, Hastings noticed; perhaps the ankle was more seriously injured than he had supposed. "But there are some things no decent woman can make allowances for, not if she wants to stay decent. You fell asleep, Mr. Wimbury!"

"I know. Sorry about that."

"Oh, falling asleep is not the point, it's where you fell asleep—on my bed is where, and in my room! You have spent the night, sir, in a lady's chamber!"

The phrase had the ring of a nursery rhyme, which Hastings found rather appealing. It gave him a feeling of pride, as though he had done something impressively mythical; he *had* spent the night in her chamber—he couldn't deny it. And saying the phrase to himself gave him a new way of looking at Miss Pine, too. Up to now she had been little more than one of the appurtenances of Halcyon House, a place where he spent few of his waking hours: she was mixed up in his mind with cane chairs and washstands and the smell of oil lamps, mutton, and cabbage. Now he saw her as a woman, and one with a lot of reddish brown hair, a snub nose with a sprinkling of freckles on it and the slightly plump figure that sometimes went with those features. She is saying, he realized for the first time, that I have compromised her. It was an exciting thought.

"It was the middle of the night," he pleaded.

"Of course it was, sir; that only makes it worse!"

"I mean, nobody can possibly have been aware of it. As soon as it was light you turfed me out and I went back to my own chamber—I mean room—to sleep the nasty stuff off. No one saw or heard us."

"Even if they didn't, sir, we saw and heard ourselves."

"We were asleep!"

"Don't try to wriggle out of it, if you please. We both know what happened, and that what has been done can never be undone. I am not thinking of my reputation, sir, though that is all a poor girl like myself can call her own, that and her employment. And her honour, which is what I *am* thinking of."

"What has been done? But surely nothing was done, really."

"You call that nothing?" Cassie gasped.

"Well, yes, I suppose I do. I mean, forgive me, Miss Pine, I am not really a man of the world, for all that I work in a theatre, but I have always understood that there is a little more involved in this matter of compromising a woman's—excuse me—I mean a lady's reputation. Certain—I don't know how to put this—actions, or, I may say, activities."

"Oh!" The noise Cassie emitted is best expressed by that vowel but was more of a squeak than a human utterance.

"Miss Pine, we are both very young, and we have much life ahead of us. I am myself engaged to be married, or at least I hope to be, subject to the agreement of the lady's family. I expect you, too, have someone you love or at least the prospect of having such a person."

"So you're engaged!"

"Well, yes and no, as I said."

"And what would your fiancée say if she could see you now, Mr. Wimbury, in another lady's room, a room where you spent the night not twenty-four hours ago?"

Hastings was confused. "Well, if she could see me, I suppose she would be here, too, which would probably make it all right, wouldn't it?"

"Don't trifle with me, sir!"

"I'm sorry. Look, Miss Pine, I don't know what it is you want. Please tell me, and then I can go to bed. I have had a long and disorientating day."

Cassie's voice, ever since the squeak, had largely escaped her control, a preliminary to crying though Hastings saw no tears in her eyes yet. Instead, the snub nose had turned red and she was gulping between words. "All my life," she was saying, "all my life."

"Please, my dear lady, if there is anything I can do…"

"You know very well, sir, what you ought to do, and it's the same thing as what you ought to want to do. And if I was only somebody else instead of me you *would* want to do it without having to be told to want to. And I was not brought up with the expectation of being humiliated. Only"—her words were coming out more as gurgles now, and with longer pauses between them, so that he had trouble following their sense— "only, now I come to think of it, that's exactly how I *was* brought up, to be humiliated, and what else can you expect if that's how you was brought up—?" Then the tears supervened.

She cried for a long time, making no further effort to control herself, and Hastings found himself in an even more awkward position. It would not be gentlemanly to get up and walk out, leaving a lady in distress, much as he longed for bed. It would be kindly, and no doubt enjoyable, to go over to her chair and comfort her, possibly by means of a discreet arm placed around the shoulders, but that would only make matters worse. The dreadful thing was that, the longer he remained on this bed, the more tempted he was to stretch out on it as he had done last night, causing all this trouble in the first place. For all his protestations of innocence, there was a part of him that did believe it was in some way his fault. She was in a sense right: gentlemen did not, as far as he knew, do what he had done last night—indeed, they did not do what he was doing now. His only excuse was that on neither occasion had it felt like something he was doing, more like something that had happened to him. But perhaps that was how one always felt when one had done wrong.

Eventually the tears and convulsions stopped, but Miss Pine did not attempt to continue the conversation. "I shall go now, shall I?" Hastings said.

She made no reply, only a shrug.

As Hastings rose to leave, a thought occurred to him that startled and horrified him more than anything that had passed in the room just now: *Well, at least if the worst comes to the worst, I can leave the country. The Count has seen to that.* He put his hand in his trouser pocket. The treasure was still there, so their conversation earlier in the day had really happened; he felt the shape and texture again, as he had done at intervals during the evening. He had been carrying it in his pocket as if it were no more significant than a pebble, but no pebble had those sharp, regular edges, that glassy feel under the fingertips. It was the Count's ruby.

# Chapter 11

The sun was shining. Flora, as she entered the breakfast room, saw the gold light flooding the table like spilled tea, and shuddered. She had promised Mr. Pilkins to go for a picnic with him in Reigate Woods today if the weather was propitious, and it was impossible to deny that it was. It was not that she had any objection to further conversation with Mr. Pilkins over the cold roast beef and plum pudding, though they were beginning to run out of neutral topics, ones that did not involve references to her beauty and accomplishments on the one hand or the pleasures and duties of being a vicar's wife on the other. But this would be a first time twice over: their first joint expedition beyond the grounds of the Rowans and the first meal they would have eaten alone together. A picnic felt like a terrible commitment, the next thing to being really engaged instead of provisionally so. And what if it was not intended as the next thing at all, but the thing itself? It was true that he was still not, as he had put it on that snowy day that now seemed so distant, in a position to marry—how could he be, as a new curate, with no hope of a living of his own for several more years?—but other men embarked on real engagements rather than provisional ones in such circumstances, and real engagements were not easy to get out of. How long would Mr. Pilkins continue to be satisfied with the distant prospect of a promise?

Flora had never discussed her attachment to Mr. Pilkins with Papa, and so, in family terms, it could not be said to exist. Mr. Pilkins had merely had dinner with them on a few occasions, as many other young men did, and as long as Papa remained in ignorance there could be no question of financial arrangements, and hence no serious consideration of marriage. All the same, Mama's attitude was a good deal too welcoming. This very picnic had been a sort of conspiracy between the two of them: Mr. Pilkins had mentioned at tea how much he enjoyed picnics and how glad he was that the improvement in the weather was making it possible to spend more time out of doors, and Mama had at once suggested (no, practically commanded) that he should take Flora to Reigate Woods. Mrs. Honeydew prepared such wonderful hampers, and it would be pleasant to get out in the pony chaise in the spring weather. Mama was perhaps a little in love with Mr. Pilkins herself, on Flora's behalf.

Dreading the thought of the picnic, Flora had lain in bed longer than usual that morning, and was the last one down for breakfast. It hardly mattered if she breakfasted on cold toast with the picnic so imminent. (Mr. Pilkins was expected at eleven.) As she took her place at table, she noticed an envelope addressed in the familiar handwriting:

*Miss Flora Burlap.*
*The Rowans.*
*Rectory Lane.*
*Reigate.*
*Surrey.*

It was heavy and lopsided, with something hard and bulky in one corner. She looked round quickly to see if anyone was present, then felt the bulge carefully with her thumb and forefinger. It was a gemstone; she could feel the angled facets through the paper. Unset, apparently, and about the size of the marbles Algy used to play with as a boy. She doubted very much, knowing how poor Hastings was, whether it could be genuine, but in any case their engagement was unofficial and she could not risk anyone knowing that she had received a present from a gentleman, valuable or not. Not feeling like breakfast all of a sudden, she got up hastily.

The door of her room was ajar, and she could hear Hannah moving about inside, tidying up and doing whatever maids did at this hour. It would not do to go in just yet. Perhaps she should return to the breakfast room and wait a little longer? Instead, yielding to one of those childish impulses that still struck her occasionally, she sat down on the top step as she used to as a girl. It was not so comfortable when wearing a bustle; she felt her skirts rise round her like waves engulfing a stricken ship. Still, no one could see her here. They would have to be going up or down the stairs to do so, and that was not likely in the late morning. Was there not something in the Bible about the secret places of the stairs? She might just open the envelope and have a look.

The stone was a ruby, or perhaps the paste equivalent, but if so it was a more than passable imitation. Flora had always had a weakness for rubies, above all that distinctive colour some of them had, a red with something of mauve in it, like the inner flesh of a cherry. A gem was at its most beautiful when it made you want to eat it. She held it up in an attempt to catch some light, but it was gloomy here, with no sunlight to bring out the sparkle. The stone was cool in her fingers. Could it be real?

The thought first excited, then horrified her. If it was indeed real, where on earth could Hastings have obtained it? A genuine stone like this must be worth a fortune. She thought of the excitable tone of his letters, his infatuation with the tawdry values of the theatre and the women of low morals he associated with there. Could it have come from one of them, from Mrs. Beveridge perhaps, presented to her by one of her aristocratic lovers? Whatever its source, it was not the kind of gift she could honourably accept. Just as she was slipping the ruby back into its envelope, she heard Hannah emerge from the door of her room and cross the landing towards the back stairs. The way was clear for her: she must go back to the room and read his letter.

My own Darling,

I enclose the letter I started to write to you a few days ago, at a time when I was in despair. It seemed to me then that my career in the theatre had reached an impasse which it could never surmount. Of all the plays that Mr. Roderick could choose with which to taunt my ambitions, Hamlet is the only one I would find unbearable. I am not to play the Ghost, let alone the Prince: I am not even to set foot on the stage, having irrevocably committed myself to the other side of the business. Or at least, that was the situation when I wrote the enclosed lines which I could not bear to finish.

I have recently made the acquaintance of a foreign gentleman, Count Nollo by name, and he has honoured me with his confidence. He comes, it seems, from a small, remote, and decidedly peculiar country. I shall not relate the details of his description of it except that it is like nowhere I have ever heard of in my life. According to him, the people of that place are hungry for British culture and science, so much so that a young man like myself, accomplished in both (or so he flatters me!), may find opportunities he would seek in vain in London. In brief, my darling, he proposes to stage a production of Hamlet there, with myself both playing the Prince and managing, with his assistance, resources, and local knowledge, all aspects of the production. Not immediately, of course. While my own performance has, as you know, been polished by years of study, as well as my spell at the Reigate Playhouse, there are many more arrangements to be made before I journey to C— to begin rehearsals in earnest. (Forgive my not naming the country: he has placed me on my honour to keep it a secret, and in any case the name would mean nothing to you—I doubt if it is even to be found in most atlases.) He is, he tells me, in constant communication with the authorities in *that land, and obtaining permission and organizing the facilities for this most ambitious of spectacles is slow and cumbersome. I am to hold myself in readiness, furnishing him the while with any scraps of knowledge or other small conveniences as I may have access to. One day—it may be without warning—he will give the word and we shall depart, not forever, but only for long enough to change my fortunes and set you and me on the road to married life.*

*You are sceptical, beloved, and how should you not be? You have not met the Count, whose very person carries conviction, and even I, who have, listened with some doubt to his outlandish narrative. (It is far more so than I have revealed to you in the above summary.) Being a man of sensitivity and intelligence, he understands this, and has offered me what he calls a small token of his veracity and good will: it is a ruby from C—, which has mines richer and deeper than any in Europe. As soon as I saw it, I had only one thought as to its destination. Please accept it, my darling, as a belated Christmas present, with all my love.*

Flora sat at the little escritoire in the corner of her room reading and rereading the letter. In between, she would hold up the ruby in the beam of sunlight from the window. This one seemed more than edible; it was edible and on fire at the same time, like a cherry flambéed in some exotic liqueur, one that burned crimson instead of the usual blue. It is not real, she told herself, any more than the story of the Count and his mysterious far-off country are real. When Hastings left Reigate, he gave up all that was genuine in life for a land of make-believe, and now nothing that pertained to him could be trusted. And yet make-believe could be beautiful, could it not?

After all, where did rubies come from, or any precious stones for that matter? She was sure there were no ruby mines in England. Jewels came from unimaginable places like

Madagascar and Celebes, places that were no more than exotic names. Any jewel he could have presented to her would have a mysterious and exotic provenance—why should she baulk at this one?

She had forgotten her arrangements for the day, when she realized that she had for some time been aware of noises in the background: footsteps on the gravel, a knock at the door, Mr. Pilkins's exchanged words of greeting with Thomas, the footman. And now that her mind had caught up with all these, there was a knock at her own door, and Hannah entered to announce his arrival.

The ruby was clutched in her hand, where she had concealed it when Hannah entered; she locked it quickly in the drawer of the escritoire and got up to change. Just as she was leaving the room, however, a thought struck her. She returned to the escritoire, unlocked it, and slipped the ruby into the hidden pocket in the bosom of her dress.

# Chapter 12

**M**r. Pilkins must have scouted out the land they were to ride over in advance, so well had he chosen the clearing for their picnic. It was on a sandy slope surrounded by silver birches, and the only place they had encountered all morning that was not thickly carpeted with mud and decayed leaves. Sloping though it was, there was a sheltered dip just off the main ride that was the perfect size for their picnic blanket. He took down the hamper from the chaise, then they left Thomas and the pony in the road, picked their way through the birches and spread the blanket on the sand. Mr. Pilkins was unable to restrain himself from rooting through the hamper.

"Sir, that is my responsibility," Flora said, and was surprised to notice an almost flirtatious tone in her voice.

"Forgive me, Miss Burlap, but…" he said without raising his head from the interior. "Oh, how very thoughtful! Claret I had expected, but here is a half bottle of champagne, too!" He emerged, holding it up in triumph. "Now, that, you will acknowledge, is my responsibility."

The champagne had been shaken up during the ride and sprayed over the blanket and their clothes when he opened it. "Oh, excuse me," he said breathlessly, scrabbling for a glass, while Flora delved in beside him in search of a napkin to wipe up the mess. By the time the emergency was over they were both laughing as the most socially acceptable way of covering the confusion, and there was enough champagne left for a glass each once the foam had died down.

"It is less a beverage," Mr. Pilkins said, "than a sort of liquid firework. That must be why it is always served at celebrations."

Flora was not sure what they had to celebrate, but she was glad of the champagne anyway; its airy frivolity invaded her mouth and nose then rapidly took possession of her brain, making her feel that none of her concerns of that morning mattered. She was aching from the bumpy ride, the dampness of her skirts was beginning to seep through to chill her legs, and a cold wind found its way sporadically into their dingle. Somehow all these discomforts were enjoyable, reminding her that she had a body, which cared little for the scruples and anxieties of the mind.

"You must be hungry, Miss Burlap." Mr. Pilkins had finished his champagne and was now lolling on the blanket. There was no way to sit on such a surface that was not both uncomfortable and inelegant, even indecorous, and that, too must be part of the point of such occasions.

"You mean *you* are, sir!" Flora was once again taken aback at the playfulness of her voice. "But forgive me, I am not doing my feminine duty as you have so bravely carried out your masculine one." He gave a little snort to acknowledge the teasing, and Flora returned to the basket. She retrieved the food in random order, and they stopped from time to time to consume whatever she had found: the tongue with the plum pudding, the cold beef and pickles with the Dundee cake. So involved were they in eating that Mr. Pilkins forgot the claret till they had almost finished the Stilton, but he insisted that this was in any case the best time to drink it.

"To your health, Miss Burlap," he said, raising his glass, "and to our future together."

A gust of wind arose at the same time, tearing the napkin from Flora's lap and making her once more aware of how cold and wet she was. By now the sensation had lost the charm of novelty. "Sir," she said, "I am not sure I can with complete confidence drink such a toast."

If the remark sounded crushing in her own ears, it did not dent his self-esteem in the slightest. "Say not so, Miss Burlap, say not so. Please, I beg you, look on the wine when it is red, and you will find your confidence much increased. Everything, Miss Burlap, looks rosier through a glass of claret." He drained his at a single gulp and poured himself another. "May I refill your glass?" He moved towards her on hands and knees, clearing a path among plates and leftovers as he went, and raising new escarpments in the blanket which hindered his progress.

"I have not tasted this one yet. And I do not think it is wise for us to drink too much, sir." She glanced towards the road, where Thomas appeared to be dozing in the chaise.

"Well, taste, please, I implore you. It will give you courage, as I find it is giving it to me."

"I am not sure I require courage," said Flora, but took a small sip of the claret anyway. "Do you not find the weather rather chilly, sir?"

"I did, but food heats the blood. I am now perfectly comfortable." He had halted his approach, and was sitting about a yard from her, not facing her but parallel, his knees drawn up, holding the glass in one hand and the bottle in the other. "Wine also heats the blood," he added, taking another gulp.

"So I gather," Flora said.

At this Mr. Pilkins seemed for the first time to detect the disharmony between them which had begun with his toast. "I am not inebriated, Miss Burlap, I assure you. I have drunk very little so far. It is only that your company and the pleasurable exercise, and this fine repast, and above all your delightful company…" He was stammering a little, and once again drained his glass by way of a conclusion to his rambling sentence. "There are some primroses over there under the birches," he said. "Will you excuse me a moment while I go and pick them for you?"

"Please do not," Flora said, then, aware that she sounded harsh, added, "I always think wild flowers are best enjoyed where they are, as part of nature, don't you?"

"As you wish," he said, not in the least affronted, and took another large sip of claret. "The woods are lovely in spring, are they not?"

He did not seem to require a reply other than gazing appreciatively at the ghostly trunks of the birches and the haze of new green growth around their bases, which Flora accordingly did.

"It is a lovely name, Flora," Mr. Pilkins went on. "It makes you seem part of nature yourself, the Flora of the woods."

"I have never given much thought to the meaning, Mr. Pilkins," she said.

He took another gulp of wine. "And Flora Pilkins, how would that sound, do you think?" he said quickly, not looking at her, then turned his head and stared full in her face, awaiting her reply.

"Oh," Flora said. "I think it sounds horrible!"

Probably he did not even hear her, for he had put down the bottle and glass, both of which fell over, spilling their contents over the already damp blanket, and leapt the remaining yard between them in an attempted embrace. His right hand brushed against her shoulder, his left against her skirts. Flora, her hands full (glass in one, plate of cheese and crackers in the other) was unable to defend herself and collapsed, scattering comestibles. Mr. Pilkins lost his purchase on her person and the rug at the same time. He landed with his head in her lap, and was immediately calm again, as if that situation had been his aim all along. Flora took a deep breath and tried to rearrange herself and sit up but only got so far as resting her upper body on her elbows. "Sir," she said, and her voice sounded strange to her, for she knew she was repeating a phrase she had only come across in novels, which made her feel momentarily like a fictional character rather than a woman of flesh and blood, "you forget yourself!"

A groan came from somewhere deep in her skirts. "Oh," Mr. Pilkins said, "you do well to reprove me, madam!"

This left her with nothing to say, so she continued breathing deeply and trying to recover her composure. Mr. Pilkins groaned again.

"I wish I *could* forget myself," he said. "Then I might not make such a catastrophe of things. Can you forgive me, Miss Burlap?"

She was not sure if he was asking to be forgiven for assaulting her or for doing so unsuccessfully, but his request did at least give her the opportunity to negotiate. "I will forgive you, Mr. Pilkins, if you will only"—she had been going to say *unhand me*, another phrase she had read in novels, and then realized just in time that his hands were no longer in contact with her—"unhead me," she concluded, to her own dismay.

"What?"

"Um, if you could lift your head, and allow me to resume my normal posture, I'm sure… That's better."

"I am afraid I have made everything rather damp," he said, struggling to his feet and brushing at the crumbs on his trouser-legs.

"Oh, it is nothing." She looked round: the blanket had twisted over on itself and resembled a large ribbon incongruously imposed on the forest floor. A large and a small red wine stain disfigured the tartan. Crackers and cheese were scattered among the dead leaves. "I suppose I had better tidy up."

"I will help you." They worked in silence for a few minutes, then Mr. Pilkins exclaimed, "Hallo, what's this?"

She turned and saw him holding out his hand towards her. On the palm was the ruby she had received from Hastings. "Oh," she said, "it must have fallen from the pocket of my dress in the confusion. Thank you, Mr. Pilkins, I should have been sorry to lose it."

"Yes," he said, giving it up to her, "but what is it?"

"I believe it is a ruby. In fact I am almost certain."

"But how did you come by it? Not, I realize," he added hastily, "that it is any concern of mine. It is just such a queer thing to find among old leaves and the crumbs of a picnic."

"Well, as a matter of fact, I was going to show it to you, Mr. Pilkins. Before events overtook us."

"I see." His tone suggested that he did not see at all, but suspected that whatever she was about to say would be bad news for him.

Flora held the folded blanket in her arms, almost as if she were embracing it, damp as it was. "I have not told you, Mr. Pilkins, that I knew, no, that I was already attached to, a young gentleman before I had the pleasure of meeting you. The ruby is a present from him."

"Attached, Miss Burlap? And what form did this attachment take?"

"We are engaged to be married. Or I suppose we are, but we have never asked my father's permission, and none but ourselves know of it."

"That is still more than I have achieved," Mr. Pilkins said. "In my case, everyone knows of it, but there is nothing for them to know. I had hoped, Miss Burlap, that today would have been the day—"

"I know what you hoped, sir, and I'm sorry. I do not think it can ever be."

"You love this other gentleman?"

She nodded.

"I see. Then all this has been a waste of time." He made a sweeping motion with his hand around the wreckage of their picnic.

"I am sorry."

"You need not be. The fault is mine." He continued staring for a moment, then sighed once and seemed to recover his composure, with unflattering rapidity, so Flora thought. "I could not compete with a present like the ruby. Though, come to think of it, it is a rather odd one. Does he intend to have it set later?"

"That," Flora said, "is what I hoped to ask you about. There is no one at home I can talk to on this subject. My brother and sister know about Hastings—"

"That is his name, Hastings?"

"Hastings Wimbury, yes, but they cannot be said to approve of him, though being young their approval is not necessary. At all events they are not persons I could approach for counsel. You are wise, sir."

Mr. Pilkins snorted.

"Yes, you are wise, and I think it must have been God, or if that is too blasphemous, then a kindly Fate that sent you to me. Sir, you cannot be my lover, but may I entreat you to be my advisor? I am sorely in need of one."

# Chapter 13

"It distresses me to see you like this, Miss Pine," Dr. Farthing said, fingering his beard.

Cassie shrugged. If there was one thing she hated worse than being unhappy, it was other people bothering her about it.

"No, no, really, I assure you," he continued, "I do my best work in a tranquil atmosphere. I am, as any spirit investigator must be, a person of some sensitivity. One must be alert in all areas of cerebral activity, the emotional as well as the rational, in order to make the accurate distinctions between hoax and true manifestation that are my stock-in-trade. Unless I am at my most acute, how can I distinguish between ectoplasm and luminous vegetable fibres, spirit voice and puppeteer's swozzle? And there is a sympathy in my nature that vibrates in time to your own despondency and makes it hard to concentrate."

"I can't see as that's my fault."

"I did not say it was." He gave one of his unfocused smiles, that always seemed to radiate outwards in all directions rather than being aimed at her, as if he was pleased with the world in general. "Would you perhaps like to talk about it?"

"No, sir, if you don't mind. Can't we just get on with the work?"

"Very well, if you are sure you can give it your full attention. I have a meeting tomorrow morning with Inspector Dollis on this affair of the Acton Ghost, which seems to be interesting the police suddenly, I have no idea why. I'd be grateful if you could look out our files on prowling ghosts generally: Spring-heeled Jack, the Hammersmith Ghost, that sort of thing? It seems such a long time since we had one, I should be glad to think they were coming back into fashion. I, for my part, will prepare my faculties with a short sleep, and when I awaken I would like you to brief me on their principal characteristics. You are sure…? Never mind."

He removed his shoes and jacket, and lay on the couch in the dramatic posture he always assumed, which sometimes made Cassie wonder if his sleep was feigned, lying on his back with one arm dangling over the side of the couch and the other flung across his face, palm upward. In this position, though his eyes were closed, he did none of the things Cassie normally associated with sleep; there was no snoring or sibilant breathing, no sighing, moaning or restless changes of position. He made her think of a gaslamp that had been suddenly extinguished, though there were no gaslamps in this windowless room. She was always tempted to stand over him making faces or waving her arms to see if he retained any awareness of his surroundings, but lacked the courage. Instead she would get on quietly with the task he had given her to do, feeling his silence and immobility as a companionable presence until he woke exactly half an hour later, after which he usually seemed more querulous than before, as if the sleep had made him feel worse.

She walked over to the filing cabinet and started sorting through it. There was very little relating to prowling ghosts in the lower drawers, which were the ones she had tamed with her personal filing system. That meant she had to open the top one, which contained files from before her period of employment, still in the chaotic state she suspected Farthing really preferred. Some were records he had collected in his Oxford days, the cuttings out of order and sometimes not even labelled with date and source. Some were pasted to sheets of foolscap, others now floated free, with just the yellowish accretions of hardened glue on the obverse to show where they were once attached. Here, too, was the decanter of brown sherry he kept for entertaining clients and, beside it, the small revolver that had given her such a shock the first time she opened this drawer. It was another memento of Oxford, what Dr. Farthing called his werewolf gun, and still, he assured her, kept loaded, in case he should ever be called on to investigate a werewolf. The bullets were sterling silver—he had melted them down himself from the snapped-off figures of the apostles on an old set of spoons, as he had explained with a mixture of pride and embarrassment that made her see what he must have been like as an undergraduate. He had never been called upon to use it, but you never knew.

She took the files over to her desk and began to look through them, peering in the dim light which made this room feel more like a bedchamber than an office. The Hammersmith Ghost had only one file, which was convenient, although manifestations had occurred during at least two distinct periods, in the first years of the century and again in the 1820s. Here were the files relating to the Peckham Ghost, the Dundee Ghost and the New Forest Ghost, together with several slimmer files, and another labelled Ghosts, Miscellaneous, which she could search for mentions of prowling habits.

Here was a cutting yellower than most, almost brown, and so brittle that fragments of it broke off between her fingers as she picked it up. The antiquated typeface was still readable, though:

> On the 15th of December last, about ten in the evening, some servants belonging to a brewhouse in the neighbourhood were returning with a friend from the outskirts into the town, when they were met with the Ghost, dressed in what they described to resemble the hide of a calf, with a pair of enormously large horns and cloven feet. The men not altogether liking the appearance of the intruder turned about and ran off, but the Ghost was too nimble for the drayman whom he overtook, seized him by the throat, and nearly choked him. The fright, together with the ill usage, threw the poor fellow into a fever from which he is but lately recovered.

The man had apparently been assaulted by the ghost of a cow! Though it was clear that it had the figure of a human along with its horns, hide, and hoofs, and it had tried to strangle him with unbovine hands. It seemed a transparent imposture, and it was hard to imagine what it was designed to achieve. There were animal ghosts, Cassie knew, faithful dogs that howled over their masters' graves, the horses that pulled phantom coaches, but she had never heard of a ghostly cow before, so the impersonator was pretending to be something new to supernatural science. She was inclined to think she would be more afraid of the living specimen.

Here was another, a little less discoloured and relatively intact:

> Two or three nights ago, the Monster made his appearance at Bradmore, which is at the back of Hammersmith, towards Shepherd's Bush. It opens to the fields, many lonely paths leading to it; but as there are no lamps, any person may soon be lost in the surrounding darkness, and elude the most vigilant pursuit. He went to a small house kept by a gardener named White, opening the front door by lifting the latch. The wife was there—the front parlour being a species of chandler's shop—and she was not a little affrighted to behold in the door-way a strangely and ghostly dressed figure with a large ugly mask and glaring eyeballs. Some flame was then emitted, after which the Ghost exclaimed, "Good night, farewell!" and decamped with supernatural rapidity.

Again, it was an obvious impersonation, as even the writer of the newspaper account suggested, with the use of the word "mask". "Some flame was then emitted" was an enigmatic phrase: did it emerge from the mouth, as if the Monster were a dragon, or from some other part of the body? And how did the impersonator generate it: with a gas lamp, perhaps? In any case, the ghost, for all its fiery appearance, was remarkably well-mannered, wishing the woman goodnight instead of trying to strangle her.

And here, correctly labelled, was an account of the New Forest Ghost from the *Hampshire Telegraph* of 26 December 1824:

> He said that a tall man dressed in a rough frieze coat, with a mask on his face representing the head of a

swine, walked alongside him, through Houndwell, for a considerable distance, without addressing him. Suddenly stopping, he threw open his upper garment, and shewed his body, clad in a tight white jerkin, with ribs and all the paraphernalia of death traced on him with phosphorus. The figure stood a moment fronting him, then, before he could recover from his surprise, suddenly darted off with great swiftness.

Another animal-headed monster—these ghosts from earlier times had something of the character of pagan gods. But how to explain the victim, who had walked with this pig-headed being beside him "for a considerable distance" without thinking to challenge it or try to escape? Had he thought there was nothing out of the ordinary about a little supernatural companionship? Perhaps it was no more than you expected if you chose to walk along lonely country roads at night. Once again though, the author of the article had no doubt that the apparition was counterfeit, the bones painted on to his costume with phosphorus. Were any prowling ghosts real?

Dr. Farthing gave a short sigh, replaced his spectacles and sat up. "So, Miss Pine," he said, his voice manifesting no vestige of sleep. "What is your conclusion?"

She had been daydreaming over the files rather than studying them, she realized guiltily. "I hardly know," she began, then, seeing that his face showed a slight disappointment, hastened to qualify her ignorance. "I get the impression that there aren't all that many prowling ghosts nowadays."

"No, that was what I suspected. Anything else?"

"Well, sir, from what I can see, none of them was, well, real."

"Real ghosts are rare, Miss Pine. We have established that—that is, if they exist at all."

"That isn't what I mean, sir. I mean more that they don't even try to be, and nobody thinks it of them, which is a queer thing to say of any ghost."

"It is indeed. Go on."

"There was one of them with the head of a cow, horns and all, and another with a pig's head and one with a mask and flames coming out of it, and I don't know what else besides. And all I can say is that I never heard of a ghost that looked like that, and it's hard to understand what they were trying to be a ghost *of*, if you understand me. If I saw a man with a pig's head I wouldn't think it was, I don't know, the spirit of my dead grandfather."

"No, but would you be frightened?"

Cassie thought about it. "I don't think a person can know in advance whether they'd be frightened or not."

"Because there is an element of surprise in fear? True enough."

She continued examining her inner being, an exercise that had been foreign to her before she started working with Dr. Farthing, but which he seemed to regard as one of the duties of her employment. "But when I read about them, I feel, I don't know, a sort of shiveriness, which I suppose you might call fear. Fear in advance, you might say."

"Good, a foretaste of fear. In spite of the fact that these beings are evidently illusions?"

"No, sir, *because* of that."

He frowned, and she wondered if she had been more subtle this time than he expected of her. "People more terrifying than ghosts?" he said finally. "Yes, I suppose there is something in that."

"People pretending to be what they aren't. Real people making themselves unreal. It's like you can't trust anybody's reality at all any more."

"Well, you are right about one thing: the theatricality is part of the power. It is as if the whole thing is a performance, don't you think? And perhaps one reason these onlookers are afraid is paradoxically because they are *expected* to be afraid. It is the part assigned to them in the drama." He reached for his shoes and began putting them on. "As for the animal heads, they are not as unusual as you might think. Supernatural animals are a tradition of long standing in rural areas, and particularly to be met with by night-time travellers. Did not the man with the pig's head walk beside his victim on the road?"

Cassie nodded.

"There you are, a night-time traveller. These spirits are often companionable in that way. Turn your head to one side and you may see a fiery ball the size of a pumpkin rolling beside you, or perhaps a roaring flame, a round bowl, a goose, a dog or a lovely young woman. Or indeed a fellow with the head of a pig. It is all part of the masquerade of rural life."

"But mostly it wasn't rural," Cassie said. "One of them was in the New Forest, but most of the others were in places like Hammersmith and Liverpool and Dundee."

"Ah, but one does not get away from the countryside merely by moving to the town. Or indeed by building houses over the fields. As the town grows, it absorbs the life of the country, spirits, goblins and all. Tell me something, Miss Pine—were there any thefts associated with these impostures?"

"Thefts, sir?"

"I wondered if the ghosts stole anything, or if they were content with a little physical assault now and then?"

"To tell the truth, sir, I don't really know yet. I haven't finished studying the files."

"Well, then, let us proceed. I'll take some of them and we will look through them together." He rubbed his hands. "I do enjoy a change of ghost occasionally, don't you, Miss Pine?"

# Chapter 14

When Hastings opened the door to the upper room at the Duke of Buckingham, he found that the Count had not yet arrived. A bottle of wine stood on the table as before with the cork placed on a saucer beside it in case, he assumed, either of them wished to sniff it to gauge the wine's condition. Unsure whether it would be bad manners to pour himself a glass in the absence of his host, but feeling in need of a drink, he did go over to the cork and sniff it as a compromise. The smell of the sticky residue was even stronger than he remembered; there was something rotten about it, an odour of ink and stale fish mingled with the cloves he had detected before. He shuddered and then, oddly, felt a little better, as if braced by the olfactory shock. At least it isn't Chlorodyne, he thought, and the memory of those nights in Miss Pine's chamber floated briefly before his mind's eye, remote and harmless, as if they had happened to someone else. He reached for the bottle; the glass had a grainy feel unlike that of a civilized claret or port bottle and the label had an archipelago of black stains on it, no doubt from some long-ago cellar catastrophe.

Before he could pour, he heard a footstep outside, and put down the bottle quickly. The Count hurried in and took Hastings's right hand in both of his own. "Pardon, my friend, a myriad pardons! There are many calls on my attention at present."

"It is nothing, Count."

"Oh, but it is a great deal. I have been consulting with persons of importance from my country, but there is no one of greater importance than yourself. You are not drinking? You should not have waited. Let us sit."

With a full glass before him, Hastings felt slightly sick at the thought of drinking it, but forced himself to take a small sip when the Count proposed a toast to "The Melancholy Dane." The taste was not as bad as the smell.

"You are still more sad than previously, I think?" the Count said.

"I will not burden you with my sorrows."

"It distresses me that you have any, a young man of such gifts. But in truth I wonder if you will really make such a fine Hamlet as I have always thought if you are not prepared to regale an audience with the minutiae of your misery." There was something a little savage about his smile that had not been apparent in their earlier acquaintance.

Hastings took another sip. "I don't think the troubles of a very ordinary young man can be of much interest to you, Count. Here, I return this, with my thanks. I have no further use for it now."

He reached in his pocket, took out the ruby, and looked at it for a moment before placing it on the table between them.

"But this is yours, Mr. Wimbury!"

"Thank you, Count, I do not want it. When you were so kind as to make me a present of it, I was overjoyed for one reason only. I wished to give it to… to a young lady of my acquaintance."

"And she has given it back?"

"She writes, and I cannot blame her for it, that it would be wrong of her to accept it from a gentleman to whom she is not officially engaged. It stung me rather. From the way she writes it is as if all that we have been to each other is as nothing to her."

"I see." The Count picked it up quickly and slipped it into the outer pocket of his jacket. "But come, it cannot be so bad. You are young—"

"You keep saying I am young, Count, and excuse me, but I wish you wouldn't. It is not something I can help, and I don't think I will feel any better about it when I am older. In fact, I dread getting old, alone and unloved as I am now." He broke off, remembering that he could not exactly call himself unloved. Miss Pine was another of the causes of his distress; indeed, much of it could be attributed to the exhaustion consequent upon delaying his nightly returns to Halcyon House as long as possible in the hope, usually thwarted, of avoiding another encounter with her on the landing.

The Count reached across and patted him on the hand. "I see I am no help. But you have another love, do you not? The stage. Would you like to know what I was discussing with my Cimmerian friends that delayed me so badly? They are most exhilarated to hear that you have accepted my invitation to come to our country. I believe the whole population, or at least all those of any importance, the Dwellers in Darkness as we call ourselves (only it sounds better in Cimmerian) will soon be awaiting your arrival with the greatest impatience."

Hastings shrugged, but said nothing.

"Does not Hamlet himself know the pains of love? You will be able to express your passion all the more vividly when you are with your Cimmerian Ophelia, a fine actress, I assure you—as a matter of fact she is my own daughter, and has been studying the part for several weeks."

"Yes, I shall be expressing my passion for her in the dark!"

"Not the least appropriate place to express passion, my friend, as I perhaps know better than you. But as I have told you, it will not be wholly dark, and the contrast between brilliance and obscurity is the whole point of this unique production, of *your* unique production, I should say. Or do you prefer the Villiers *Hamlet* and your important responsibilities in that?"

Hastings snorted. "For the ghost scene, they have made some magic lantern slides of Mr. Barnes, and now we see him walking on the battlements some ten feet tall, with the stones of the wall clearly visible through his armour. It is an impressive spectacle, I admit, but then the real Barnes has to come on to speak his lines, and the effect is as if the poor chap has shrunk. But he still comes off better than Mr. Rowlands. No amount of green fire and limelight can make up for the dullness of *his* performance! If I am a little down in the mouth, it is this, as much as anything, that accounts for it. ''Tis not al-one my ink-y cloak, good Mo-ther,' " he recited in a hollow singsong. "He goes through the whole performance without changing the tone or volume of his speech, up one syllable, down the next, just like that: 'Whe-ther 'tis nob-ler in the mind to suf-fer / The slings and ar-rows of out-rage-ous For-chin.' "

The Count nodded. "And you would be so much better?"

"Do you doubt it?"

"I, no, but it seems you do."

Hastings sighed and took another sip. "I have already agreed to take part in your production, Count, rather against my better judgement, but you have the word of a gentleman. I don't know what more you can ask of me. I will make love to your daughter and tell her to get her to a nunnery, though as she has spent her life to date in a cave I am not sure she will see much of a difference. It is just that I still do not understand how this production is going to work."

"The wine is growing on you, yes? I knew that it would. A little more? Not yet? You are right, of course, that the obstacles are formidable, but you, I am convinced, are the man to overcome them. Who else could I have found with both the talent to act the part and the technical knowledge to light it?"

"You overrate my abilities in that area, Count. I am merely an apprentice."

"But you work with light and fire every day, indeed every night. Besides, I know you to be a man of quick intelligence, and one, moreover, whose motivation will drive him to overcome all obstacles."

"But I have never been to your country! It would be hard enough for me to manage the lighting of an entire theatre in the West End, but in—forgive me—a little out-of-the-way place on the edge of Europe… Do you even have a gas supply?"

"Ah, now you are talking business, I like this. Yes, there is gas in my country—do you think it only exists in England and France and the other nations that call themselves civilized? Where does gas come from, do you even know?"

"Coal, I believe. I have never given it much thought. I think they burn the coal and collect the gas from it somehow."

"Precisely. And where does coal come from?"

"From underground—oh, I see."

"Yes, Mr. Wimbury, I *live* underground. My people have spent centuries, millennia, in the interior of the earth. There is not much we do not know about its contents. That ruby I gave you is almost valueless to us, for we have so many like it, and other treasures, far greater, diamonds, sapphires, emeralds, gold, silver. Coal is the least of them, and we have never cared for it much because the smoke produces a rather choking and unsavoury effect, but we are learning better now. To tell the truth we do not need to rely on it solely, for there are great reservoirs of gas in some deep and remote regions of our subterranean empire. We have been looking for some time now into ways of tapping them, and we are close to a solution. Oh, my dear friend, do you believe that you and I are the only persons involved in this project? No, you are important, as I said, and I am most happy to have found you, but I have colleagues working for me everywhere. There are Cimmerian agents all over London, all over Great Britain, in fact, negotiating for the resources we need. Scientific and industrial assistance will not be wanting; we are consulting experts at Oxford and Cambridge as well as in your great industrial corporations. All in support of a production of *Hamlet*, you say? No, of course not, that is merely the first beacon that will start the chain of fires that light up the Cimmerian night. It is my dream, the dream of the party I lead, the Party of Light in Cimmeria, to bring the wonders of gaslight to our entire empire. *Hamlet* will show that it is possible. And you will be the man on whom that first miraculous ray falls."

Hastings gulped at his wine without thinking, and did not even notice the taste. "It seems impossible to believe. But what can you want from me, apart from my histrionic ability?"

"As I said, the greater part of our effort is taking place elsewhere, in academe, in factories, in the offices of great leaders and politicians. But any small contribution you can make will help us. The plan is an ambitious one, and there are many sceptics in my country who must be impressed if they are to give us their support. If I, or my collaborators back home in

Cimmeria, could demonstrate to them some of the brilliancies of which your science is capable, it would aid us greatly. For this, I would need—" He stopped and looked quizzically at Hastings, as if doubting whether it was worth proceeding.

"Say on, Count, I implore you."

"A box of green fire would be most useful. For a start."

# Chapter 15

The cab dropped them off on the corner of Woodbridge Street. The scene of the incident had been roped off, so that they could not get any closer, and the cabbie had to turn his vehicle round in order to leave. It was a cold morning with fog lingering in the air, and Cassie was regretting that the investigation was taking place outside; she would have been glad of a nice cosy séance in these conditions. A constable greeted them at the boundary and raised the rope for them with some ceremony. The roped-off area comprised portions of several streets, and it was not easy to see where to go, since there were little knots of constables scattered around, looking intently at pavements and walls, and no sign of Inspector Dollis in any of them. Dr. Farthing did not seem to care; he was sniffing in the way Cassie had seen him do on their earlier investigations.

"There, do you smell that, Miss Pine?"

"Fireworks, sir?"

"Yes, the dominant aroma is that of saltpetre, one of the principal constituents of gunpowder, and used also in pyrotechnics. The hoaxer has been deploying his coloured fires again. I wonder which one—not the green, I think; I know the distinctive coppery savour of that by now. Probably the mauve one that was reported in Highgate last week. Of course, there is no reason why they should not use any colour they like, but I have a feeling the hoaxer will continue to avoid reds and yellows as being too warm and comforting. Oh, hallo, Inspector. You have summoned us for another haunting?"

Inspector Dollis had indeed come over from somewhere to greet them, but had been distracted by a succession of constables coming up to ask questions. He was now consulting with an assistant in plain clothes, that is, the same fawn greatcoat and bowler hat that Dollis wore, as if plain clothes were only another kind of uniform.

"Oh, sorry, sir. Yes, I think we may fairly say it was our most extensive haunting yet as well as our most metropolitan one, as it were. Clerkenwell, sir, Clerkenwell," he repeated with great satisfaction, no doubt feeling that the central location of this apparition made both it and him more important.

"What colour fire?"

"Purple, sir."

"I thought as much. We've only had one haunting of that colour so far, and the hoaxer must have a supply to use up. In any case, I think I'd prefer a purple haunting to a green one given the choice, wouldn't you, Miss Pine?"

"He could use both, sir."

"I doubt if he has unlimited supplies. Anyway, I think that extravagance would have ruined the chilling atmosphere he was seeking to establish. He may be using fireworks but not for the purpose of entertainment. How did it begin, Inspector?"

"He started in Wynyatt Street, as far as we can make out, at about eleven o'clock, where he was seen by three witnesses, moved along there to St. John Street, and then by way of a couple of linked alleys to Gloucester Way. We lose sight of him for a while then, and indeed I should say that his appearances was always somewhat sporadic, sir, until at about ten to midnight the spirit manifests himself in a little courtyard off Clerkenwell Road where he burns quite brightly for some ten minutes."

"Any burglaries associated with this one?"

"None reported so far, sir. I get the feeling this was a sort of trial run. There was a pedestrian robbed in Gloucester Way, but he insists that it wasn't the spirit as robbed him. Said he was running from the spirit and banged into some other fellow, an accomplice I dare say, who took the opportunity to relieve him of his wallet. He says, and this is peculiar, that the phantom was not such as would have any use for money, as having no substance to speak of. He seemed a good deal more distressed by the ghostly experience than he was put out by having his money pinched."

"So the apparition on this occasion was not obviously a man in animal costume or wearing a sheet and a mask? A more realistic ghost?"

"I don't know whether you'd say more realistic or less realistic, sir, seeing as a ghost isn't real in the first place. The way he told it, this ghost was less real than normal, and in that respect more like a ghost, if you take my meaning. He says, and the other witnesses confirm it, that the figure was such as you could see right through it. And it wavered, that was our Gloucester Way witness's word."

"Wavered? Now that is interesting. What does that make you think of, Miss Pine?"

"Ectoplasm, sir?"

"Most of the ectoplasm I have come across in my work has been a material substance, manufactured from cotton. Could this have been some kind of gauzy fabric, do you think? It would not have been difficult to manufacture. The hoaxer would use luminous paint to make it glow, then it would just be a case of imparting movement. It did move, didn't it, Inspector?"

"It did, sir, but only a few yards as far as I can make out. Then it would disappear and turn up again somewhere else a little later on."

"A puppet, perhaps, mounted on wheels, and given a bit of a push. No, more probably towed by means of a rope. What form did it take, Inspector?"

"The phantom was that of a man, sir, exceedingly tall, and wearing what appeared to be a suit of armour. He wore his visor up and his face was chalk-white, as they describe it. And all witnesses agree that you could see the walls of the neighbouring houses quite distinctly through his body, metal and all."

"That don't sound like ectoplasm," Cassie said.

"No, you could hardly make armour out of gauze, nor anything quite so detailed. But the imagination will often amplify the experience. Perhaps the witnesses saw something much vaguer in the darkness, and then added the other details themselves. It was dark, I take it, Inspector."

"Yes, sir. The gaslamps had gone out as usual."

"But did all the witnesses describe the same figure?" Cassie asked.

"Pretty much so, miss."

"Then it cannot have been their imagination, can it, Dr. Farthing?"

"I suppose you're right. We are dealing with a quite sophisticated hoaxer, by the look of things, and one who has gone to a lot of trouble, coloured fire, elaborate puppet show and so on, for rather small financial gain on this occasion. Are you still convinced that this mastermind of yours is behind it?"

"Mastermind?" Cassie said. "You never said anything about a mastermind, sir."

"We don't know his name," Dollis said. "We really don't know much about the fellow at all, not even whether he is a home-grown villain or a foreigner. Our sources indicate that he was a stranger to them until very recently. He arrived on the scene with a good deal of ready money, which he started splashing about to build up an empire, so to speak. You must of read about the Bond Street jewel robbery, miss? He, or rather his associates, got away with 10,000 guineas' worth of gems, set and unset."

Cassie nodded.

"Well, that was the first job he ran. We think he did it mostly to impress the underworld, since he's never done anything on that scale since, and I don't believe he needs the money. I think he's an amateur criminal, a man as has money by right. That's always been our nightmare, a gentleman mastermind, born to rule and using his natural authority for criminal purposes."

"Hm," Dr. Farthing said, "he must be quite an impresario. I should so like to meet him. I wish just once I could manage to be present for one of his performances. So ingenious the way he contrives to have the gas fail at the right time. He must have agents at the gas company, as well as in the underworld."

"That's the worst of it, to my mind," Inspector Dollis said. "Well, I am interviewing their employees, and if I find anything to the purpose, I will nip round to your office and let you know. I always appreciate a drop of werewolf's blood, as you know, doctor." This was his regular joke about the contents of the top drawer of Farthing's filing cabinet—he regarded the werewolf gun as a benign eccentricity, and was always glad of a glass or two of the sherry on his visits. "A ghost is something and nothing, if you ask me, and I wouldn't normally bother myself with investigating it, especially as the sums taken has been no more than is lost in the normal course of London criminality, and on this occasion considerably less. But if you can't trust the gas supply, what can you trust?"

# Chapter 16

Hastings had finished the first glass and was about to pour himself another when he heard the Count's footsteps outside. It was true that the black wine was an acquired taste. Hastings would drink half the bottle now at their regular meetings. It did not seem to make him drunk, or no drunker than he felt most of the time these days. A note would be delivered for him at the theatre stating the day and time, and he would arrive at least ten minutes before his host, and pour himself a glass and try to focus his mind on the project they were to talk about. Most of their conversations were about the forthcoming production of *Hamlet*, which was both irritating and embarrassing, since Hastings had given little thought to it. Sometimes the Count would ask him to recite a speech, and then his reaction was most gratifying. "Yes," he said once, "I feel the nuances you bring to the role. This is not mere bombast, but a real man trembling on the border between sanity and madness. You will be the supreme Hamlet of your generation." Even praise such as this was beginning to pall, however. The lines had long been automatic with Hastings and he was not trying out any new interpretation. If he did sound as if he was going mad, that was perhaps because he was. *Well*, he said to himself, *that is the sign of the true artist—I am bringing the anguish of my soul to the part.* All the same, he could remember what it felt like to play Hamlet without any anguish at all, and he had preferred it.

As for the Cimmerian production, how could he plan it? The Count would occasionally drop hints about the facilities available, the size and shape of the theatre ("It is a natural amphitheatre of rock, greater than any the Athenians would have known. And just think, Wimbury"—he had dropped the *Mr.*—"your Ophelia will have a real river to drown herself in!"), and the likely response of the audience, but it was still impossible to picture it. The stage would be constructed from stone, since wood was in short supply and mostly reserved for fires; that meant there would be no trapdoor for the Ghost to rise out of and disappear into, but as the Count said, what need was there of trapdoors when there were so many tunnels? "You must think of the production," he said, "as an arrangement of stone, light, and voices. Oh, do not worry, Wimbury, as soon as you see my country (though *see* is not exactly the right word), all your plans will become clear to you."

This meeting would be a difficult one. Stage-fright was a thing almost unknown to Hastings: in his Reigate Playhouse days, he had merely been aware of a heightened intensity in all his sensations before going on stage, as if a gas burner had been lit somewhere inside him, but now he understood what those actors who sat around before a production head in hands must be going through, a hollow misery that made one want to be anywhere else but here, anybody but oneself. He knew he must speak before the Count did. He had fallen into a pattern of letting him have the first line, and dictate the course of the conversation from then on. To prevent this, he had prepared some lines for himself and learned them in bed at night. His cue was to be the opening of the door:

*HASTINGS (rising): It isn't good enough, Count. I must have the dates of the production, and I must have them at once!*

Of course, he had not been able to compose any lines for the Count to speak, which made his own responses somewhat uncertain, but he was prepared for a little ad-libbing if necessary; most of the scene was to consist of his own soliloquy, in which he insisted that he would not do any more fetching and carrying (as he put it to himself) until he had not only the production dates, but the details of the travel arrangements (preferably with tickets), the names of the cast, a full inventory of the resources of the theatre, if theatre it could be called, in fact some solid evidence that the Cimmerian *Hamlet* was really going to take place.

In the event he missed his cue, although it was really the Count's fault for speaking out of turn: "Ah, Wimbury. You are becoming a true Cimmerian!" He gave a pleasant nod in the direction of the empty glass.

"It's not good enough, Count," Hastings said rapidly.

"What? I thought you were beginning to like it. You are certainly consuming it more enthusiastically than previously."

"I don't mean the wine, I mean—"

"Wait, wait!" The Count held up his hands, smiling. "I am hardly even in the room yet, and you are a whole glass ahead of me, young man. I have the honour of my nation to uphold in this little matter of drinking."

"But I have much to say!"

"I am sure you have, and you shall have plenty of opportunity to say it, I promise." He took his seat and poured wine for them both.

"Oh, you are always promising things," Hastings said, not only deviating from his lines but slipping out of the characterization he had planned for the scene. He had intended to be forceful rather than sulky; the Count had a knack of making him both feel and act younger than he really was.

"On the contrary, it is you who are promising—more than promising, I should say." The Count nodded in appreciation of his own compliment. "But let me tell you my news: Ophelia is now perfect in her lines. I heard from her mother today. I do not think you will be disappointed in her. In fact, I must confess, I harbour a secret wish... but no, it will not be secret if I tell you!"

"Really, Count, I should expect nothing less. What is more important is—" Hastings broke off. "It is strange you refer to her as Ophelia. She is your own daughter—why do you not use her real name?"

The Count laughed. "Oh, you could not pronounce it, Wimbury. That is, if *I* were to pronounce it, the sounds would mean nothing to you. Even my own name is not truly Nollo— that is a mere approximation I use in England for the sake of convenience. Let us, for the same reason, continue to refer to my dear daughter as Ophelia. Now, what was the important matter you mentioned?"

Hastings composed himself and tried to remember his lines. But it was no use; the play he had had in his head had gone altogether. He must try to struggle on in real life, making up the words as he went along. "Count, a month ago you outlined your scheme to me in this room. In all that time I have done nothing but continue my menial existence as a gas-boy, and, and, drink wine and pilfer."

The Count looked hurt. "Pilfer, is that what you call it?"

"I do not know what else to call it. I took a box of green fire for you three weeks ago, a box of amethyst fire last week…"

"I see you have been keeping accounts; that is very efficient of you. Your theatre could well afford the loss, I think. You said yourself that they did not even notice it. But for me, for us, those acquisitions were of vital importance. We had to test the efficacy of these western chemicals in the peculiar conditions of Cimmeria, and, as I told you at the time, our experiments were a complete success."

"So you won't need any more?"

"Certainly we will need more, Wimbury. We cannot manufacture such sophisticated chemicals for ourselves, rich in minerals though we are. I hope to call on you in due course—"

"That's just it, Count. You call on me for the things you want, and this performance of yours never gets any closer."

The Count raised his glass, sniffed at it and put it down again. "You were a little distressed about the magic lantern, I think?"

"A box of fire is one thing—it is all going to go up in smoke anyway—but a magic lantern is, well, a machine, and machines are valuable. And it is not just the machine, but the slides to go with it, and the gasbags and lime cylinders to power the limelight. And those slides show Mr. Barnes as the Ghost in Hamlet. If anyone were to find them, they could be traced to the theatre, and I would be suspected. In addition to which, I cannot see what use they will be in the Cimmerian production, since when the Ghost appears in the flesh the audience will be able to see perfectly well that it is not the same person. Unless, that is, you plan to kidnap Mr. Barnes and take him to Cimmeria along with me."

"We can make our own slides," the Count said, "now that we understand the mechanism. It is all, as I told you, a matter of experiment. Have patience, Wimbury. We are nearly ready for the next stage of our adventure. There are just a few more items we need."

"I am not stealing another magic lantern for you, if that's what you mean."

"Oh, you exaggerate so, Wimbury. It is the artist in you, I suppose. Even if we grant, for the sake of argument, that it was a theft rather than a sharing of knowledge, as I prefer to think of it, it was not you who took the lantern, but my own servants. All you did was open the door to them and show them where to find the equipment. They could probably have done the same without your help—you merely made the process a little more convenient."

"Then I wish they *had* done it without me."

"You are feeling guilty?"

"No," Hastings said after thinking it over, "I suppose not."

"Of course not. There is no place for guilt in art. You have no responsibility towards the Villiers Theatre, or the laws of Great Britain, or anything else but your own talent. Now do you?"

Hastings met his eyes for a second, then looked away. He tried to reply but what came out was no more than a gurgle.

"No," the Count replied for him. "I think I will refrain from asking you for another magic lantern at present. They are useful but rather conspicuous, and a second one might be missed. And there are still plenty of lime cylinders left. It is more gasbags I need. Perhaps we could arrange a delivery for Thursday night, the same time as before?"

Mr. Eweson was waiting for Hastings at the foot of the steps to the right flies. "I been looking for you, Hastings," he said.

"I had to meet somebody."

"Anything to do with the theatre?"

Nothing to do with *you*, Hastings wanted to say, but he was experiencing more difficulty than usual in speaking his lines today. "No, Mr. Eweson."

"Come and have a chat," Eweson said. He led Hastings to his office, and fussed over him while he sat down. Hastings was reminded of his schooldays. There was, he remembered, a sort of schoolmasterly behaviour that consisted of excessive kindness and that was usually preliminary to the most unpleasant punishments. Eweson had never so much as shouted at him in all his time as a gas-boy, and yet there was something about his manner that induced nervous respect, even in one of a higher social class.

"How long have you been with us now?" Eweson asked, though he knew as well as Hastings did. It was a ritual question, the kind that preceded a dissection of one's character.

"Six months, s— Mr. Eweson."

"Six months! I bet you never thought you'd last that long, did you, lad? When you first come here, you was red-hot to be an actor, wasn't you? And gas-boy would do till that came along. I'm sorry it didn't, mind."

"So am I."

"We wasn't to know, Hastings, neither of us, when we shook hands on it that day. Seems the gap between us and them is just a bit too wide to jump across, even for a man what speaks like you do. If I'd a-known that, perhaps I wouldn't of offered you the job."

"And perhaps I wouldn't have taken it."

"No, well it's all gas down the pipe, ain't it? In a manner of speaking, boy, I am responsible for you taking a job of work what's beneath your station, and therefore I blame myself."

"It's not your fault, Mr. Eweson," Hastings said, "though, come to think of it, I'm not quite sure what you're referring to."

"What I has to remember," said Eweson, looking at the ceiling and now apparently talking to himself, "is that a gentleman don't look on a job of work the way the rest of us does. For such as us, it's what we lives by, and therefore you could say it's also what we're made of. Do you follow me, lad?" he added, waking up to Hastings's continued presence.

"Not really."

"Fish-tail burners, batwing burners, tee-pieces, pipes, valves, yes, even limelight machines. They matter to us, Mr. Wimbury, because they're *part* of us."

"But, Mr. Eweson—"

"If it was anyone else," Eweson said, suddenly stern, "I would say out you go. And if it was anyone else, that'd be the worst thing I could say, because it'd mean they wasn't a gas-man, or a gas-boy, any more, and that was *all* they was. But when a chap ain't a gas-boy in the first place, it's another matter."

"I don't understand."

"Now you, being educated, have no doubt studied the arithmetic, am I right? Me, I never studied nothing much, though I seem to remember spending some time in a classroom many years since. Not sure if the arithmetic was part of it, but I *can* count, Mr. Wimbury. A box of green and a box of amethyst, wasn't it?"

"I don't know what you're talking about."

"And I turned a blind eye to it, because I thought, well, the poor fellow is entitled to something, as we ain't paying him the sort of money he's used to. Mind you, I was a bit taken aback, as you might say, because I always thought gentlemen was above that sort of thing. Oh, I don't mean the taking what don't belong to you, because you're as human as anyone else, but selling it on the market, as it were, well that's trade, ain't it?"

"But why should you think it was me? Anyway," Hastings added, stung, "I didn't sell it."

"There you are, you see, it *was* you, I knew it was. I know everything what goes on in this theatre, and I know the characters of them as works for me. And the fact is, I like you, Hastings, only I don't think you really belongs here, as I have said more than once. So you could have a couple of boxes of fire and welcome to them as far as I was concerned, but a magic lantern is too much."

"A magic lantern!"

"Now you ain't going to lie to me, are you? I thought gentlemen was above that, too. Now the thing is, Mr. Wimbury, we're going to need that magic lantern, what with another fairy play being planned, seeing as *The Amethyst Princess* was the most profitable show we ever done. And a fairy play needs the full six lanterns, and here we've got only five, and it's me what'll have to explain to Mr. Roderick where the sixth one has got to."

Hastings thought of several things to say, and discarded all of them.

"I like you, Hastings, and it seems you like being around the theatre, even if you don't belong in it, so I'll tell you what I'll do." He patted Hastings on the shoulder. "You bring back that lantern and the lime cylinders and the couple of gasbags that went with it, and we'll say no more about it. That's on condition that you never do anything of the sort again. You so much as filch a spoonful of fire and that's it for you, my lad. Now I can't say fairer than that, can I? Well, can I?"

Hastings sat on in silence.

"Does we have a deal, Hastings?"

"I can't, Mr. Eweson," he said at last. "I haven't got it."

Eweson sighed. "But you know where it is?"

"Yes, sir. Or at least, I have some idea where. I know a man—but never mind that."

"And can you get it back for me? Because if not—"

"I don't know," Hastings said. "But I will ask him. I'm sure he will listen to reason. He is, after all, a gentleman."

# Chapter 17

For once, Mr. Wimbury was present at dinner. The other residents were bemused by the new Wimbury, the one who stared sullenly at his plate instead of letting his eyes dance round the room, and they continued to address remarks to him, even though each one elicited nothing more than a *yes*, *no* or *indeed*, grunted out in the voice of one who has just been woken from a deep sleep and is working up the energy to resent it. Miss Hartston, in particular, never gave up on him. "The weather is unseasonably chilly, Mr. Wimbury."

"Yes."

"I do hope you are not susceptible to colds? I myself am not susceptible to colds, having worked in the emporium so long. One becomes used to everything the public can inflict on one. On the other hand, my little nephew and niece are frequently ill, and of course when they get it my sister and her husband get it also. It is one of the misfortunes of family life."

"No."

"You must often be exposed to infection, working in the City?"

"Indeed."

Cassie said nothing, but looked pointedly at Miss Hartston from time to time, willing her to leave the poor gentleman alone. Could she not see that he was distressed? Cassie was torn between pity for his grief and anguish at the thought that his unfulfilled responsibility towards her was the cause of it. She had no desire to marry a man who would be made miserable thereby, or rather, she would think that any man who was made miserable by marrying her deserved everything he suffered, if it were only some other man whom she loved less that she did this one, which, of course, it wasn't. Still, it was some comfort that they were sharing their gloom this evening instead of her having to endure it on her own as she usually did. She just wished the others were not so insensitive to it, so... the only word she could think of was *irrelevant*, a favourite accusation of Dr. Farthing's. Observe Mr. Flewitt, chewing a mouthful of cod with every appearance of enjoyment. What was the use of cod at a time like this? If indeed it was cod, which she doubted: there was a slippery greyness that extended from the skin, which had a right to be slippery and grey, deep into the flesh, which ought to be white all through, and surely the Atlantic codfish should not have so many bones? Every diner, with one exception, was obliged to stop between mouthfuls and remove a little quiverful of them from between their lips, disguising the action as a thoughtful rub of the face or the flourish of a napkin. Only Mrs. Makepeace crunched through them in her Presbyterian way, a labour which, to judge by her expression, she regarded as penance for everyone else's sins. So dinner was undoubtedly a struggle; what Cassie resented was the relish with which her fellow residents gave themselves to it.

Retiring to the other room at least removed the irrelevancies. (The tapioca pudding had been even more of an ordeal than the counterfeit cod.) Cassie and Hastings sat on opposite sides of the room. Mr. Flewitt engaged in debate with Miss Hartston on the subject of employment. Was it seemly, he wanted to know, for a woman to neglect her family and go out to work? In so doing, he said, with a chuckle at his own logic, she was only taking the bread from another family.

"Some of us," Miss Hartston said sharply, "have little choice in the matter."

"Oh, you must not take it personally, Miss Hartston."

"I am employed, sir."

"Yes, but not by design. You said so yourself. I am referring to the women the newspaper tells us of"—and he waved his own paper to emphasize the point—"who are not satisfied with getting married and so forth."

"All the same," Miss Hartston muttered, "I wish you would not say *women* at all."

"I can't help it, ma'am. It is in the paper." He waved it again, and some pages fell out. Without rising from his chair he bent forward and began to gather them together again, reading as he grovelled in an effort to find the article he was referring to.

Cassie thought she saw a way to involve Hastings in the conversation. "For myself," she said, "I don't for a moment regret having a position. It has made me the w—, beg pardon, Miss Hartston, it has made me who I am. I was only, and I'm not ashamed to say it, the daughter of a tobacconist in Penge, and now I feel, I was going to say somebody in the world, but I don't mean that, not in a vainglorious way. I mean I know something *of* the world, which I wouldn't of if I'd of stayed home." Mr. Flewitt was now bent double, reading a detached leaf of his paper on the carpet, and holding his pince-nez in place with one hand. Miss Hartston was watching him with the expression of one who expects a renewed attack at any moment. Neither of them was listening to Cassie. As for Hastings, she could not tell what he was thinking as he sat staring in front of him with unfocused eyes. Nevertheless, honour demanded that she conclude her line of thought, which she was in danger of losing. "And I do think that a man, if he is a man, will respect that in a, in his chosen, I think the word in the Bible is *helpmeet*, isn't it?" she concluded.

"Hmph," Mr. Flewitt said. "I see there's been another of these ghost chappies walking the streets. Clerkenwell, this time. Wish I'd been there. A diaphanous, gauzy substance, it says here. We'd soon see how diaphanous it was once I'd had a go at it with my stick."

"Helpmeet," Cassie repeated softly, looking hard at Hastings in the hope the message would get through to him. He showed no sign of understanding, but sat motionless, apparently asleep with his eyes open.

"Well," Cassie said, "I think, being as I've a position to be going to in the morning, I had better be getting upstairs to my bed. You'd be surprised, Mr. Flewitt, at my responsibilities." She nodded at his paper, resisting the temptation to boast that the Clerkenwell ghost was one of the responsibilities in question.

"Surprised, ma'am?" said Mr. Flewitt, getting up awkwardly and scattering the rest of the paper around him in the process. "I'm sure I should be."

Cassie gave a little curtsey in honour of his illogical compliment, and turned so that her gesture could take in Mr. Lyman, who had risen likewise. Then she turned back again in the direction of Hastings who, for a wonder, seemed to sense at last that something was happening, and slowly got to his own feet. Cassie smiled at him rather than curtsey again, but he did not acknowledge it or meet her eye.

"Well, goodnight all," she said, and then, looking hard at Hastings, she murmured for the last time, "Helpmeet. Help. Meet."

Cassie had wrapped a blanket round her shoulders, but she still shivered in her room. She had a novel on her lap, but was unable to concentrate on it for more than a few minutes at a time.

At last there was the heavy tread of a man's footsteps on the stair, and she rushed to the door. The expected candlelight rounded the corner, and the figure rounded it immediately afterwards. It was too bulky and shaggy to be that of Hastings: she had merely been trying to turn it into him by willpower. "Ah," Mr. Flewitt said, somewhat taken aback, "goodnight, ma'am."

There followed a long wait, during which she heard Mr. Lyman and Miss Hartston retire to their own rest on the floor below. Surely he would come soon?

When her clock showed eleven-thirty, she decided she would wait till midnight and then go to bed. After all, she did, as she had said, have responsibilities of her own. There were the notes of the Clerkenwell incident to write up and file, and Dr. Farthing would be embarking on further investigations. And her attempt to arrange a meeting with Hastings was beginning to seem a passing whim—he had not so much as looked at her, let alone acknowledged her coded message.

The last two minutes had gone by in the same time as the previous ten. At this rate, she would die of exposure before

midnight arrived. Surely everyone was in bed by now, even
Esmé, so what could have become of Hastings? She could not
have missed his return to his room. Had he slipped out again, or
was he still downstairs? Could he—*heavens!*—have died where
he sat? She would step on the landing and see if she could see a
light under his door, or perhaps detect some sign of movement
elsewhere in the house. Then she would go to bed.

She stood once more on the landing, candle in hand, as she
seemed to have stood so many nights these last few months.
Other women had lovers, assignations, engagements, while she
practised a sort of pre-mortem haunting, as lonely as any ghost,
waiting for a victim to scare. There was no light under his door;
it was no use waiting here: she must go downstairs.

The hall was as bright as when she had left it, all those hours
ago. Esmé was standing at the drawing room door, and turned,
hearing Cassie approach.

"I don't like to wake him, miss," she whispered. "I don't
know what I ought to do for the best."

Cassie peered over her shoulder. The door was ajar and
one hand was visible resting on the arm of the chair. Evidently
Hastings had not moved.

"Never mind, Esmé. You can go to bed. I'll see to the lights
and the fire."

"Are you sure, miss?" A whisper cannot express much
emotion, but if this one showed any doubt, Cassie thought,
it was purely to do with her ability to take over a maid's
domestic duties. It was not for Esmé to question the morality
of her betters. So Cassie just nodded and did her best to look
confident, and Esmé, taking one last look round at her place of
work, retreated in the direction of her quarters.

Hastings stirred when she entered the room, as if he intended
to rise as he had done earlier, but Cassie walked over to him
quickly and put her hand on his arm.

"There is no need, my dear," she murmured. She was
treating him like an invalid, she realized, perhaps as a way to
overcome the embarrassment of the situation.

"I'm sorry, Miss Pine. I must have—"

"I can see you are troubled, Hastings." (He winced at the use of his Christian name.) "I haven't come to upset you, any more than you are already."

"Oh, um." He gave her a frightened look and tried once more to get up but she pressed hard with both hands on his captive arm to indicate he should stay where he was.

She sat down beside him. "It is not your obligations to me that are upsetting you, is it?"

"You are very good, Miss Pine," Hastings said, "but it is not something I can talk about with someone with whom I am not on intimate terms."

Cassie felt as if all the breath had been knocked out of her. Somewhere inside herself she was screaming in a voice she recognized as her mother's: *Intimate terms Mr. Wimbury I'll give you intimate terms I will indeed and if spending the night on a lady's bed isn't intimate terms then I should like to know what is thank you very much!* Suppressing it, she forced herself to continue gently, "Sometimes, however, it can be helpful to tell your troubles to someone who doesn't share them."

"I would not inflict them on you, Miss Pine."

*Not inflict them I suppose you call it not inflicting your troubles to sit all evening in an armchair with those eyes of yours staring straight in front of you till a girl can't think about anything else and how I'm supposed to get a wink of sleep I do not know.* "You are making yourself ill. Please tell me."

Hastings smiled, and the voice of Cassie's mother was struck dumb. "I'm afraid it's a very long story."

"We have all night, sir, if need be. Everyone in the house is sleeping."

"Well," Hastings began, "I have become acquainted with a certain foreign nobleman, a Count."

# Chapter 18

The Curacy, as it was pretentiously called, was only a few hundred yards from the Rowans, so it was not necessary to ride. Flora walked up the lane. It was a cold day, and the mist of the morning still lingered. No one emerged from the Lodge to ask her business, and the Rectory itself seemed deserted. Mr. Pilkins's cottage stood in a patch of open ground. The squat cob walls and the smell of smoke rising from the chimney made it seem more like a witch's house in a fairy tale than the home of a clergyman and scholar of the Apocrypha.

Mrs. Rathbone admitted her to the leathery study, where Mr. Pilkins was sunk in contemplation of a book so large she wondered how he had got it down from the shelf. He rose with gracious surprise, as if he had not seen her for weeks, and scrambled round the desk to shake hands with her. "Pray be seated, Miss Burlap." He returned to his original position even more awkwardly than he had left it since he had to turn his back on her to do so. "You wished to speak to me, to ask my advice on something, perhaps?" He smiled shyly.

"It is about Mr. Wimbury." Flora unsnapped her reticule and Hastings's letter sprang out, having been crushed into place against the resistance of powder compact, rouge, and the other objects she kept inside. "I am, I confess, a little worried about him. He does not often mention some matters we know of, but—"

"What matters?"

"A certain foreign titled gentleman, but he has mentioned him in this most recent letter, and I am somewhat alarmed. Mr. Pilkins, perhaps it would be best if I read it to you?"

" 'I told you, my darling, that the Count—' " Flora broke off. "Oh, Mr. Pilkins, I'm so sorry. I don't think I should read Mr. Wimbury's endearments, do you? It is hardly seemly in the company of another gentleman, or, well, in anyone's company, really. It is just that when I get into my stride, as it were. I do not notice the language he uses until it is too late and the words are out."

"Think nothing of it, Miss Burlap."

"But, quite apart from concerns of decorum, I cannot help remembering that you have yourself held at one time a regard for me—"

"More than a regard, I assure you, and you are wrong, dear lady, to suppose it a thing of the past."

Flora felt a flush rise to her cheeks. "Well, we will say no more of that, sir, for both our sakes. It is only that I am sensible that to hear the tender language he uses must be, for you, like eavesdropping on our most private conversations, and that must surely cause you pain."

"I cannot deny it," Mr. Pilkins said, with what looked to Flora a somewhat smug expression, "but I must hear everything if I am to advise you properly. Let the endearments remain *in situ*, though each one is a barb in an especially sensitive part of my soul. Pray continue, Miss Burlap."

" 'I told you, my darling, that the Count warned me that I may have little notice before I must leave for his country and the performance of *Hamlet* that is to change my fortunes forever. His preparations have taken so long that I have at times doubted if I would ever see that dark country of his—oh, how I wish I could tell you its name, but he has enjoined me to preserve the strictest secrecy and I must respect his wishes. However, the time has almost come; his hand has been forced by my own actions, which I suppose I should be glad of, though the actions themselves are not such as to make me proud. O my sweetest Flora'—sorry again, Mr. Pilkins—'think well of me, whatever you may hear of me in the near future. For very shortly I shall be carrying out one last requirement of the Count's, after which the greater, the better part of my life can begin. Whatever I have done I have done for love of you, to make myself the kind of man worthy to be your husband. Some of my deeds have been—and, I should add, will be—such as are frowned on by the law, but you must always remember that an artist is not bound by the same laws as other men. So the Count insists, and I must agree with him. My hand has been forced also, for I cannot remain any longer in the employ of the Villiers Theatre, having fallen out irrevocably with the Management of that establishment. When I return from C—, they, along with every other theatre in the West End, will be crying out for me, and not, any longer, in the capacity of gas-boy.

"'When I leave the Villiers for the last time, in the company of certain of his subordinates who are needed for my final commission there, the Count has promised to meet me in a hansom cab. We shall drive to Bayswater, where I shall collect my baggage, enough for a long journey and far more than that—indeed it will be a challenge getting all the things downstairs without waking the household. There is a person there, a fellow resident, to whom I wish I could say goodbye, but, though I have confided a little of my situation to her, she must not know of my departure. Forgive me, darling'—and forgive me, too, Mr. Pilkins—'but I could not any longer refrain from speaking to one who was present in the flesh, so to speak, and who was willing to lend a sympathetic feminine ear to the troubles which have weighed so heavily on me of late. I know you are not jealous, nor have you reason to be!

"'Despite all the Count has told me about his country, I cannot imagine my arrival there, let alone the labours I must undertake subsequently. It must be so much worse for you, who do not even know where I am going! It is late. I must try to sleep, though I doubt if I will succeed. At any rate, bed is the most comfortable place to pass my hours of sleeplessness. Farewell, my darling! Do not believe I have forgotten you. With all my love, from your adventurer. Hastings.' So, you see, Mr. Pilkins, why I am so greatly in need of your advice. My beloved has as good as told me that he is about to commit a crime. There is probably not sufficient time for me to write to him and forbid it. Is it not my duty to go at once to London and intervene?"

Mr. Pilkins pressed his hands together under his chin. "This is indeed a dilemma, Miss Burlap."

"I am sure that this Count he speaks of must be a bad influence. Hastings was always a headstrong and, shall we say, eccentric person, but it seems to me that the change that has come over him dates from his meeting with this gentleman."

"If you can call him such, Miss Burlap."

"He has a title, sir, though I suppose a foreign one is not quite the same. I am not sure what a Count is."

"It is the equivalent of an Earl, as I understand it."

"If he had come under the influence of an Earl, I should be much less concerned. I cannot think an Earl would do him any harm, but a Count! There is something devious in the very word."

Mr. Pilkins nodded.

"And whatever it is this Count has persuaded him to do he says is for my sake! Surely that makes me—what is the word?—his accomplice?"

"Oh, I should not go so far as to say that. You can hardly be an accomplice in a crime when you do not even know what it is. Indeed, you have only Mr. Wimbury's word that it is a crime at all, and he was evidently not in the most lucid state of mind when he wrote the letter."

"But, sir, I cannot help remembering the words of the General Confession: 'We have left undone those things that we ought to have done, and we have done those things that we ought not to have done, and there is no health in us.'"

"Beautiful words, Miss Burlap."

"Yes, sir, but they fill me with despair now, for I fear that I am in danger of leaving undone something that I ought to have done."

"It is only a *General* Confession. You must not take it personally. Indeed, there is something comforting, is there not, in the fact that the whole congregation must say it every week? As this suggests, we *all* leave undone those things that we ought to have done, so in the end we must simply accept the fact. The letter is disconcerting, Miss Burlap, but I think you should consider it a warning. This man Wimbury, for all his charms—and I must admit he writes well—has the subtlety of the serpent. Pay him no heed! You have seen, very astutely if I may say so, that he plans to commit some audacious act, perhaps even a crime. You have seen, too, the danger of making yourself an accomplice in that act, but you cannot do so if you stay away from London, where it is to be committed. It is our modern Babylon, my dear madam, and we must remember what is prophesied of it in Scripture: 'Babylon is fallen, is fallen, that great city, because she made all nations drink of the wine of the wrath of her fornic—' oh, excuse me."

It was Mr. Pilkins's turn to redden. They sat in silence for a moment, while Flora tried to imagine what it would be like to venture, a woman alone, into that Babylonian city.

# Chapter 19

Hastings passed the open doors of one or two public houses in his nocturnal perambulations; light flooded out on to the pavement, accompanied by the sound of singing, but he was in no mood to enter. Even after midnight, the broader streets of the West End were far from deserted, and the pedestrians he shared them with were all in jovial mood, the men especially jostling and calling out to each other, and occasionally even to him. He was used to travelling home late after his evenings at the Villiers, but as the time wore on he grew first astonished then irritated at having to share these dark spaces with so many others at a time when he wanted to be alone with his thoughts. So he turned off the busy streets into the darker, narrower ones that led off them. Even here, he would sometimes encounter another person, skulking in a menacing way or walking with the frantic gait of someone who is only just suppressing the urge to run, and, when he did so, he would at once seek a street still narrower, where he could escape even this less congenial company. He was not afraid. He was the one to be afraid of now.

At last he came out on to Victoria Embankment, which was brighter even than the Strand. It was everything he had been trying to avoid, a broad space where many people still milled about under the brilliant lights. He should by rights have fled back into the darkness, but something about it fascinated him. It was as if London itself had been turned into a theatre, with the Embankment its auditorium and the Thames the stage, with its scenery of moored boats and barges, and the steps arranged along it as entrances to that impossible space. He sat on a bench and looked at the reflected lights, a show like those he had helped to put on at the Villiers. These were not gaslamps but electric lights, Yablochkov candles as they were called, that used the same mysterious power as Mr. D'Oyly Carte's electric fairies at the Savoy. He looked at the nearest of them; above the base with its coiled black dolphins rose a tall iron post with a globe on top giving off an intense white light. The whole structure crackled and hissed, and seemed to shake slightly; he was sure that if he were to go up and touch it he would feel those vibrations flowing through his own body. One night soon, Hastings thought, there will be enough of these celestial candles to eliminate the shadows altogether. Then there will be only day, the yellow day of the sun alternating with the pure white day of electricity.

At the appointed hour, he approached the Villiers once again; by now there was hardly a soul about in Charing Cross Road or the Strand. He turned down the side alley as usual, and there were the men the Count had told him to expect, six of them, dressed in the jackets and flat caps of ordinary workmen. He felt disappointed—somewhere in a part of his mind he had not used since childhood he had hoped for masks.

The foremost of the men had an elfin look that reminded him uncomfortably of Mr. Eweson. "For this relief much thanks," he murmured, then added a word Hastings had not heard before, but whose import was easy enough to guess.

"'Tis bitter cold, and I am sick at heart," Hastings replied, inwardly resenting the Count's choice of password, which made him feel ridiculous.

"Thought you'd be here ahead of us. We been here ten minutes already."

"I have been walking about to pass the time." Hastings took out his watch. "It is exactly two o'clock."

The man sniggered. "Present from Daddy, is it? Shouldn't take that out here, mate, lot of thieves, ain't we?" Seeing that his insolence met no response, he continued, "Got the keys, then?"

Hastings unlocked the door. "Stay there till I call you. I am going to light some of the gaslamps to make things easier. The Count said that one of you would have a lantern for me, is that so? Thank you. I will be back in a few minutes to show you where to go."

The men knew their business. Indeed, Hastings reflected, it was not all that different from that of their legitimate counterparts, the Pickford's removal men, as his own intervention with keys and lights had relieved them of the most underhand necessities of their work. The only difference was that they spoke in whispers and refrained from singing and whistling. In not much more than an hour, they had taken out the five remaining limelight machines, the boxes of green, amethyst and red fire, the lime cylinders and the gasbags, enough equipment for the most sumptuous production of *Hamlet*. Nevertheless they could not be quick enough for Hastings; after showing them where everything was, he felt redundant, and longed for it to be over so that his adventure could begin. As the Eweson-like man was carrying out the last box, Hastings, having already extinguished most of the lights, followed him, trying to hurry him up by practically treading on his heels. "Is the Count here yet?" he asked.

"Search me."

Hastings had to turn aside to deal with the rest of the lights. By the time he got into the alley and locked the door behind him, it was empty, and he thought for a moment the men had all gone. He found them in the Strand, however, loading the last of their acquisitions on a cart, with the blinkered Shire horse standing motionless in front. "Is the Count here?" he asked again.

"Didn't send any message to us about coming here in person, governor. All we know is we has to take this lot to Hampstead. So leave us be, will you? The bluebottle comes by at twenty past the hour, by which time we has to be out of here, understood?"

Hastings looked up and down the street. It was entirely empty now: he could not imagine the approach of the expected policeman, let alone the Count's hansom cab.

"Get out of my way, mate! Got to clear off."

"Sorry." He realized he had been obstructing them half-deliberately, not wanting them to go and leave him alone waiting for a cab that would never come. But they were finished now:

the cart was loaded with their loot, which was not piled as high and precarious as the typical Pickford's load and did not look enough to justify the use of the Shire horse. The driver cracked his whip and the horse lumbered off. The cart's progress along the empty road was slow and noisy, so that he could not believe that every policeman for miles around did not hear it. He took out his watch, and saw that it lacked but three minutes of twenty past; the policeman would be along soon, and the cart was turning ponderously to the left, escaping the main road just in time. Hastings could not be found here with no story to tell, and, as he considered the prospect of ducking down the alley again, he was swept by a conviction that, when the officer had been and gone, he would be alone again for the rest of the night. He ran down the road after the cart, and caught up with it fifty yards down the next street.

The driver cursed him as he seized the horse's harness, and the elfin man put his head up from behind the bulky gasbags. "Get out of it!" He used another word Hastings did not know.

"You must take me to the Count!"

"Didn't say nothing about that, mate. Just the stuff from the theatre, that's all."

"He was due to meet me there, but something has gone wrong, or he has forgotten. He will want to see me: his whole scheme will be a failure if I do not go to him!"

"Nothing to do with me, mate."

The driver shook the reins and cracked the whip, but the horse continued moving at its steady pace, no faster than Hastings could comfortably walk. They turned another corner with him still attached.

"Look, let me on, will you?" There was no reply. "Do you know who I am?"

"Some actor bloke."

"I am the close friend of the Count; almost, you might say, his partner in this enterprise. He will not be pleased to find you have left me behind."

"And he won't be pleased I've brought you if I wasn't supposed to, will he? Can't win either way."

"I am not letting go of this horse, damn your eyes, so you might as well let me on."

"Keep your bleeding voice down. You'll have every copper in the West End on top of us. Give him a flick with your whip, Ferret."

"If you do, I'll shout louder. And I'm coming with you anyway, on the cart or not. I hardly think your horse can outrun me."

"Bleeding gentlemen," the man said. The horse stopped and Hastings clambered on, finding himself a seat on one of the boxes of lime cylinders. They were still only a quarter of a mile or so from the Villiers—it would be hours before they reached Hampstead, and even then there was his luggage to go back for. Had he panicked too soon? Perhaps the Count was even now waiting for him in the hansom outside the Villiers. Why had he been so certain that he had been left in the lurch? Deep in his heart, he realized, he did not trust the Count, who was too well-mannered, too intelligent, too foreign above all, to be entirely honourable. And yet this was the man he was travelling through the night to see!

# Chapter 20

Hastings awakened from his doze as the cart began climbing the hill on the approach to Hampstead. He consulted his watch when they passed a streetlight, and saw that it was a few minutes past five. He was facing the rear of the cart, and the lights of London were spread out below him in constellations. It was cold now, and a keen wind was blowing against the left side of his face. The leader of the gang was sitting on a box a little behind him, just his trousers and boots visible, so Hastings turned and asked when they were due to arrive.

"Why," the man said, "there is the Count's house now."

Hastings stood up, bracing himself on a box, and turned to face forward. The road they were on swept round to the left in an arc of gaslamps, and almost directly in front of him was an irregular patch of darkness like a ragged hole in a starlit sky, which must be the Heath. On the near edge of this was a large house, almost big enough to be called a manor; it gave a lopsided impression, since the lower right side of the building was illuminated, with a couple of additional lights where there appeared to be a sort of outhouse, while the rest of the house was not. Approaching such a grand residence in what was still deepest night, he was not anxious, but embarrassed. The Count would surely be asleep, and not at all prepared to welcome an uninvited guest. But then he had in a sense been invited: not that there had been any mention of where he was to spend the night, and indeed the arrangements for his journey had been vague in the extreme, but he had been given the impression everything was taken care of. It was the Count who had failed to keep his promise, he thought, trying to block from his mind the possibility that he had after all kept it.

The cart pulled into a turning in the road and stopped at a pair of wrought iron gates, where a muffled servant met them with a lantern. He and the driver exchanged passwords, the same quotations from *Hamlet* that had been used in the earlier rendezvous, and the gates swung open. They trundled for some fifty yards along a winding, paved drive before turning off again and stopping at another pair of gates, wooden this time, which were opened from inside. They entered a courtyard brightly lit with lanterns, and with a barn or warehouse standing open at the far end. The workmen, as Hastings continued to think of them, jumped up and began to busy themselves with the boxes, handing them to the men who gathered round them and carried them into the warehouse. Hastings, finding himself an encumbrance, eased himself down from the tail of the cart, and spoke to one of the strange men.

"Is the Count here?"

"I don't think so," the man said, and then, after a baffled pause, added, "sir."

Hastings slipped away in the direction of the main house. He found a door in the wall of the yard, and passed through into a dim alleyway which contained a couple of dustbins but otherwise seemed tidy and salubrious enough. There was a savoury smell in this region, and he soon traced it to a door which stood ajar, light and warmth flooding out of it.

He pushed the door wide and found himself face to face with a plump girl in the dark dress and white apron of a kitchen maid. She smiled at him. "Finished already? The food's almost done."

"I was, um, looking—" Hastings began, and then reflected how absurd it would seem to be searching for the Count in his kitchen at that hour of the morning.

"Sit yourself down," the maid said. "I'll get your beer. Or would you prefer coffee?"

"It is still night for me. I will take the beer."

He hung his coat and hat behind the door and sat at the long oak table, and the girl brought him a mug of beer. A cook and a scullery maid were working behind him, and he gazed into his mug feeling simultaneously pampered and in the way. The servants were too busy to talk to him, though the girl he had first seen made an effort to catch his eye every time she arrived at the table with plates of bread, bottles and mugs. He was ready to doze off again in the warmth when the men came in from the yard, chuckling, rubbing their hands and talking with the self-conscious exuberance of those who are not quite at home in their surroundings. They took their places around him, and the girl brought platters of sausages and bacon.

"You'll be hungry after all your work," she said, and caught Hastings's eye again.

"It was a long journey," he said, helping himself to the food, as the chief of the gang, seated across the table, snorted and looked the other way. The maid started to move away, but Hastings plucked her by the sleeve. "I wonder…?" he began.

Something about his manner or voice seemed to strike her for the first time, and she looked puzzled. "Yes, sir?"

"Is your master about?"

"I wouldn't know nothing about that, sir."

"Well, is there someone who would? Could you send someone to me?" He reached in his pocket in search of a shilling, then thought better of it. "The food," he concluded, "is magnificent."

"Thank you, sir. I'll go and see."

Hastings had finished his plateful, and was contemplating the last sausage on the platter before him when he felt a hand on his shoulder.

"You are full of surprises, my dear fellow." The Count was dressed for the outdoors in coat, Ulster and soft hat, and, seeing Hastings looking at him, seemed to feel the need to explain it away. "I have been walking on the Heath. I am not a man who needs much sleep. I am sorry for the humble entertainment. I would have wished to receive you more appropriately."

"The entertainment has been delightful, and just what I needed after my journey."

"Quite." The Count seemed ill at ease. Hastings was almost sure that he had failed to call at the theatre last night, but he did not feel able to come out with the accusation in such surroundings. "Have you finished? Let me, at any rate, take you somewhere more private."

They passed through a long, bare corridor and up a dim flight of stairs to the first floor. The walls were papered in a dingy grey pattern, and there were no pictures. They entered a drawing room with worn leather chairs, one of which Hastings was invited to occupy while the Count rang for his butler.

"I live very simply, as you see. I have not been here long, and you must remember that my real home is elsewhere. It is a curious time of the day or night, though I have always enjoyed such times myself. Would you prefer coffee or brandy? Or perhaps both?"

"I do not think you called for me, Count."

"What makes you say that?"

Hastings was saved from the need to decide how to respond by the arrival of the butler.

"Coffee and brandy, Briggs."

"Did you forget, or was it never your intention to fetch me?"

"My dear chap, I was there, I assure you, just as I had promised. I was deeply disappointed to find the street deserted. I waited in the cab for a good half-hour before concluding, reluctantly, that you had changed your mind about our project, as you had every right to do."

"As if I would change my mind when I had just assisted you in carrying out a robbery! I see it all now, Count: there is no production of *Hamlet*, no Cimmeria—I doubt if you are even a Count! You are merely a criminal, the leader of a gang of thieves, and it suited your purposes to enlist my assistance. What do you do with the equipment you steal, sell it to the provincial theatres?"

"Oh, this is preposterous!" The Count was smiling. "You have had a long night without sleep, or you would be aware how ridiculous your accusations sound. Do you think I would go to such lengths to obtain a few items of machinery, merely to turn a profit like a tradesman? You and I are gentlemen; it is art, not money that motivates us. Ah, here is Briggs with the refreshments. And after that, I am sure you will be ready for a sleep. We can talk about *Hamlet* later."

# Chapter 21

Hastings awoke in the dark. That is, he experienced many of the phenomena he usually associated with waking: a lucidity of thought, a rush of memories from the previous day, the bodily sensations that told him he was lying in a bed with the covers pulled up over him and his head on a soft pillow. But this was like no waking he had known in his life. It was not the dark of a bedroom with curtains drawn and doors closed that allows the faintest suspicion of light to leak through the cracks round the edges, but a dark that eliminated all the world except the parts of it he was in contact with. The space around him might be a cupboard, a field, the dome of St. Paul's Cathedral or an endless void with no solid surface to stand on should he be unwise enough to leave the safety of the bed. And this uncertainty made him doubt the memories and sensations he had woken up with. Was he Hastings Wimbury, and had he ever moved through a world that contained Flora Burlap, Cassie Pine, the Villiers Theatre, horses, hansom cabs, steam engines, gaslamps, top hats, horsehair chairs, mutton chops, pints of porter, the endlessly varied paraphernalia of life? It took only a little darkness to rid the world of all of it, and most of himself, too.

Still, the thoughts continued, and that was something—was there not a philosopher who concluded that he must exist because he was thinking? Hastings decided to marshal whatever information he had about his situation: he had gone to the Count's house in Hampstead, eaten breakfast in the kitchen with the men who had burgled the theatre, had an unsatisfactory interview with the Count himself, then retired to bed, having been up all night. How long had he slept? Though he was used, in the profession he had so recently abandoned, to keeping late hours, there was something disorientating about sleeping through the hours of daylight and waking up at night, standing time on its head as it were. No wonder he was unsettled.

"How do you like Cimmeria?" the Count said.

Hastings gave a yelp and tried to start up, as if to flee from the bed, but the covers held him fast. Anyway, he had nowhere to run to.

"I am sorry to startle you, but I could see you were awake and I could not resist the experiment. Forgive me; my sense of humour can be rather unkind at times, so I have been told."

"You could see…?"

"It is not really dark for me, more a kind of twilight that I find very restful. There is a fire burning only a few hundred yards away—perhaps you can smell the smoke?—and a little of the light has penetrated the room, even though your eyes are not yet sensitive enough to be aware of it. As I was saying, this is your new home. Shall I describe it to you? You are in one of numerous rocky chambers that have been hollowed out partly by time and the action of water, partly by the hand of man, that flank one of the minor streets of Cimmeria, which you would probably call a passage or tunnel. We are perhaps a mile from the Great Hall of my country, which serves as its main square as well as its royal palace and seat of government. When you are accustomed to moving around you will soon get to know the street plan and be able to find your own way to the Great Hall. Meanwhile, I suggest you get used to your chamber. It is high enough that you can stand up straight in the centre, more or less where I am seated at present, but at the edges of the room you will have to stoop a little. If you stretch out your right hand about as far as you can reach you will touch a wall."

Hastings did so, encountering first the bed curtains, then empty air, then—. He started. "There is wallpaper!"

"Certainly there is wallpaper—we are not barbarians. I told you, the chamber is a natural formation that has been much improved by the hand of man. The walls have been chiselled smooth and covered with plaster—we have, of course, all the necessary minerals in our mines—and then papered."

"Count, this is absurd."

"But perhaps you were expecting stalactites, and minerals in the walls? If so, I am sorry to disappoint you; you will not find them in this part of the city. Such things do exist, of course, if you travel further afield, to what we think of as the countryside. Why that ruby I gave you, and which you were so ungrateful as to give back to me, was merely a trinket I picked up one day on one of my country walks."

"I cannot be in Cimmeria. Only this morning I was eating breakfast in your house in Hampstead. I don't know how much time has passed since then, but—"

"Much more time than you imagine. The brandy I gave you contained a powerful sedative. You slept for almost twenty-four hours, and when you showed signs of reviving I injected you with more. Do you feel a soreness in your arm? No? That only shows how skilfully I performed the operation. I expect you are hungry, though. In all, your journey to Cimmeria took the best part of a week."

"Of course I am hungry. I am also very much out of temper."

"It is only to be expected. I must ask your pardon, but I really do not think you would have enjoyed the journey. And, to be entirely honest, it does not suit my purposes or those of my countrymen that strangers should know the way. We are a secretive people, and it is a trait that has served us well over the millennia."

"Count, you have kidnapped me. You are keeping me a prisoner!"

"No, no, I assure you—you are perfectly free to go whenever you wish. Only you would not want to be seen like that."

"What are you talking about?"

"You are naked except for your drawers." Hastings felt about under the covers and found this was true. "It is another thing I am sorry for, but we did not have time to send for your belongings. In fact, I did not even know your address, and could not ask for it when you were unconscious. It all happened very quickly. Anyway, the clothes you arrived in are here; they have been washed and pressed, and are now laid out for you on a chair next to the foot of the bed. I thought you would prefer to wear them rather than the national costume of Cimmeria, which is practical but might strike you as outlandish. On the other hand—"

"I wish you would cease this nonsense!"

"I am afraid my life, and those of others like me, must always seem nonsense to a truly civilized European gentleman like yourself. As I was saying, I shall leave you shortly and you will then be free to rise and dress yourself, though I suppose you are more used to having a servant to help you."

"I have been living in a boarding-house and working as a gas-boy."

"Of course, you are capable and resourceful, as all good Englishmen are. And I daresay you will find it easy enough to dress by touch. Perhaps you would like me to send you some breakfast first, to give you strength for your ordeal?"

Hastings remembered the sausages and bacon with a pang— could they really have been a week ago? He could almost taste them. But he knew very well this was a trap. Once he accepted the Count's hospitality, he was accepting everything else: the drugging and kidnapping, the enforced darkness, whatever other nefariousness he might have in mind. "I have had breakfast already," he said.

There was a silence.

"I am sorry," the Count said. "I was nodding to indicate my acceptance of your decision. I forget you cannot see my gestures. I admire your spirit of independence. I shall leave you to dress and find your way out. Turn right when you reach the street, or passage, and that will take you to the main thoroughfare, where you must turn right again. You will find many people there, and there will be some illumination from cooking fires and the like, perhaps even some torches. It is our Piccadilly Circus, so to speak. From there the journey to the outside should not be so difficult for an adventurous spirit like yours. It may be some time before you meet a Cimmerian who understands English, but that has never impeded your compatriots much. Communicate by means of gestures, indicate that you are looking for the way out. I know from having, through necessity, acquainted myself with your belongings that you have nothing much to offer by way of a fee to any guide you may find, but that should not stop you. We are a kindly, if rather shy, people and do not encounter many strangers. What worries me more is what you will do when you find yourself on the side of a mountain in, well, never mind where. How will you find your way back to civilization? Still, once you have left Cimmeria, your safety will be your own responsibility. Goodbye, my dear fellow."

There was the sound of a chair being pushed back on a wooden floor. Not a rock floor, Hastings thought, but then he was not sure what such a floor would sound like. Then footsteps, with the distinctive sag and creak of floorboards. Then a muffled thump and a word Hastings could not make out uttered under the breath. A swearword, perhaps foreign? He wasn't sure. What he was absolutely certain about, though, was that the Count had bumped into the open door.

The clothes were where the Count had said they were. Hastings found dressing by touch a clumsy process: he had an awkward moment when he buttoned the bed curtain into his shirt, and his tie got lost at an early stage of the process. The effect would not be elegant to any spectator, but of course there would be none until he found his way to the light. He was still picturing Cimmeria as the Count had described it, with its tunnels and Great Hall, even though he was by now almost sure it did not exist.

Nevertheless he set his feet to the floor, feeling with pleasure the familiar sensation of walking in shoes. His walk to the clothes had informed him of the position of the bed and the two chairs, and he knew he must guide himself by them as far as possible before striking out on his own. He still walked right into the Count's chair, which was nearer the bed than he had pictured it, and had a brief flare of anger and panic. Then he controlled himself, stood upright again and continued his progress in the direction of the door. He knew it to be open, and that he must not make the Count's mistake of walking into it. It was time to leave the guidance of the bed, but he remembered the *sotto voce* curse and did not think it could have come from more than five or six paces away from his present position. He struck out, hands held out before him, and found it.

The corridor was longer than he had expected, no doubt because he was not used to walking so slowly. He tended to drift towards the wall, so that after a yard or two he would be clinging tightly to it, a position from which it was an effort to detach himself. If the turning was to the right, as the Count had said, he could not miss it. Eventually, he more or less fell into it when his hand encountered no resistance. There was no sign of pedestrians, no noise of commerce, no change in the temperature as might be expected in a wider, draughtier street. He sniffed the air, and could not detect the smell of smoke the Count had mentioned.

Abruptly he came upon another gap in the wall. If this was the entrance to Piccadilly Circus, it was a disappointment, since there was no firelit throng here. Nevertheless, he decided to take it, because the thought of losing his guiding wall for a yard or two was unpleasant. He grasped the corner of the wall and stepped into nothing.

It was only a step—his foot descended some four inches further than he had anticipated—but it was enough to throw him forward, full-length into the void. As he fell he must have let go of the wall and stretched his hands in front of him, because they made the first contact with the stairs and saved him, most likely, from more serious injury. The rest of his body followed, and he rolled most of the way down the flight, not knowing which way was up or what was happening. Every part of him hurt and he could not breathe at first. He must have cried out when he fell, and he was aware of an answering commotion somewhere below him. And lights. That was even more of a shock than the fall had been.

He was lying in the shape of an inverted question-mark, his legs, higher than his head, forming the straight part. He hurt everywhere, but he was beginning to be able to breathe. Somewhere at the lower end of his being people were talking and fussing. The closest of them was the Count.

"My dear Wimbury," he was saying, "I never thought you would take me seriously. It is all my fault, as usual. Come, we must carry you back to bed."

# Chapter 22

The sign on the door could do with repainting, but the flowing script undoubtedly read Halcyon House. Flora tugged on a handle which almost came off in her hand but was apparently attached to some device worked by string, since a bell sounded distantly inside a second later. Snippets of many-coloured light fell all round her from the stained-glass panels in the door. It was a raw night with a cruel wind penetrating all the layers of her clothing, and it began to seem as though she would stand all evening on the doorstep. She tugged again, shaking the handle to make the bell ring for longer. Finally she heard footsteps on the tiles of the hall and the door was opened by a maid.

"Yes, ma'am?"

"I wish to speak to Mr. Wimbury."

"Follow me, ma'am."

She waited in a chilly room, where the fire was not yet lit. The smells of the house were as Hastings had described them in his letters, stale mutton, horsehair, dust and lamp oil layered together and more intense than one would have expected in this high-ceilinged, draughty space. Sounds could be heard in other parts of the house, a tread on the ceiling above her head, some clanking noises suggestive of a kitchen, a woman's voice saying something scornful which she could not make out. At last she heard footsteps approaching, and a woman entered. She was above average height, and dressed in the black of a widow. Her hair, too, was black, unnaturally so, Flora thought, examining the folds of that unsmiling face.

"I am sorry, ma'am," Mrs. Makepeace said at once. "You come at a busy time. I can spare you two minutes, no more."

"I must apologize for intruding on you," Flora began. "It is Mr. Wimbury I wish to speak to."

Mrs. Makepeace sniffed. "Perhaps you can tell me where he is? His bed has not been slept in for a week, and the rent is due on Friday."

Flora had been expecting to hear something of the kind, and had rehearsed this scene dozens of times in the train on the way to London. "I wonder if I might sit down, ma'am?"

"Certainly, if you wish." Mrs. Makepeace remained standing, making Flora repent of her own weakness, which put her at a disadvantage in the ensuing conversation. "May I ask what your interest is in the gentleman?"

"He is my fiancé."

"I see." Her tone was one of grim resignation, as if Flora had just admitted to some weakness of the flesh, which in a sense she had. "Then I suppose, miss, you ought to have some idea of where he has got to?"

"Oh, Mrs. Makepeace, I had hoped that he would be here."

"Here is where he ought to be, there is no doubting that. But I assure you he is not, and whether or not he sleeps in his bed, that will be another week's rent he owes me come Friday. He has no business to be sleeping anywhere else without prior notification, not while he resides in this house."

"I am sorry. I came here in the hope of finding him."

Mrs. Makepeace sniffed again. "Then you came in vain, miss. And in any case, had he been here your visit would have been strictly against the rules of the house. So…" She made a gesture to indicate the visit was at an end.

"At least," Flora said quickly, "I can offer to pay my fiancé's outstanding rent, if that would be agreeable?"

Mrs. Makepeace gave a start. From her expression it was clear that it would indeed be agreeable, but not, perhaps, altogether respectable, and that struggling between these considerations she was momentarily lost for words. "Well, miss—"

"And indeed," Flora continued, "I daresay it was incumbent upon him to give notice before leaving, was it not? And in default of that, to pay a certain number of weeks' rent?"

"Four weeks', miss. But—"

Flora had been vaguely thinking of her offer as a bribe with the intention of securing Mrs. Makepeace's attention for a little longer. But with what benefit? Mrs. Makepeace did not seem the sort of woman who was interested in the personal lives of her guests and an examination of Hastings's room would probably reveal nothing she did not know already. Most of all, Flora was dreading the thought of being turned out on to that windy street, to find a cab and make her lonely way back to the hotel, a woman abandoned by her fiancé, or, worse, one who had abandoned him to an unknown fate. She had only one clue to follow: Hastings had written that he had confided some of his concerns to a fellow resident, a lady. If only she knew the lady's name she could use her bribe to secure an interview.

As if in counterpoint to the conversation, Flora had been aware of the preparations for dinner going on in the background, a clanking of pans, a smell of frying onions and the faint accompanying sizzle. "Perhaps?" she said tentatively.

"Yes, miss?"

"I was thinking I could take over my fiancé's room while he is not using it. It would save you the trouble of finding a new tenant."

Mrs. Makepeace drew in her breath sharply. "Oh, that would hardly be proper, miss!"

"Why not? He is not there."

"No, but it is a gentleman's room. It contains items of a… masculine nature."

"What do you mean exactly?"

Mrs. Makepeace became almost coy. Being dark in complexion, she did not blush, but she had an expression on her face as of one who would blush if she could. "There's a razor, miss, and a shaving brush, very fine quality, of badger hair. My late husband always said they were the best." She broke off, looking more embarrassed than ever, having inadvertently given a glimpse of married life to one not yet initiated into it. So this was the sort of thing husbands and wives talked about when they were alone together!

Flora was more interested, however, in the revelation about the contents of the room. So Hastings had been away for a week without taking even his shaving things. That suggested his departure was unplanned, perhaps against his will. She knew she should be frightened, but for some reason she was more excited than anything else. It was more imperative than ever that she find out anything she could about his behaviour in the days leading up to his disappearance, and she could not do that without taking more time to investigate. "And I suppose there are clothes and other belongings in the room, too?"

"Yes, miss. It is out of the question that you should sleep there."

"I cannot see the difficulty. You need only have the things moved from the room, as you would have to anyway in order to let the room to another tenant. I am simply proposing that your next tenant should be myself."

Mrs. Makepeace had entirely lost her authoritative manner and was almost pleading. "So you think Mr. Wimbury won't return, miss? Then what am I to do with his belongings?"

"Certainly he will return, and when he does I shall move out again." Then, seeing the landlady still looking dubious, "I understand your scruples, Mrs. Makepeace, and they do you credit. I promise you he and I will never be in the room at the same time. As for the belongings, your servant will pack them away and you may store them in some suitable place until he reclaims them. It is purely a temporary arrangement." Then, seeing there was still no response, "It is business, ma'am. There can be nothing more respectable than that."

That evening, Flora found herself sitting down to dinner in the company of a group of people she knew only from Hastings's letters. Mrs. Makepeace introduced her merely by name without making any reference to her acquaintance with Hastings, but looked up at her rather guiltily as she did so, still

apparently thinking of the secret as a stain on the good name of
Halcyon House. Mr. Flewitt said grace in a manner both grave
and diffident, and the rumblings which he emitted occasionally,
and which Hastings had described as "some volcanic inner
hilarity" (Flora knew all his letters by heart) she diagnosed at
once as indigestion. Mr. Lyman was the only person who ate
with gusto, or at least like one in a hurry to be finished with the
strange brown food. (The casserole was followed by something
called a guards' pudding.) Flora had expected him to be more
talkative from Hastings's description, but perhaps he was cowed
by her presence. Miss Hartston told the latest episode of her
conversations with Mr. Roscoe the shop-walker. Miss Pine,
the younger female guest, whom Hastings had described in an
early letter as belonging to some obscurely technical profession,
seemed to be studying Flora intently, but said very little. Of the
two possible candidates for Hastings's confidante, Flora thought
this one was probably the more likely, simply because she was
younger, and might, if viewed from some angles, be described
as pretty, but she did not give much impression of intelligence,
and could hardly be a lively companion.

Afterwards they retired to the drawing room, where a fire
was now lit, though burning smokily and giving out very little
heat, while she debated with herself how she was to broach the
subject of Hastings. She was spared the difficulty of deciding
by Miss Pine, who, as soon as she sat down, came up to her and
touched her on the sleeve.

"Oh, Miss Burlap, I wonder if you would care to come to
my room for a few moments? I have a collection of curios I
should like to show you." There was a twist of her features as
she spoke, so that Flora guessed she had some ulterior motive
and rose readily.

There being only one chair in Miss Pine's room, she offered
it to Flora and sat on the bed herself, looking uncomfortable.
The smell of lamp oil was stronger here, and the orange light
made everything in the room seem uncanny; Flora fixed her
eyes on a pair of china spaniels over the bed, whose illuminated

features gave them a sinister air. Perhaps these were the curios Miss Pine had had in mind; if so, she made no attempt to draw Flora's attention to them, and seemed at a loss as to how to begin. Finally Flora thought it was up to her to start.

"You had something to tell me, I think? Was it about…?" She hesitated over whether to say *Mr. Wimbury* or *my fiancé*, unsure whether Miss Pine knew of their engagement. She had just decided on *one we know of*, when Miss Pine interrupted her.

"You see, miss, I know who you are." Despite this disconcerting directness, she did not look Flora in the eyes; instead she raised her right hand to her face and scrutinized the fingernails. "And I know that you and Mr. Wimbury, my—. I know that you have, in the past, been closely acquainted."

"We are closely acquainted now."

"Well, yes, I suppose you think so. But you can't be really, can you, because he isn't here?"

"I don't see what that has to do with it."

"Mr. Wimbury told me all about you, and I know he used to write you letters, and believe me, I feel for you very deeply."

"Thank you. I am a little confused."

"I don't blame you, miss. That is the effect Hastings, Mr. Wimbury, has on me, too, sometimes. But for myself I quite enjoy being confused as long as it don't go on too long."

"What are you saying?"

"Of course, I understand he had to write you letters, because he said he would, and now I expect he'll write them to me, because, as I said, he isn't here any more…"

"Are you implying, Miss Pine, that there is some sort of understanding between yourself and my fiancé?"

Miss Pine smiled in a sad, but knowing way. "Oh, but Miss Burlap, I don't think you can call him your fiancé any more. If anything, he is mine!"

At midnight, Flora gave up trying to sleep. She had been right to cut Miss Pine dead after the intolerable presumption of her pronouncement about Hastings: leaving the room without

another word, just the most disdainful of parting looks, had been
the only option compatible with her pride and the difference
between their stations in life. However, it had not got her any
further in her researches. What was she doing in this lumpy bed
with its inadequate covers, breathing the odours of the house
that were even stronger in the dark, and listening to the creaks
and bangs that it seemed to generate of its own volition, if she
had abandoned her intention of finding out what had become
of him? She was angrier with Hastings than with the woman he
had confided in, and, in the process, so completely misled about
his feelings. But surely she could not avenge herself by leaving
him to his fate? Quite apart from the fact that she still loved him,
she was curious.

She rose from her bed and felt for the box of matches on the
washstand. The flare of the match hurt her eyes, then the glow
of the candle took its place. It was absurd to cross the landing and
wake Miss Pine at this hour, but then everything she had done in
the cause of her devotion to Hastings had been absurd. Besides,
Miss Pine would leave in the morning to go to her employment,
and Flora would be unable to talk to her again until evening.
There was no time to lose if she really wanted to find Hastings.

She crossed the landing and tapped on the door with one
knuckle. It opened, and Miss Pine appeared and beckoned her in.
She was respectably attired in nightgown, nightcap and dressing
gown, so that Flora felt almost naked in her shift. "I wondered
if you would come, Miss Burlap," Miss Pine said in a low tone.
"You must be cold in that"—gesturing to the shift—"and I'm
afraid there's no fire in the room. Pray get into bed while we talk.
I am quite comfortable here in my dressing gown."

It seemed pointless to argue when they had so much else
to discuss, and Flora was indeed beginning to feel the cold, so
she did as suggested. Miss Pine sat in the wicker chair at her
washstand.

"You did not bring any nightclothes?"

"They are at the hotel where I went when I first arrived in
London. I shall send for them in the morning."

"You wanted to ask about Hastings? I am sorry, I can't call him Mr. Wimbury."

"You may call him what you like, I am past caring about such matters. Yes, I came looking for him."

Cassie nodded and pursed her lips. For the first time it occurred to Flora that she must be sad, too. Perhaps she loved him almost as much as Flora did. "I keep thinking he'll come back," Cassie said.

"He wrote to me that he was planning to go abroad. But if that is so I will follow him even there."

"You must be mad. You must realize how difficult it is for a woman on her own to go to foreign parts? It isn't like London, and London can be bad enough if you don't know it well. The men don't always respect women in those places, not even British women."

"You seem to know a lot about it."

"I read a good deal. And my employer is a gentleman of wide experience and talks to me about such things sometimes, when there hasn't been much spiritual activity going on."

Flora was puzzled. "He is a clergyman?"

"More of a scientist," Cassie said, "but that's beside the point, as he would say. It takes money to travel."

"I have some, and can send for more. My brother Algernon came of age in December. We have always bickered a little, but he is devoted to me. I shall write to him at once and ask for a loan which I can pay back with interest when I am reconciled with my father."

"And there are so many things you'd have to arrange. Forgive me, Miss Burlap, but you don't strike me as a lady who's used to making her own arrangements. Besides, you don't even know where you are going, do you?"

"That," Flora told her, "was what I came here to ask you."

When one talks all night the familiar notions of the daylight hours lose their reality. At a certain time just before dawn one no longer knows whether one is awake or asleep, and all ideas seem equally likely and equally preposterous. Flora found herself warming to her companion on the dubious grounds that they had a fiancé in common.

"We must go to the police and see if they can trace him," Flora said.

Cassie shook her head. "I wouldn't do that, Miss Burlap. Hastings has his own way of doing things, you might say, and the police might not appreciate it, not the way we appreciate Hastings. I have had some dealings with the police, in the course of my employment. They are excellent men, but not always very imaginative."

"What do you mean, 'his own way of doing things'?" Flora said. When there was no immediate reply, she spoke more gently. "He hinted about something he was going to do in his last letter to me. He said an artist is not bound by the same laws as other men. Do you know anything about it?"

"He told me he had taken equipment from the theatre sometimes. The way he put it, they wasn't all that bothered about it at first, and then they said enough was enough and he'd to give something back, only he couldn't because he hadn't got it any longer."

"Hastings, a common thief!" Flora bit her lip.

"It was the Count who was to blame. He would never of done it without the Count preying on all his hopes."

"But to be in love with a thief!"

"He isn't just a thief, though. He's also an actor, and according to him the one cancels out the other. That's men, though, ain't it? At least the ones I knew when I was in Penge was generally such as you had to make allowances for. I thought when I left it would be a bit different, and, to be fair, it has been. None of the men in Penge would of been able to work in a theatre, or play Hamlet, or even know who Hamlet was. And that's something."

"I have never been to Penge," Flora said, and there was silence for a few moments.

"That wasn't all," Cassie said. "When we spoke that time, and he told me what he'd done, he said he had to go back one last time. He was leaving anyway, on account of the stuff they wanted back which he couldn't give them, but before he went he was to do something else. He was worried about it but he wouldn't say what it was."

"He wrote something similar to me. That is why I came here."

"Yes. Miss Burlap?"

"Yes, Miss Pine?"

"I think I know something more of the world than you do, with all the respect, miss, that is due to a lady of your position. I am not a lady, not in the way you are. But I have learned to find my way around the city, and I dare say I can help with your investigations here. But if it should come to travelling abroad, even I would be doubtful. You have never even been to Penge— have you so much as consulted a Bradshaw?"

"I have heard of them."

"How you expect to travel to Cimmeria, I cannot imagine. It is not somewhere civilized like France or Germany or the Austro-Hungarian Empire. He never said exactly where it was, but I doubt very much if it is even in Europe."

"Cimmeria, is that what it's called?"

Cassie nodded. "He said it was always dark. I don't know what he meant by that."

Flora yawned. As if in counterpoint to Cassie's last words, a grey light was spreading through the room.

# Chapter 23

The Reading Room of the British Museum was a grand circular space that made Flora think of an enormous hat box containing, not a hat, but a many-layered silence. It was lit by windows all round the perimeter, with another in the domed ceiling, and yet it did not seem bright, for shadows gathered at ground level, where many desks were arranged like the spokes of a wheel, the hub of which was formed by a double ring of desks for the librarians, as though they had fortified themselves against assault from the readers all round them. One of the librarians led her to a long table, separate from the spokes. "This is reserved for ladies, madam," he whispered.

"Oh, but there is no one sitting at it," Flora said. "May I not be placed at one of the smaller desks like everyone else? Look, there is a lady at that one." She gestured to the place where an earnest middle-aged woman in spectacles was making her way through a pile of books that reached to her chin.

He sighed. "Very well. I don't know why we have this table at all. None of the ladies wants to sit at it. I'm sure if one did, you all would. May I bring you the catalogue, madam?"

"I only wish to consult the *Encyclopædia Britannica*."

"You need hardly come to the British Museum Reading Room for that!"

"I am sorry. I did not know where else to go."

"You will find the encyclopaedias round the outside of the room, madam."

He stalked off, heron-like, on his long thin legs. Flora made her way as noiselessly as she could, in a room that seemed to magnify the least sound she made, to the bookshelves at the end, found the eighth edition of the *Encyclopædia* and carried the volume BURNING-GLASSES–CLIMATE back to her desk, painfully aware that she had only one book instead of the piles that her neighbours had.

There was no entry for Cimmeria, but her heart gave a single monumental thump then seemed to stop completely for a few seconds when she found one for Cimmerii. She began copying it directly, in the notebook she had bought for the purpose, not really taking in the words as she wrote them:

CIMMERII, the name of a mythical people, represented by Homer as inhabiting a remote region of mist and darkness; but they are localized by later writers near Lake Avernus, and also in the Tauric Chersonese, and in Spain...

Flora reread what she had written, expecting somehow that it would make more sense in her own handwriting. Sadly, she found that it did not. The article assigned the Cimmerii to three possible homes. In addition, the author seemed to assume that they were no more, which, if Count Nollo's was one of them, could not be true. She wished that Mr. Pilkins were here; though his scholarship was of the biblical rather than the classical kind, she felt sure that he would be able to make something of these strange names. Still, she could at least look them up, so she returned to the shelves for the relevant volumes, from which she found that Lake Avernus was in Italy and the Tauric Chersonese in southern Russia, on the Black Sea. Spain, Italy or Russia! This would never do.

She returned to the central desk and sought out the heron-legged librarian. He separated himself reluctantly from the file of ancient brown index cards he was doing something to.

"I am interested," Flora whispered imperiously, "in Cimmeria."

The librarian looked quickly behind him as if seeking support, someone who knew more about Cimmeria than he did, but, seeing that all his colleagues were burying themselves in their work, was obliged to return his attention to her. "Indeed, madam?"

"Can you tell me where it is, please?"

He sighed. "I believe it is in Homer somewhere. May I recommend a translation? I assume you are unable to read it in the Greek."

"I do not mean where it is in a book. Where is it in real life?"

"Well, nowhere, I suppose." He was now looking both to right and left and would perhaps have turned and run if there had been any room for running in his circular enclosure. "You would not wish to look for Troy in real life, madam?" he pleaded. "I am a librarian, not a geographer."

"Read this." Flora handed him her transcription of the *Encyclopædia* article. He read it, and looked enquiringly at her. "Cimmeria cannot be in three places at once," she said.

"It does not exist, madam. It is a figment of the poet's imagination, or if it existed once it does so no longer."

"But I know it does exist," Flora said, conscious of people at the surrounding tables looking up from their work in repressed disapproval, disturbed not so much by the noise as by the awareness of any human communication taking place at all. "My fiancé is travelling there, on, on business, and it is imperative that I follow him." Then, seeing that he still had nothing to say, "The important thing is the darkness—a land where it is always dark."

"Ah." He moved his lips as if he were chewing something or talking to himself, then looked at Flora before finally making up his mind to speak. "There is another dark country I have heard of," he said, "but its name is not Cimmeria."

"You look tired, Miss Flora," Cassie said. They were meeting in her room, as they had done previously, and Flora wondered idly why they should automatically make their way there after dinner, instead of to her own almost identical one. It seemed to put Cassie in charge of the situation by making her the hostess; on the other hand, Flora was still unable to rid her mind of the association between her own room and Hastings, even though it retained no traces of his occupancy, and she was glad that Cassie did not set foot there.

"I am, a little. It has been a long day."

"I wish I could offer you a glass of brandy. I have some smelling salts, if those would revive you?"

Flora shuddered. "No, thank you."

"Oh well." Cassie went over to the medicine chest in the corner and took out a small blue bottle, from which she sniffed deeply. She screwed up her eyes and tottered for a moment, then smiled, put a handkerchief to her nose and returned the bottle to its place. "Mrs. Makepeace's mackerel wasn't all that fresh this evening," she said, "but I think that's seen off the last of it. And my day has been a tiring one, too, but then maybe I'm more used to that than yourself, miss. Did you find any information about Cimmeria?"

Flora had copied out the relevant passage from the book the librarian had brought to her.

And that contré is covered al with derknes so that is no lyght. And men ther der noght go in that contré for hit is so derke. And yit men of that contré that beth ther sayen that they may here somtyme therynne voys of men, and of hors, and of cockes crowyng, and therfore men wyteth wel that men dwellen therynne.

"The land was called Hanyson," Flora said. "A man called Sir John Mandeville wrote about it in the Middle Ages. God caused it to be perpetually dark."

"It don't sound very scientific. I don't know what Dr. Farthing would make of it."

"But did not you yourself tell me that your profession is the investigation of ghosts and spirits? This is no less scientific than that, surely?"

"Most of them are frauds, though."

"But some are not, I assume? In any case, we have nothing to go on at present but this information, which might explain why the Count said that his homeland was always dark. There need not be an unscientific cause. Perhaps it is a phenomenon of the weather, storm clouds or something similar."

"And you think the Count has taken Hastings there?"

"It was what he promised to do, was it not? I questioned the librarian about its location, and he eventually informed me that the land of Abkhazia, which is described in the book as bordering on Hanyson, is in the Near East, on the shores of the Black Sea. That confirmed to my mind that it is identical with Cimmeria, which was also said to be on the Black Sea."

"And do you propose to go there, miss?"

"I will do everything I can to trace him here in London first," Flora said. "Meanwhile, we must prepare to set forth on our travels; that is, if you are willing. Are you with me, Cassie?"

# Chapter 24

Dr. Farthing was in a distracted mood this morning. Cassie had arrived late in the office after her long talk with Flora the previous evening, and he had found himself more than usually in need of tea.

"John Carpenter Street!" he said, when she brought him his cup. "A ghost passed just outside this very office, and I was not here to see it! I had only to work a little late, and I would no doubt have bumped into him on my way home."

"Never mind, sir," Cassie said. "I'm sure he'll be back."

"Oh, I doubt it very much. They have the knack of being wherever I am not. Perhaps they even know I am investigating them, and wanted to taunt me."

"Are we not going to go outside and collect evidence, interview the witnesses and so on?"

"Inspector Dollis can do that. I am tired of the whole thing. We know what we will find: the gaslamps went out, there were green fires or purple fires or both, and a tall figure in rusting armour was seen looming over the house fronts by a few lucky pedestrians. At the same time, a number of robberies took place, whether by the hoaxers, or any other criminals who happened to be in the vicinity."

Dr. Farthing reclined on his couch and asked her to leave, saying he wished to think. Cassie put down the filing she had been doing and stepped into the dazzle of the street. A policeman was standing with his back to the door as if on guard, and as she tried to slip past him, he turned with a start and wanted to know what she was doing there.

"It is my place of work," Cassie said. "I am running an errand for my employer."

"And your employer is?"

"Dr. Farthing, the psychic investigator. He is an acquaintance of Inspector Dollis."

"That's as may be, miss, but what was this Dr. Farthing, if such is his name, doing at seven o'clock last evening, may I ask?"

Cassie had some difficulty dissuading the constable, who was clearly anxious to establish his detective credentials, from going in and interviewing Dr. Farthing directly; Inspector Dollis would take care of that, she assured him.

She took the omnibus to Piccadilly, where she bought a copy of *Bradshaw's Continental Railway Guide* and, finding them irresistible, the two volumes of the same publisher's *Hand-Book to the Turkish Empire*, though she was not entirely sure that Hanyson was part of that empire, asking for them to be delivered at Halcyon House. From there, she made her way along Oxford Street to Marshall and Snelgrove, where she purchased a portable stove called an Etna, two leather hot-water bags for warming the hands and feet (more convenient to carry on a journey than the usual earthenware hot-water bottles), some items of luggage and a small picnic hamper, all of which she charged, following Flora's instructions, to Mrs. Alfred Burlap. "Mama is very vague in matters of accounting," Flora had said. "She is most unlikely to notice what she has purchased till Papa questions her about it at the end of the quarter, by which time, God willing, we will be safely out of the country." No one in the two shops questioned her identity; they accepted without question that she was a maidservant in the employ of the Burlap family of Reigate, Surrey.

She went on to Victoria Station, where she ordered two tickets for the boat train in a week's time. They would be arriving in Calais at seven o'clock in the morning, but the clerk assured her that it would be easy to purchase tickets for their onward journey, though he seemed a little puzzled that Cassie did not know where exactly her destination was. "My advice to you, miss," he said, "is to go to Messrs. Thomas Cook and ask them to plot out a full itinerary for your mistress. It is always as well for ladies travelling alone to be sure of their overnight hotel reservations."

"Oh no," Cassie said, "my mistress likes to be free to travel wherever the fancy takes her. And we won't be travelling alone, sir—we'll be travelling together."

It was the middle of the afternoon when she returned to John Carpenter Street. The policeman had gone from the door, and there was no sign of Inspector Dollis's investigations. She found Dr. Farthing pacing around his office. "There you are, Miss Pine. I did not expect you to be gone so long—wherever did you get to?"

"I'm sorry, sir, I had some errands to run, for my mother. I thought as you did not seem to need me—"

"You are not supposed to have a mother during the hours of business."

"I'm sorry, sir," she said again, "I couldn't help myself. And besides, you looked so peaceful there in the candlelight that I thought it would only disturb you if I came back too early."

"That is all very well, but Inspector Dollis disturbed me instead. He drank three glasses of my sherry."

"I thought you seemed agitated, sir."

"How should I not be agitated? It is"—he looked at his watch—"eighteen minutes past three, and I have not yet had any luncheon."

Cassie realized that she had not had any either. "You could of gone out to the chophouse."

"Of course I could have done, but it seemed unwise with policemen all round the door and the Inspector watching my every move, especially as I had no secretary to deal with any enquiries that might be made in my absence."

"I will go and fetch your pie, sir."

"Yes, please do." And then, seeing that Cassie had not yet moved, he added, "I trust there is nothing the matter with your mother, Miss Pine?"

"Oh no, sir," Cassie said, feeling guilty that she had dragged her mother into this business, just as Flora had dragged hers, "she is the same as she ever was."

"Inspector Dollis seems to consider me a suspect now that the ghost has begun operating in my vicinity. As if I would haunt myself!"

"Well, he did say the man at the bottom of all this was a gentleman."

"Yes, he did." Dr. Farthing sat on the couch. "You know, I should like to meet this mastermind of his, if only to find out the motive for his strange behaviour. Inspector Dollis has the advantage of me there; he is the one with the resources of the Metropolitan Police at his disposal, the network of informants and so on, and he is undoubtedly not telling me all he knows. Think of it, Miss Pine: a man with agents in the gasworks, who can turn the lights of London on and off at will, and who uses this unheard of and infernal power not mainly for robbery, or, say, to blackmail the authorities into handing over money, but, as far as I can tell, for entertainment, for the pure fun of the thing!"

# Chapter 25

"You can't stay here," Cassie said.

Flora was inclined to agree. This morning she had been to the offices of *The Times* to place a notice in it requesting information as to the whereabouts of Mr. Hastings Wimbury, then on to the Villiers Theatre where she found Mr. Eweson sick with anger and disappointment. He kept repeating, "I thought better of him, Miss Burlap," and "If you ask me you're better off out of it." She thought of going back to the British Museum, but she hardly knew where to begin searching through those books for odd mentions of Hanyson or Cimmeria. So by mid-afternoon she was back in Halcyon House, where she passed the time reading the volumes of Bradshaw that Cassie had brought back on Friday.

There was no mention in them of any country answering to the Count's description of his homeland. The proposed expedition was beginning to seem like a fool's errand. What was the point of setting off across Europe, crossing one empire after another (Austro-Hungarian, Ottoman, perhaps even Russian) in search of a country whose location was uncertain, whose name was changeable and whose only known characteristic was that it could not be seen? Her heart would have failed her, and she would have gone back to Reigate to weather her family's reproaches, had it not been for Cassie's enthusiasm. Much of this, Flora suspected, was for the mechanics of the journey itself, her Bradshaws and boat trains, Etnas and hot-water bags—in the short time they had known each other, she had become familiar with Cassie's passion for organizing herself and everyone else—but it was fuelled, too, by her love of Hastings, and this was one accomplishment in which Flora was determined not to be outdone. But now that Cassie had made the arrangements and the tickets were booked, there was nothing for Flora to do, nothing to look forward to except Cassie's return from work and the dubious pleasures of dinner.

"Look," Cassie said. "The evening paper."

Flora found the article on an inside page. It stated that a young lady, Miss Flora Burlap, aged twenty-three years, was reported missing from her home and that her parents, Mr. and Mrs. Alfred Burlap of the Rowans, Reigate, had offered a reward of twenty-five guineas for information leading to her restoration to the bosom of her family. "It is most inconspicuous," she said. "I doubt if anyone will notice it."

"But you know Mr. Flewitt reads every word of the paper. It is a mania with him. He likes to read bits of it aloud. Oh, Miss Flora, why did you not give an assumed name when you came here?"

"It never occurred to me. And you really suppose——?"

"For twenty-five guineas, I have no doubt he would contact the police. I'm sure anyone would."

Flora, who, only a few minutes ago, had been contemplating returning to Reigate of her own free will, now felt cold all over at the mention of the police. "And would you, Cassie?"

Cassie put her hand on Flora's arm. "Miss Flora, how could you think it?"

"We are rivals, after all."

"I don't see us as that, somehow. I mean, I know we are, but you can't exactly fight over a man who isn't there, can you, miss? We have to find him, don't we, and then we can fight all we like?"

"I shall not fight at all."

"Well, then, he can choose between us. Either way it don't make any difference if we can't find him, and we can only do that if we work together." Then, as Flora continued to avoid her eyes, "I've bought the tickets, miss, and everything! And we are going to be mistress and maid all across Europe. We couldn't do it alone, we couldn't indeed."

Flora lifted Cassie's hand off. "No, Cassie, but we are mad to contemplate it. We do not even know where we are going."

"You can't go back now. Not if you love him!"

They looked at each other for a moment, and Flora made a convulsive movement, something between a shudder and a shrug. "No. But it seems I may have no choice in the matter, not if Mr. Flewitt's reading habits are as you say."

"That's what I said, you can't stay here. You'll have to leave straight away, before dinner. That gives you half an hour to pack—think you can manage it? I'll help you."

"But where shall I go?"

"There's only one place I can think of."

They walked through the hall together, Cassie carrying Flora's carpet bag. The door of the dining room was open, and Esmé could be seen laying the table; she did not look up as they passed. On the other side of the hall was the drawing room, where the fire was not yet lit, and only one figure could be seen. He was invisible behind his newspaper but they recognized him by the smell of his pipe. It was Mr. Flewitt. Quietly as they tried to walk, he lowered the paper as they passed, and half stood, just enough to make it clear that he would have done so completely if they had entered. "Good evening, ladies," he said from his crouch. "I think it's a little warmer. Spring in the air, eh?"

Cassie smiled. "We're just going…" she said vaguely.

"Taking the air before dinner?" Mr. Flewitt had not noticed the carpet bag, let alone spotted the notice in his paper. "Good idea. I'd join you myself, but…" He took the pipe out of his mouth and looked at it as if puzzled by its presence and the unwelcome responsibilities it imposed on him. "Watch out for those prowling ghost chappies. If you see one, just give a little scream, and I'll come running." He chuckled and sat down.

Then they were outside, in the many-coloured light of the stained-glass door panels. It was strange to think she would probably never go back there; somehow as long as she had been in his room at Halcyon House, she had felt close to Hastings, as if he could return there at any moment. And now this bustling young woman with the uncouth vowels was taking her away from him, perhaps for ever. "Where are we going?" she said.

"Keep your voice down, miss. Only to the bus stop."

"Yes, but after that?"

"To work."

Cassie produced a large key from inside her clothing, and unlocked the door. The narrow street around them was silent and empty. Flora had not known there could be such tranquil spaces in the centre of London; she had had an image in her mind of a city that grew louder and more populous at a consistent rate as one travelled in from the perimeter. There was a gaslamp a couple of yards from where they were standing, and it seemed a waste that it should shine all night on a few feet of cobbles on the off-chance that someone would pass by who needed its illumination. The loneliness of the place made her shiver. In her oversensitive mood it seemed more frightening than a dark country lane would have been, with the buildings crowding round them, all of them designed to be thronged with industrious humanity, and now abandoned to the routine desolation of night.

There was hardly any hallway. Cassie took a candle from the basket by the door and led her up a steep staircase of crumbling grey wood, past several landings with passages leading off them. Dr. Farthing's office was at the top of the building. They stood on a landing that felt more like a platform, and Cassie unlocked this door too. Once inside, she lit several more candles. The furniture loomed into view: a couch, an occasional table, two desks, a couple of chairs and a cabinet that filled most of one wall. It smelled of candles, sherry and damp. Flora took one of the candles in its saucer and walked round the edges, examining everything.

"There are no windows," she whispered.

"You can speak up, miss. There's nobody here but the two of us."

"Oh, but it's frightful!"

"It's my place of work," Cassie said. "I sit on this chair here, and Dr. Farthing sits on that one, or on the couch. He uses that for a bed sometimes. He likes everything peaceful and quiet, almost the atmosphere of a bedroom, which is why there are no gaslamps."

"But how can you bear it?"

"I don't know what you mean by *bear*, miss, it's just what I do."

Flora would rather be a maid, like Esmé or Hannah, than be cooped up in such a space with a snoring gentleman. She was not even sure it was entirely respectable.

"Look, here's a blanket," Cassie said. "Good thing it's not cold at the moment—there was only room in the bag for the one. You'll be sleeping on Dr. Farthing's couch."

"Oh, but I can't. Suppose he comes in and finds me asleep on it?"

"He don't come in till ten o'clock, by which time you'll be long gone. You can stow your belongings under the couch—he won't find them there. Of course you'll have to clean everything up before you go, and not leave a scrap of evidence behind. Dr. Farthing is a regular demon for evidence."

"But, Cassie, I can't live in a place like this!"

"It's only for a few days, miss, till we catch the boat train. You'll have to live rougher than that when we're on our way to Cimmeria."

"I don't think I'm brave enough to go to Cimmeria after all."

"Nonsense, of course you are—it's too late to go back on it now. There's a public baths round the corner in Tudor Street, where you can wash in the morning, and, this being the city, there's lots of places you can buy food. You'll have to find something to do to pass the daylight hours. Dr. Farthing keeps odd hours, but he should be gone by seven o'clock and I can meet you here then. I'll just go out and get us something for our supper. You must be hungry by now."

"And what then? Can't you stay here with me? I should feel much safer in your company."

Cassie sat down on the couch and, after a moment's hesitation, Flora sat beside her. "I can't, see?" Cassie said. "They don't know anything against me, not for certain. It's a shame Mr. Flewitt saw us going out together, and I'm going to have to think up some excuse why I wasn't in for dinner, but I've not done anything they can pin on me. I've got to carry on living at Halcyon House and working for Dr. Farthing as if nothing had happened, otherwise they'd have the police on the both of us, and trace us to here in no time. And if Hastings replies to your advertisement in *The Times*, I need to be there to receive the news. One of us has got to go back and carry on being respectable, and it can't be you, not now."

# Chapter 26

Hastings spent most of the time in the dark now. The Count said he must get used to it if he wanted to adapt to the normal conditions of Cimmerian life. "Yes, it is true we have cooking fires and torches, even candles in the most modern and sophisticated houses, but you cannot be a real Cimmerian until you have trained your mind to our natural element. In time you will find your other senses growing far more acute, and not only those, but your intellectual faculties also. It is a great weakness in the European mind that you write everything down to help yourselves think. No wonder your memories are atrophied."

"My memory is particularly acute," Hastings said, blinking. The Count now turned up for their meetings equipped with a small lantern, whose orange light stupefied him after his hours of privation. As before, Hastings was lying in bed while the Count sat in a chair beside him. His injuries made it inadvisable to move too much, though in fact he had no broken bones, only bruises.

"Because of your acting experience? I suppose so. Let me test you. Can you recite the opening speech of Act 3, Scene 2? 'Speak the speech as I pronounced it to you—'"

"Speak the speech, I pray you, as I pronounced it to you, trippingly on the tongue: but if you mouth it, as many of your players do, I had as lief the town-crier spoke my lines. Nor do not saw the air too much with your hand, thus, but use all gently; for in the very torrent, tempest, and, as I may say, the whirlwind of passion, you must acquire and beget a temperance that may give it smoothness. O, it offends me to the soul to hear a robustious periwig-pated fellow tear a passion to tatters, to very rags, to split the ears of the groundlings, who for the most part are capable of nothing but inexplicable dumbshows and noise: I would have such a fellow whipped for o'erdoing Termagant; it out-herods Herod: pray you, avoid it."

The Count applauded gently. "Most impressive, and a salutary corrective for all over-emphatic actors. And you know the whole part in this way?"

"Count, I know every part."

"Good, for you are to be a manager, not merely an actor, are you not? Nevertheless, I advise you to go over the lines again and again while you lie here. On the third, or the tenth, or the thirtieth, or the three hundredth repetition, the whole play will take shape in your mind as you have never seen it on the page. Such is the extraordinary effect of darkness."

For an hour after he took the light away, Hastings watched the scar it had left in the dark. Or perhaps it was only five minutes—time did not have much meaning now. When the scar had healed, he began reciting the play from the beginning.

"Now, my boy," the Count said, "how would you like to see daylight? I could take you to the slopes of the mountain and show you the bothies and vineyards of the outer Cimmerians."

"Daylight? Oh, I shouldn't think so. I've seen enough daylight to last me a lifetime. I much prefer darkness now."

"Oh, really?"

"Indeed," Hastings said, "I find I have a much better variety of daylight inside my own brain. The normal kind strikes me as a bit, well, prosaic, somehow. A little watery and insipid. It seems strange, Count, that in the workaday world you have to wait for the sun to rise. I wish you would take that lantern away. It gives me a headache."

A hand came from somewhere and patted him on the shoulder. "You are ready, Wimbury. You are a true citizen of Cimmeria. Very well, we shall not venture out on the mountain, or not now, at any rate, for there is much work to be done. Are you perfect in the play?"

"I really think I am. Of course, I used to think so before, but all I meant was that I had learned the text. Being perfect in the play is another matter entirely."

"I told you it was."

"You did, and you were right. Now wherever I go I shall have the play within me, fires and limelight and all. It almost seems a shame to put on a production."

"But a production we must have, for the poor people who do not know the play as you do. What about your bruises—are they better?"

"Much better."

"Good, for you will have to get used to standing and walking about. Do not worry, you will have me with you at all times, so you will not fall again."

"I don't think I should fall anyway. My senses are a great deal sharper than they were before—you were right about that, too. Now take me to this hall of yours, or Piccadilly Circus, as I like to think of it, and we can begin rehearsals."

The Count chuckled. "No, no rehearsals yet. First we must take some photographs."

Hastings had some difficulty at first in understanding why the Count wanted him to dress up in armour and impersonate the Ghost.

"You wanted to play Hamlet, did you not? And the Ghost *is* Hamlet. The old Hamlet."

"I know that, of course, and I remember telling you that I hoped for the part at the Villiers. It was you who told me that the Prince was more suitable for one of my age. And there is no need now for me to start small and build up to the principal role, since this is my own production."

"Here, put this on." The Count handed him a helmet, and Hastings ran his fingers over the visor; although the room they were standing in was brilliantly lit, with a great fire burning, a chandelier hanging from the ceiling and flaming torches in the walls, he had lost the habit of identifying things by sight, and did not like to look for long at them. He used his eyes now as a probe, to be applied briefly after he had used all the other senses.

"I believe this is the very helmet Mr. Barnes wore in that production."

"Of course. Since we were losing you as our agent at the Villiers, we took the opportunity on that last adventure to acquire as many props as possible. You are not still feeling guilty about that, are you?"

Hastings had put the helmet on with the visor down. Being made of papier mâché, it did not entirely shut out the light, but filtered everything to an orange blur, which he found much more agreeable than the dazzle of the lights. "Not at all, Count."

"Of course not. You had worked for them all those months and they had not given you a sniff of a part—that is the idiom, is it not?"

Hastings nodded.

"I like it. Sometimes the English language sounds almost Cimmerian. In any case, you owed them nothing—the debt was all the other way. Do put up your visor, my dear fellow, or how will the audience know who you are? That's better. I am not suggesting you play the Ghost *instead* of Hamlet."

"You mean I can double? But that is impossible—they are on the stage at the same time!"

"You can double, treble, quadruple—you can in fact perform the entire dramatis personae. Has your time in the dark taught you nothing? The whole production is in your own head—you are every part in the play."

Hastings shook his head, making the helmet swivel too with a slight time-lag that made him feel as if he had two heads. "I must admit I cannot understand it."

"There is no need, you must simply do as I say. Here is a sword for you. Hold it like so, good! Now, remember you must stay perfectly still for at least a minute while Briggs takes the photograph. Are you ready, Briggs? Now!"

The flash that followed was the brightest thing Hastings had seen since those evenings he had spent between the sunburner and the limelight.

# Chapter 27

"An odour from another world," Dr. Farthing said. It was late afternoon, and Cassie was feeling simultaneously restless and exhausted. Dr. Farthing had not lain down that day, though several times he had gone over to the couch as if he intended to, and then thought better of it. Each time, Cassie would glance at the rectangle of shadow underneath it, sure that if she stared hard enough she would be able to make out the outline of Flora's carpet bag. Of course, she must not do so, but the temptation, stretched out over the course of the day, had become painful. She had noticed the odour with dismay the moment she stepped into the office: it was the smell of violets that always clung about Flora's person, no doubt from some expensive scent she used. When Flora was there, it was subsumed in her general aura, but now in her absence it was painfully conspicuous. Perhaps it accounted for Dr. Farthing's unusual mood—he had been dismissive earlier when Inspector Dollis had called to drink sherry and ask him about the exceptional ghost activity of the previous night: reports coming in from Moorgate, Clapton, St. John's Wood, even as far away as Ealing. "Don't bother me with your ghosts," he had said, "they are all transparent impersonations!"

"That's the very thing," Dollis had replied, "the transparency. It makes it so much harder to dismiss them as hoaxes."

"Find your mastermind," Farthing told him, "and the hauntings will cease, transparent or otherwise!"

It was not like him to be so curt, but when Dollis had gone Farthing had muttered, half to himself, half to her, "I don't see why the police expect me to do their work for them, *pro bono*. I am supposed to be a professional."

Farthing was not really working that day, nor did he expect Cassie to. He would pick up a book, read a few pages, wander about the room and engage her in conversation. By mid-afternoon, he had at least settled down enough to remain most of the time on the couch, which was a relief to her because from that position he could not possibly see anything unusual stowed underneath it. He was reading only one book now, a volume of poetry which he would put from him then pick up again.

"Do you read poetry at all, Miss Pine?"

"No, sir, I don't think I would understand it."

"You are missing a great deal. Poets are often granted insights that are denied to the rest of mankind. That is why they must express themselves in verse, I suppose, because the language of prose is not fine enough to convey it."

"What is the book?"

"It is a recent poem by one of our modern poets, a man who called himself B.V., though his real name was Thomson. He died only last year, a great loss to all of us who love the night. Listen to this:

'Although lamps burn along the silent streets;
Even when moonlight silvers empty squares
The dark holds countless lanes and close retreats;
But when the night its sphereless mantle wears
The open spaces yawn with gloom abysmal,
The sombre mansions loom immense and dismal,
The lanes are black as subterranean lairs.' "

"It doesn't sound like he loves it, sir. I should of said it was gloomy, and I can't think as it's doing your spirits any good to read such stuff."

"Ah but spirits are the point, Miss Pine. The man must have known London uncommonly well, must have walked its streets and squares almost every night encountering all the queer sights that are to be met with at no other time, even down to its prowling ghosts. Here, this is what he writes of them:

'Some say that phantoms haunt those shadowy streets,
And mingle freely there with sparse mankind;

And tell of ancient woes and black defeats,
And murmur mysteries in the grave enshrined:
But others think them visions of illusion,
Or even men gone far in self-confusion;
No man there being wholly sane in mind.' "

Cassie shuddered. "What's it called, this nasty poem?"

*"The City of Dreadful Night."*

"There you are, you see, he didn't love it. He made a poem out of what he didn't like, which if you ask me is a thoroughly contrary thing to do. I don't know much about poetry, sir, but I always heard it was about flowers and love and suchlike, not ghosts and blue devils."

Dr. Farthing smiled. "Much of it is, you are right. But I think you wrong the nocturnal hours, Miss Pine. They have their uses. Indeed, if there is one fault in our modern world, I would say that it is the perpetual and futile war we wage against night. Have you never wondered why there are so few daytime ghosts?"

"I don't know, sir. I think I supposed they were shy and didn't like coming out when there were a lot of people about and everyone could see them."

"Hm, you put it originally, as you so often do. But now you can hardly say that there are no people about at night-time, not in a great city like London."

"There are still not so many as there are by daylight. Indeed, there are times when it feels awfully lonely." She realized she was thinking about her journey to the office with Flora last night, and glanced quickly at Dr. Farthing in case he could penetrate her thoughts, but his gaze had returned to the book. Seeing her look, he tore himself away.

"It is meant to feel lonely. In fact it should be lonelier still. It is only because we try to force it to compete with daylight that it makes us unhappy. Would B.V. have been so melancholy wandering round the streets at night if there had been no gaslamps gleaming on the river and the houses?"

"He wouldn't have been wandering at all, most likely."

"Precisely. The night is for sleeping, for ceasing to be for a while, so that the human world can rest. And that is something our poor friend B.V. was unable to do—did you know he wrote another poem called 'Insomnia'?"

"I don't sleep all that well myself, sometimes," Cassie said, "but I don't think I'd want to write a poem about it."

"It is our modern malady, Miss Pine—we all suffer from it to a greater or lesser extent, because of the outrages we have committed against the night. Why, in the Middle Ages, no one would have dreamed of venturing out of doors after dark. If a man happened to be out late on some business or other when night fell, he was filled with panic, not just because it was hard to find his way in the absence of any light other than that of the moon and stars, but also because the dark hours were the preserve of brigands, and worse, those nocturnal manifestations I told you of before: the fiery ball, the flame, the ghostly goose—everything, in fact, that did not make sense to the daylight mind. They even had a word for being caught out in this way: they called it being 'benighted'. It is a word we now associate with a state of ignorance and desperation, but for our ancestors it simply meant overtaken by darkness, and now everyone is benighted regularly, and then we wonder why we can't sleep."

*Benighted*, Cassie thought. *I have been benighted, as I am every night.* It was in fact only just twilight, and, as she returned furtively to John Carpenter Street, the lamplighter was moving ahead of her, stopping at each lamp to light it with a long pole. She was reminded of a bee settling briefly on one flower after another, though in this case the bloom only appeared after the bee had settled. As each flame appeared, the street seemed to grow a degree darker, so that by the time the lamplighter had turned the corner at the end it was night indeed, though a night that still had the bluish tinge of early evening. Cassie had left at five o'clock as usual, but stayed close to the office, returning discreetly at intervals of roughly half an hour to see if Dr. Farthing had left yet. In setting the rendezvous at seven o'clock, she was trusting to Flora's good sense not to hang around the door too conspicuously, for she was not entirely sure what time Dr. Farthing went home at night, and it would never do to have him blunder into a strange woman, especially not one who smelled of the violets that had been haunting him all day. If he did not emerge before the appointed hour, she would just have to take Flora somewhere else. Finally, as she watched from her corner she saw him hurry out of the door, lock it hastily after him and almost run in the direction of Fleet Street where he would be able to catch a cab home. For a man so torpid in the hours of daylight, he seemed remarkably energetic now, holding his hat on with one hand against the breeze. Cassie looked at her watch; it wanted five minutes of seven o'clock, and it was safe now to stand outside the door.

She did not have to wait more than a minute, for Flora had had her own nook at the other end of the street, and now came out of it to greet her. "I thought he would never leave," she said.

Cassie unlocked the door and they climbed the stairs as they had the previous night. When they were seated in the office with the candles lit, Cassie asked Flora how her day had been.

"A very tedious one. The hour I passed making myself respectable at the bath-house was the most exciting part of it. I have never been to such an establishment before—it is like a temple dedicated to the twin goddesses of soap and water. For the rest, I spent the day in the British Museum, but I have no further news of Cimmeria, indeed I did not know where to look. I have read *The Travels of Sir John Mandeville* from cover to cover, only because I had to read something to justify being there. Cassie, I am not at all sure that Cimmeria exists, or that if it does we shall be able to find it."

"No, but we've got to look for it. At least we've got to look for Hastings."

"Have you heard anything?"

"How could I have, miss, when I haven't been back to Halcyon House all day? If he sees the advertisement in *The*

*Times*, he will call there. Or maybe he'll send a letter, which will take a day or more longer."

"Don't you work with the Metropolitan Police Force?"

"Inspector Dollis was here today, but I can't exactly ask him to his face about my lost fiancé—excuse me, I mean the one we have both lost. If we wanted to report him missing we could have done so, but you know as well as I do why we haven't."

"No, I suppose you're right. But Cassie, this is unbearable. You can't imagine the night I spent. That couch is the most uncomfortable bed I have ever slept on, indeed I hardly slept at all in this horrible place with its queer noises and queerer odour. There is a quality to the very darkness that I have seen nowhere else. It comes of having no windows. I was always getting up to light a candle and then putting it out again for fear of going to sleep with it lit and burning the place down. How can you work here in such conditions?"

"Dr. Farthing says it is more peaceful. There was a window in the room when he first took over the premises, but he had it bricked up."

"Forgive me, Cassie, but this Dr. Farthing of yours sounds insane."

"He is a very brilliant man, miss."

"Then, Cassie—"

Cassie glanced at her quickly. The same thought had occurred to both of them, so Flora hardly needed to ask her next question, but she did so anyway.

"Why don't you ask him where Cimmeria is?"

# Chapter 28

"Violets again," Dr. Farthing said, "and if anything they are stronger than yesterday. Do you smell them, Miss Pine?"

"No, sir. Why are you so sure it's a ghost, being as you're always so sceptical in your investigations?"

"Because I can think of no other explanation. And because no one is trying to make me believe it is one."

"It could be," Cassie said, "something to do with myself. A scent I'm wearing or a soap I wash myself with. Or I could keep dried violets pressed among my clothes."

"Good, you are thinking logically. These thoughts had occurred to me, of course, but no, Miss Pine, you have worked in this office for more than a year. I know your distinctive odour, and this is quite different from that."

"Oh."

"Have I said something to upset you?"

"It don't matter, sir. I wanted to ask you—"

"Yes?"

"Have you ever heard of a place called Cimmeria?"

Dr. Farthing sat down on the couch. "Who has been talking to you about this?"

"So you have heard of it then? Only a friend of mine would like to find out about it."

"Why?"

Cassie had not thought this far ahead, having assumed that she would simply ask for the information and he would provide it—he did not normally need any encouragement. "Well, sir," she began, and found the words of the lie formed themselves in her mind without any effort. "She has received a proposal of marriage from a gentleman of that country, er, region, and she wants to know if it is wholly respectable, and what it would be like to live there."

"Respectable? I don't know much about it. It is mentioned by Homer."

"Yes, I, she has heard that, but you don't have any more recent information by any chance?"

"It is, um, quite a dark country, I believe. That is, if it really exists." Dr. Farthing got up again and began pacing around the room, staring at the floorboards. "Do you know, Miss Pine, this ghostly smell in the room has unsettled me somewhat. I cannot keep my mind on anything. It is as if that one unfamiliar sensation has spread its contagion to the surrounding area and now nothing seems familiar, not the desk, not the chair, not the couch, not even your good self. Do you know, even"—he stared at the couch—"even the configuration of shadows cast by the candles seems queer to me now, though I have always found their light so comforting. I could almost swear—"

"We know the land is dark, sir, that is, she and I have heard that it is. We were wondering if you knew how we could find it, whether there were any railways that went in that direction?"

Farthing was standing behind Cassie's chair now, and not being able to see him made her feel uneasy. "Railways?" he said. "Why on earth would anyone build a railway there? And why should anyone want to go there now, in these modern times? Even the Greeks avoided the place. Those shadows really are queer, Miss Pine. It's almost as if there's an object underneath."

"I told you, sir, she has been proposed to by a gentleman from those parts."

"Then she should refuse him! She cannot possibly wish to live in such a benighted country!"

"You used that word yesterday, didn't you? When you were talking about that poem by the man that used only his initials. I thought then that you were all in favour of night."

"Well, so I am: night is all very well in its place. It's just that I cannot see why any modern, educated young British lady would want to live there. Hallo, do you hear that?"

There were usually doors banging and footsteps coming and going in this building, which was shared by the offices of many professional establishments, so Cassie would have been more likely to notice if they had ceased. But now that he called her attention to them, she became aware of a set of footsteps that had detached itself from the rest and was climbing the last flight to their office: a visitor, and a female one. They stopped on the landing, and there was a pause. Then the knock came, very gently, a well-bred knock.

"You may admit her, Miss Pine."

"Come in," Cassie called, and the door opened.

The visitor was Flora.

"Curious," Dr. Farthing said. "You give every appearance of being a living woman."

Flora smiled into her teacup, no doubt taking the remark for a joke.

"And yet you have been haunting me. You have, if I may say so, a distinctive odour of violets, which I have been smelling for some time now. May I ask if you have been in this office before, quite recently?"

"I have, sir."

"Last night, perhaps?"

"And the night before that."

"Oh, Miss Flora," Cassie said. "You didn't ought to of come back. I could have found out what we wanted to know on my own. I didn't mean him to know everything."

If Dr. Farthing was offended by being spoken of in the third person in his presence he showed no sign of it. Flora gave Cassie a cold look. "It is no use, Cassie. There is no point in my wasting another day at the British Museum. Only Dr. Farthing can help us now." She turned to him. "And I feel you have no cause to do so, sir, unless I am prepared to be completely honest with you."

"Quite, madam. So you have been sleeping on my couch. I hope it was comfortable?"

"Not in the least, but I had no right to expect comfort, not having been invited."

"Indeed. And what brought you to these unsuitable premises, may I ask?"

Dr. Farthing had listened to many outlandish stories in the course of his career, and was accomplished at disguising any surprise or incredulity he might feel. He did not even object when his pointed glance at Cassie to indicate that she should be taking notes met with no response. Perhaps he understood that there was no need for her to take notes, since the story was as much hers as Flora's, or perhaps he was too absorbed in it to pay her any further attention.

"So," he said when she had finished, "the country really exists!"

"You have heard of it?" Flora asked.

"I have heard stories, in my time at Oxford. But I was never quite sure."

"And you believe everything I have told you?"

"You do not exhibit the characteristics of an accomplished liar. I am not so sure about this Count you refer to, however. He may very well be lying, though not, I think, about coming from Cimmeria—his story is too precise and detailed for that. But as for putting on a production of *Hamlet* and needing to steal equipment from a theatre to do so, that does seem a little far-fetched. No, I suspect he wants Hastings—Mr. Wimbury, I mean—and the limelight and magic lanterns for some other purpose, though I cannot think what. I have to admit Cimmeria is a long way outside my territory. I have always concentrated my attention on our humble British hauntings, in fact on London itself, which contains enough peculiarities to interest a hundred investigators."

"Do you know where it is?" Cassie asked.

"Why do you ask?"

"Because Miss Flora and I have made up our minds to go there and fetch Hastings back, only there's no sense in us going until we know where to go, if you follow me. All we know is that it's on the Continent somewhere, or maybe beyond the Continent altogether, so we've bought the tickets as far as Calais, and after that we're on our own."

"I have looked it up in the encyclopaedia," Flora put in. "It may be in Spain, or Italy, or Russia, on the Black Sea Coast. I incline to the latter, on the grounds that it is farther away, which would explain why we hear so little of it in this country. But we know nothing for certain."

"It seems a rash journey for two ladies to undertake. Besides, Miss Pine, you are my employee. I have not given you leave to do any such thing."

"I give you my notice, sir, as of this moment."

"As simply as that." Dr. Farthing sighed. "I have always regarded you as more than an assistant, Miss Pine. You have been, in a manner of speaking, my apprentice in this queer profession that no one much follows except myself."

Cassie nodded.

"It is usual to give a month's notice. How long are you giving me?"

"We are leaving on Friday evening, sir."

"I see. I see. So little time. Well, if you must, you must, I suppose. I should still advise against it, but—"

"I'm sorry, Dr. Farthing."

"Yes, I dare say you are." He paused. "At any rate, it would be madness to go unless you know where you are going. Cimmeria: it is a challenge you have set me, but I have always enjoyed a challenge, and you must have noticed I was getting a little tired of those prowling ghosts with their silly pyrotechnics. I am a scholar in my small way, though I have spent the latter part of my life in more practical investigations. I shall go to Oxford, to the Bodleian, and perhaps also to other, less widely known repositories of information. What time are you planning to leave on Friday?"

"The boat train departs from Victoria at five minutes past seven," Cassie said.

"I shall need nearly all that time to find the information you need. Miss Pine, you may take the rest of the week off. Miss Burlap, you are welcome to continue your uncomfortable residence in my office until your departure. I shall meet you both here at five o'clock on Friday, when, God willing, I shall have all the information you need to plan your journey."

# Chapter 29

After each of her morning visits to the bath-house, Flora felt that it was not just her own body that had been scrubbed clean, but the whole city. It was not at all like washing back in Reigate, which was a private ritual known only to herself and Hannah. Here, even though she paid the extra fee for a bathroom to herself, there was still the queuing with dozens of other women for towels and soap in a building that was oppressively hot and draughty at the same time, echoing with distant splashes and laughter. It gave her the sense of being processed by a vast engine powered by all the fires and waters of London. And coming out again was like stepping from a dark church into the light of a Sunday morning, a mingled sensation of physical cleanliness and spiritual purity. It was in such a mood, as she turned the corner from Tudor Street into John Carpenter Street, that Flora came face-to-face with herself.

She remembered the photograph well. She had given one of the prints of it to Hastings at his own request, though she did not like it. It made her look a good deal older than three-and-twenty, and the stern expression on her face looked like what it was, a failed attempt at dignity by one who had been holding herself motionless too long for comfort. And all to reduce herself to an arrangement of grey shades on paper! Photographs were not lifelike—they bore much the same relationship to real people as a newspaper did to a novel. So here she was, pasted on a wall, a lady made of the same stuff as newsprint, and with a printed text underneath, describing her as missing from her home and requesting that any information as to her whereabouts be reported to the nearest police station. At least the poster was new—she had not been notorious, probably, for more than a few hours. And today was Thursday. Tomorrow evening she would be on the boat train, and by the next morning out of the country altogether, beyond the reach of police and parents.

There was a fresh shock as she was climbing the last flight of stairs to the office: the sound of voices within, Cassie's and a male one, deeper and less cultivated than Dr. Farthing's. She thought at once of the poster she had just seen, and hesitated on the step, almost ready to turn and run, till she was able to convince herself of the absurdity of such an action—not only was it highly unlikely that anyone knew she was hiding here, but even if they did, there was nowhere for her to run to. She crossed the landing and knocked.

Cassie's visitor was a broad-shouldered bald man who evidently had no intention of staying long as he was standing with his hat in his hand and still wearing his fawn overcoat. "Inspector Dollis, this is my associate, Miss Brown," Cassie said.

The visitor held out his hand, and Flora, hardly knowing what she was doing, fluttered her fingers over his. The man was a policeman! Surely he must have seen her image, if not in the street below then on the wall of his own police station! And why did Cassie have to choose such a transparent assumed name, and one, moreover, that began with the same letter as Flora's own? She did not like to look at his face, certain that if she did she would see in it some sign of recognition. And she was, apparently, an associate. What was an associate supposed to say, if questioned about the details of her work?

"So," the Inspector said. "Dr. Farthing's not satisfied with one lady assistant no more, Miss Pine—he's got to have himself another one. It's a very small space for the three of you. And you can't enjoy working by candlelight, when there's a nice bright day outside, Miss Brown."

"One becomes accustomed to it."

"Already? You ain't been here long. And I don't know how he has enough work to keep two assistants busy, though I must confess, ma'am, I've never really understood the ins and outs of Dr. Farthing's profession, except in so far as it touches on my own." Seeing that Flora made no reply, he continued, "I've just been telling Miss Pine here that I came with a bit of good news for Dr. Farthing, only it appears as he's not at home, from what she tells me." He looked at her questioningly as if the evidence of Cassie and his own eyes were not enough.

"No," Flora said, seeing that some reply was called for, "he is, as my colleague has told you"—she looked desperately at Cassie but no help was forthcoming—"away," she concluded.

"Yes, she told me he was off doing research in Oxford or some such place. Shame, that, as I would have liked to give him the news today, but I may drop in for a glass of werewolf blood tomorrow. In any case, you can tell him that by the weekend I trust a certain friend of ours will be behind bars."

"A certain friend of ours will be behind bars," Cassie said.

"That's it exactly. He'll know what I mean."

"Yes," Flora said, "but we don't."

"Oh it's secret, ma'am, though I dare say Miss Pine has some notion of who we're talking about. We don't know his name yet or where we can get our hands on him, but I know a man who knows a man, and he should be able to lead me to him. That's how we do things in the Yard, knowing men that knows men, and it's a deal quicker than looking it up in libraries, you may tell him. Or not, as you prefer. Good day, ladies. It's been a pleasure, Miss Brown."

As he was leaving, he noticed the pile of luggage in the corner of the room, which had grown a little each morning as Cassie brought a new batch on the omnibus from Halcyon House. "Going on a little trip, is he? When he comes back from this one?"

"Yes, that's right," Cassie said, looking to Flora for reinforcement.

"Indeed," Flora added, "to France."

The Inspector tutted as if to say it was just what he would expect from a man like Farthing.

"I have drawn the map myself," Dr. Farthing said next day. "I could find none that showed Cimmeria at all, which is not surprising, since it is not only mostly subterranean but known by a number of different names, a nightmare for even the most scientific of cartographers. In addition to that, I wished to show the route you will take, and none of the maps I consulted was on the appropriate scale or had the right level of detail. You were right, Miss Burlap, to suggest it was near the shores of the Black Sea. It is not, however, in the Tauric Chersonese, as your source suggested. That is here, on the northern shore: it is another name for the Crimea, the remote peninsula of Russia that was the scene of our war with that Empire some thirty years ago. No, Cimmeria is about twenty miles inland from the southern shore, so my researches have saved you a tedious diversion. It is here." His map was spread out awkwardly on the desk, its corners held down by the teapot, milk jug, sugar bowl and slop dish. As there were only two chairs in the office and the couch was too far away, Dr. Farthing remained standing. He was in one of his nervous moods and several times came close to dislodging the supports of his map as he swept his hands over it with unnecessarily extravagant gestures. "Sadly the rail connections are poor or non-existent after Vienna, as your Bradshaws have no doubt made clear to you. I would suggest that from Paris you travel south to Marseille and thence proceed mostly by sea: Naples, Athens, Smyrna. Then you are in the right country, for Cimmeria is, nominally, part of the Ottoman Empire."

"I can hardly see it," Flora said.

"Here, where my finger is. I have labelled it with its proper name, or at least its modern one, Hemshin. You will have to cross almost the whole of Anatolia to get there. Perhaps again a steamer along the Black Sea coast to the point where you have to strike inland might be the best approach rather than hiring camels or mules or whatever they have in those parts. In any case, I doubt if any European woman has made the journey before. Are you sure you have the courage to undertake it?"

"I have the courage for anything," Flora said. To be honest, she was not sure she had—it was simply that the obstacles in her path, like the rest of the details of their journey were not apparent to her yet. "We have heard nothing in response to the advertisement we placed in *The Times*. The gentleman in whose well-being we are both interested has been unable to respond to us, and we are convinced that he is now in Cimmeria. It is our duty to follow him there."

"I envy you," Dr. Farthing said. "They are a very ancient people, almost a mythical one, and their way of life has not changed much since Homer's time. You will be pioneers, perhaps the first great female explorers the world has ever known. Miss Pine?"

"Yes, sir?"

"I think you are being very foolish."

"I know I am, sir, but I hope to be foolish in the most efficient way possible."

"I am not sure where I shall find another assistant like you. To think I will have to solve the case of the prowling ghosts on my own."

"Oh."

"Yes, Miss Pine?"

"All the excitement of the map and your researches put it out of my mind, sir. Inspector Dollis called yesterday. He said to tell you that a certain friend of ours will be behind bars."

"A certain friend..." Farthing passed a hand across his brow as if to wipe away the traces of Cimmerian blackness that still lingered there and clear it for contemplation of this new topic.

"Yes, because he knows a man that knows a man, which in his opinion is quicker than looking things up in libraries."

Farthing had lost interest in the map. He wandered over to his couch and sat down. "Did he say when our friend will be behind bars?"

"He said by the weekend."

"I see. Well..." He sat in thought till Flora began to wonder if he had gone to sleep with his eyes open.

"At least," Cassie said, "the business is over, even if it isn't yourself that solved it, sir."

"Yes, that is a comfort, I suppose." He continued to sit there as if stunned, as Cassie got up to clear away the tea things and take them downstairs to be washed. She did not seem to be in any hurry, but Flora had no need to look at her watch to know that it was almost time to leave.

# Chapter 30

It had been a grey chilly day and the evening was setting in as they alighted from the hansom and Cassie began negotiating with a porter to take their luggage to the boat train. Flora, wondering if she was always going to feel as useless as she did now, a mere appendage to the expedition in which it was her servant who was the true explorer, stared through the open doors at the crowded station interior. The lights made it seem welcoming, as if she were about to step into a great house with a fire blazing in the hall, an impression intensified by the smell of smoke in the air. So many people were coming and going around her that, despite the width of her skirts, she felt the pressure of their bodies pushing her first one way and then another, though most were too respectful to jostle in the true sense of the word. A second aspect of this involuntary intimacy was that she was constantly finding herself right up against a stranger's face: a man with white whiskers and a spot on his nose, a woman with a smudge of rouge on her cheek. Sometimes they met her eye and she flinched—once so sharply that the woman in question muttered an apology to her. Would Cassie never finish her conversation with the porter?

It was herself again, her head and shoulders pasted to a pillar beside the door, the embarrassing, inescapable likeness of a Flora who no longer existed, if indeed she ever had, appealing to every person to track her down and hand her back to her family. A gap-toothed young fellow, hands in pockets, was staring at it now. Just as Flora passed him he gave a shrug and turned away, almost bumping into her. Flora gathered her skirts and tacked to the right to avoid him, nearly tripping Cassie, who had been following a yard behind.

"It's this way, miss."

As soon as they had left the man behind, Flora fell back and muttered in Cassie's ear. "Did you see the poster at the entrance?"

"No, miss."

"They are probably all over the station. Oh, look, Cassie, there is a constable over there!"

"There's always a constable at stations, to look out for pickpockets. He's not interested in us, miss."

Crossing the crowded space in pursuit of the porter, who wheeled his trolley with an elusiveness they could not hope to match, Flora was convinced that everyone was staring at her, comparing her with the photograph they must surely all have seen. She tried to look at the ground to make herself less conspicuous, but that only meant bumping into people more often, with the consequent disruption to their progress and increased exposure to scrutiny as she and the stranger separated and apologized to each other. Somehow they reached the platform, where the train had not yet arrived. There were fewer people here but space was more restricted. The other passengers took no notice of them, as they were all staring along the track to the arch of gloom where the world beyond the station began, as if trying to conjure the train into being.

"Should be here by now," Cassie whispered.

Once it appeared, they would be safe. The process of boarding the train and taking their places in the compartment, the departure from the station, these were mere technical details: as soon as the fire and smoke of the engine appeared in the distance, the chain of events would have started which would take her outside the jurisdiction of Great Britain and into the world of their adventure. But something was preventing this from happening. As she continued to wait, this obstacle came to seem like a physical thing inside herself. She felt it so strongly it was almost a pain, somewhere in the region of her abdomen. And at last she recognized what it was.

"Cassie," she said, "I must go…"

"What, miss?"

"You know." Flora indicated the far side of the station with a twitch of her bonnet.

"Oh, but you can't, miss, not now. The train will be here any moment. Can't you wait?"

Flora tried to picture the facilities that were available in trains. With another internal pang she realized that she was about to leave civilization behind, perhaps for ever. If only her body could cease its functions for the duration of the journey! Murmuring something to Cassie, she turned back the way they had come.

She emerged a few minutes later with a new feeling of peace in her lower regions, while the rest of her was more agitated than ever; above her, only a few yards away, hung the station clock, already showing two minutes past seven. It was not their fault that the train was late: surely, it could not now leave at the scheduled hour? It would have to wait long enough to give all the passengers time to board. The crowd seemed thicker than before as she made her way through them, more reluctant to step aside. She started to appeal to them, first with simple *excuse me*s, then with gabbled explanations of her lateness, finally with direct instructions: "*Would* you be so good as to make way?" These began to have an effect; people nudged each other, enjoying the spectacle of a lady in flight, flushed and out of breath, but stepped aside anyway.

When she reached the entrance to the platform, the train was there, and most of the passengers had already boarded. The engine was releasing puffs of smoke from its funnel, which gave it an impatient look, like a horse snorting when looking forward to a gallop. Cassie was almost where she had left her, but had approached a little closer to the train to supervise the porter who was loading their luggage into the guard's van. She turned, saw Flora and made an agonized face to indicate the urgency of the situation. Flora, giving up any pretence of dignity, picked up her skirts and ran. Her eyes were still on Cassie, however, and she overlooked a figure who moved in front of her at the same instant, surging into him at full tilt. He nearly fell, but steadied himself, pushing back against her so that his shoulder came into painful contact with her bosom. Both of them cried out, and clutched at each other, so that for a few moments they were embracing awkwardly before they recollected themselves and began the process of apology.

Flora recognized him first—it was the gap tooth. Her gasp startled him and made him look at her face for an explanation. Then he knew her.

"Here, it's you, ain't it?"

"Will you excuse me, please?"

"It's you!" The delight on his face suggested that he had encountered an old friend. He seized her by the shoulder, and looked round for someone to share his good fortune with. There was no one except the population of the station as a whole, so he announced it to them: "It's her! The lady in the picture!"

"You are mistaken. Will you let me go, please?"

"No, you've got to come with me. Sorry, ma'am, but you're wanted. I've got to take you…" He stopped, realizing that he was not immediately sure *where* to take her.

"Unhand me," Flora said, finding an opportunity to use the expression at last, and, as she did so, perceiving the possibility of bringing others to her aid. "This man has laid hands on me. Help." The last word did not come out so forcefully as she had intended. It was more of a statement than an exclamation, and caused little stir, only a few curious glances among the people meeting friends from the train or hurrying past to other platforms. Even Cassie, still engaged with the porter, did not glance again in her direction. Flora tried a second cry, "Help." The volume was greater this time, but it could not be called a shout, let alone a scream. Nevertheless, it did catch Cassie's ear. She turned now and looked at the two of them, her expression from this distance a caricature of puzzlement. "Cassie!" Flora called, and at last the sound came out with urgency.

Cassie turned, called something and ran towards them, but, instead of stopping to remonstrate with the man, she continued past them, leaving Flora struggling in his grip. Flora thought at first that she had given the whole adventure up and was about to return to Halcyon House. Then she saw the logic of Cassie's disappearance: she had gone for assistance. Through the occasional gaps that appeared in the throng, Flora could see her engaged in conversation with the constable they had observed earlier. "Cassie!" she called again, this time with a pleading note; a policeman was the last thing she needed. In desperation, she resolved to struggle with the man herself before the constable arrived. He was still only holding her with one hand while he continued looking round for others to come to his aid; he did not seem to have noticed either Cassie or the policeman. Flora seized his wrist with both hands and tried to wrench it away, but he only held her more painfully, and pulled her towards him, grasping at her waist with his other hand to secure her properly. He was no taller than she was, and Flora now found herself inches from his face, which smelled of hair oil and tobacco. She put up one hand in defence, and then conceived the idea of pushing the face away in the hope that the rest of him would go with it. This was more successful—at least, the face tilted to an uncomfortable-looking angle, though he was still holding her as tightly as ever. Flora continued to push, until her little finger found its way into his open mouth, which caused her to cry out in disgust. The man tried to say something at the same time, so that his teeth briefly clamped her finger. It was not exactly a bite, but Flora perceived it as such, and screamed still more. At the same time, she brought her other hand up and clawed at his face to make him release her. She felt the plump wetness of an eyeball beneath her index finger, and the man cried out and let go.

She must have run right past Cassie and the constable; if so, she did not see them. If there were people round her or standing in her way, she was not aware of them either. Nor did she hear the shouting of the crowd, or the hiss of the engines in the background, or the echoes of wheels and hoofs in the street as she approached it. For all she knew, she was running across an empty field, though one that was lit by gas rather than sunlight. As for where she was going, she had no more idea of that than a horse does when it bolts. And, just as the bolting horse must do, she felt in running an exhilaration independent of the danger that caused it or the consequences that must follow. Probably she banged into several people; she was aware of buffets and sudden changes of direction imposed on her. But she never allowed these to slow her for more than a moment—it would take a much greater obstacle than these to stop her.

The approved method of stopping a runaway horse is to place one's hands over its eyes. And Flora was stopped in the same way, by the disabling intervention of darkness. The lights in the station had gone out.

# Chapter 31

It is dark in Victoria Station. In the forecourt where the hansom cabs wait, the horses are whinnying in panic. One of the hansoms had just set off, with an elderly gentleman aboard; when the streetlamps went out, the cabby's first reaction was to pull on the reins and stop half in the road and half out of it. "Oh, for heaven's sake!" his passenger says, no doubt late already, but the cabbie refuses to move until he has lit the lamps on his cab and can see where he is going. And he is not wrong: already, a few hundred yards along Vauxhall Bridge Road, an omnibus has mounted the pavement as the horses were panicked by the sudden change and missed the turning; it has skewed round, blocking most of the road, and disorientated passengers are beginning to clamber out, and walk this way and that with no thought for any traffic that might still be moving.

It is not only the streetlights that have gone out. There are no chandeliers glittering behind the windows of the grand houses of Belgravia, no gaslamps warming the curtains of Pimlico. The familiar nocturnal islands of darkness, the twin rectangles of Eaton Square Gardens, the shapeless expanses of Green Park and St. James's Park have been swallowed. The processions of lights along Birdcage Walk and Constitution Hill and the Mall have vanished, and Buckingham Palace, which rose between them every night like a magic lantern projection in a pantomime, has gone out. In the West End, the dresses in the window displays are invisible now, the theatres and restaurants are closed for the night, the late shoppers and early diners and playgoers are wandering together, undecided whether to go home again or to wait till normality is restored—either way they would have no notion which way to go. Some of them are singing.

Through Barnes, Hammersmith, Fulham, Putney, Wandsworth, Battersea and Chelsea the Thames passes, not bearing its usual freight of reflected shore lights, though the lanterns of the small boats and barges that continue moving make of it a spectral highway to replace those that have been lost. Downstream from the Tower, in the Docks, the great ships are illuminated monuments, and the commerce of small lights between them is busier even than that upstream. The eclipse of the land has given substance to the river by contrast with the formlessness it moves through. Only in one stretch has the land retained its character: this is Victoria Embankment, still lit by the dazzling white of its electric Yablochkov candles. These have drawn people down to the waterside so that it is more thronged even than usual. Stranded between black river and blacker London, the crowd looks like a freshly arrived crew of souls on the banks of the Styx, and displays the nervous exhilaration one might expect from the new dead. Someone is playing waltzes on a violin, and many people are dancing, moving in and out of the crowd of pedestrians.

In the houses people are stumbling around in search of candles, oil lamps and lanterns. Pockets of light are appearing here and there in the residential districts, dimmer and warmer than the gaslamps; there is something introverted about them, visible from the street but not sharing their illumination with it. On this cold spring evening many houses have fires in their hearths, and these have now taken on a different character, each one a small earthbound sun to the family gathered around it.

In some places, coloured fires are beginning to appear, flaring and dimming irregularly and giving out thunderclouds of smoke: the green fire that turns everything around it ghostly; the purple one with spits and streaks of yellow in it like a field of crocuses; the red like a regiment marching into the thick of battle. People are drawn to them on the principle that any light is better than none at all, and the firelit areas, Piccadilly Circus, Marble Arch, Trafalgar Square, are the places where the prowling ghosts congregate, too. There is something inhuman in their outlines: they may be taller than an ordinary mortal, perhaps furry, perhaps surmounted by a vast pair of cow horns. They move with a sense of purpose that marks them out from the crowd, going swiftly from one person to another. If you come face to face with them, you are confronted with a skull, or fangs and staring red eyeballs. Let them come too close and they may threaten you with a knife or a pistol. Some ghosts don't even bother to threaten, tearing at your clothes to get at your valuables as you stand there stupefied.

Outside the west front of St. Paul's the figure of a man appears, not directly in front of the pillars of the portico but a little to one side, against the wall of one of the towers. He is at least ten feet tall, and the impression of height is exaggerated by the fact that his feet are not touching the ground. They are clad in silvery metal, and the rest of him, too, is armoured, with hinged plates over the knees and hips, a vast ridged breastplate, more articulations at the shoulders and elbows, a helmet with the visor raised. The armour is silver with brass or gold buckles; in places it seems to be rusting slightly. He wears a long sword in a scabbard at his hip. He has a white beard, and a stern, wrinkled face, and stares slightly downwards. The overall impression is of a wispy paleness, and things are visible through his body: a window behind his head, the stones of the wall through his chest. For a long time he does not move, and then, abruptly, he raises his right arm. He turns his head with equal suddenness, and makes a beckoning gesture, as if wanting the assembled populace to come inside. This is too much for many of them: they scream and run, crashing into the people behind, stumbling on paving stones and the kerb of the road at Ludgate Hill, falling and being trampled on.

In Trafalgar Square in front of the National Gallery, another figure shimmers, not touching the ground, in front of the solid wall at the side rather than the pillars in the centre. This time it is an old woman, the eyes hollow, and with a gaping red wound in her chest. A brazier of red fire is burning on the gallery steps, causing people to cough. The woman lifts her hands; her mouth opens and closes and blood is seen running from her wound.

# Chapter 32

When Flora ran past, Cassie broke off her discussion with the constable and ran after her. She had never seen a lady run like that, heedless of the people she collided with, causing panic and outrage as she went. It was all Cassie could do to stay a few yards behind: Flora, being both longer-legged and in the grip of a temporary insanity, was the faster runner, but was clearing obstacles out of the way as she went, so that Cassie had some hope. When the lights went out, Flora was just passing through the open doors of the station. Cassie was struck motionless; it was almost completely dark, only alleviated by a hint of orange in the black which no doubt originated from some of the engines drawn up by the platforms. She called out, "Miss Flora! Miss Flora!" but others were calling all round her, so she had little hope of making contact that way. There was a picture in her mind of Flora as she had been at the moment of extinction, a whirl of dark green skirts in the doorway. If she had been mad enough to carry on running, she would surely have come to grief within a few yards—there were horses and carriages out there as well as pedestrians. Cassie knew she must try and get as far as the doors at least, though all her instincts demanded that she stay where she was. She overrode them and took a step forward without harm.

Her second step brought her in contact with a leg. She did not stop but took a further step in the hope that it would move away of its own accord; she had no choice but to continue in a straight line to the point where she had last seen Flora. The leg did not move, however, and Cassie now found herself pressed against an upper body. "Here," it said in a man's voice, "what are you up to?"

"Will you excuse me, please?" Cassie said.

"Don't know as I will," the man said, sounding pleased with his wit, or with the novelty of the situation. Cassie clutched him in the region of the arms and wrenched him to the right as hard as she could, causing him to cry out in alarm. The leg was no longer in front of her, and she was able to push past. She heard the man curse, but if he attempted any reprisal he must have missed, for she was free of him now, and moving recklessly fast. This night-walking was just a matter of having faith, the belief that she would be able to deal with any solid objects that blocked her path as she had with this first one.

The second object she encountered was another leg, though whether it was a man's or a woman's, stationary or in motion, she could not say. She felt a heavy blow in the middle of her right shin, which did not immediately cause her to fall. As she struggled to maintain her balance, however, a third object, definitely moving this time, caught her in the left hip, pushing her further in the direction she was leaning to recover from the previous impact, and this time she could not save herself. A fall for a grown-up person is always catastrophic, since we do it so seldom that we have little practice at falling harmlessly. It is worse if one is trammelled by skirts and corsets, and worst of all when it happens in the dark. Cassie felt she was being smothered, strangled and assaulted all at once. A knee struck the ground, then a hand and wrist, then her forehead and right eyebrow. Then there was nothing for a while, and she lay there in a kind of relief, thinking, *at least it has stopped happening*. There was some pain, but it felt far away, as if it were being experienced by another person entirely. She was more bothered by her inability to breathe properly. She hoped she had not injured any internal organs. There was a little bottle of Chlorodyne in her reticule, which should help if it had not been smashed, but she was not sure where her reticule was.

Cassie's fall had not gone unnoticed among the benighted crowd. They were calling out a repetitive commentary on it: *Here, watch out, somebody's fallen, who is it, a lady's fallen, I think, is that you, love, oh thank God, are we all here, make way somebody, anyone know where she is, over here, I think*. At least, Cassie thought, nobody *saw* me fall; they will never know me again, that's one consolation.

She would present a most undignified spectacle if anyone could see her, her clothing in disarray and no doubt blood and dirt smeared over her face. She knew now that she was lying on her side, having fallen forwards but turned somehow on or immediately after her impact. She was not in contact with any of the people, but she could hear that some of them were quite close, and also that the commotion she had caused was widespread, because others, further away, were talking about it.

"Has anyone seen my reticule?" she asked.

"What did she say?"

"I think she wants something."

"You just lie there, love. You've had a bit of a shock. Not to worry, no bones broken." The speaker gave an elderly chuckle, quite close to her face, as if bending over her. *How on earth can he tell?* Cassie thought. *He cannot even see me.*

"Should we leave her there?" a woman asked.

"She's perfectly comfortable," the man beside her said, chuckling again.

As if in answer, Cassie cried out. Someone had stood on her hand.

"There, there," the man said, "you're all right now, love." Other noises around her suggested that not everyone in the crowd agreed, and they were bewildered about what had happened to her now. Cassie tried to explain what had happened, but the man shushed her.

Then there was Flora's voice. "Cassie, is that you?"

"Miss Flora! I've lost my reticule."

"Where are you?"

"Over here, miss. I thought I'd never see you again."

When Flora spoke again, her voice was much closer, and Cassie had the impression she had got down on her hands and knees. "Are you badly injured, Cassie?"

"I don't think so, miss, just a bit shook up. Took a knock over my right eye, that's the worst of it."

"Excuse me," Flora said to the world in general, "could you keep still? There is a person in distress here. Is this it, Cassie?"

"Thank heavens, miss." Cassie felt the reticule pressed against her hand and snatched at it. She fumbled inside. That one would be the smelling salts, those were the cephalic pills, here was a little pot of rouge, and here, unmistakably, was the bottle containing Chlorodyne. There was no possibility of measuring it, so she unscrewed the cap and took a swig, then another, till she felt the glow spread through her. At once, as though the memory had been contained in the bottle, she remembered that the reticule also contained a box of matches for lighting the Etna. "Miss Flora, I'm going to strike a match. Are you ready?"

The flare of the match did not light up much of the scene. It was mostly legs, a part of the anatomy that Cassie had had enough of by this time. The chuckling man who had been beside her head was no longer there, but Flora was, her face quite close to Cassie's. Her body was not visible, but Cassie guessed she was on her hands and knees. "I'm going to try and stand up."

"I'll help you."

They rose together, and Cassie struck another match, to general appreciation, as if she had let off a skyrocket. "Will you make way there?" she said, and the two of them moved arm in arm through the station door, Cassie holding the match aloft like a miniature torch. When this one went out, she decided not to light another, but to see if she could make out any of the prospect before them without their help. It was at first entirely dark, but after she had waited a minute or two for the impression of the match flame to fade, she became aware of a paleness in one direction. She was looking east, towards the Thames, and there was some light leaking into the sky that way.

"What shall we do?" Flora asked. "We can't go to Cimmeria now. The train has probably left already, with our luggage on it."

Cassie felt the Chlorodyne burning within her. When she answered, it was with a certainty that did not come from any rational process. "Don't you see, miss? This is Cimmeria! It isn't some place in Turkey; it's all around us."

They made their way along Victoria Street and Cassie, lighting matches at regular intervals, explained. The criminal mastermind Inspector Dollis spoke of needed darkness for his operations, and achieved it by cutting off the gas supply at night. Now, as far as they could tell, the darkness was general, with the exception of the small patch of light they were heading for, which was growing more definite as they advanced. What if the inspector's mastermind was identical with Hastings's Count? Both were said to be gentlemen, but came of obscure origins, and both had an obsession with darkness. "It's as if, I don't know," Cassie said, "as if Cimmeria is a place he invented, out of his own imagination."

"But Dr. Farthing said it exists. He showed us where it is on the map."

"Well, then, suppose there is such a place, but the Count is trying to turn London into it. Maybe he comes from the real Cimmeria and wants to make London more like home. Either way, the inspector said he would have him under arrest by the weekend, so if he is the Count we'll soon know."

"Neither of us has ever seen the Count," Flora said.

"Anyway," Cassie said, "I don't think this is a good time to be travelling across Europe with an Etna, do you, miss?"

"We have no choice in the matter."

Outside Westminster Abbey, they came across a source of light too small and local to be the one they had seen from Victoria Station, but fascinating enough to have drawn a crowd. It was green, and fizzed, filling the air with a sulphurous smell. "That's a chemical fire," Flora said.

"Oh, you know about that, do you? That's one of our chap's tricks. Should be a prowling ghost not too far away, I shouldn't wonder—maybe several."

"They use the coloured fires in the theatre. Hastings wrote to me about them. He—" Flora suddenly remembered her conversation with Mr. Eweson after Hastings's disappearance. "Oh, Cassie! I think this is some of the stuff Hastings stole! You must be right, it was not for a performance in Cimmeria, but a performance in London. Hastings must still be here somewhere."

So preoccupied were they with their conversation that they walked straight into the prowling ghost without seeing him. He was a man of normal height dressed in a dark close-fitting suit with the outline of a skeleton painted on it in luminous paint, the very design Cassie had read of in one of her newspaper articles. The skull face was unmistakably a pasteboard mask, and the whole effect was comical rather than terrifying.

"Hand it over," the ghost said in a tone of resignation mixed with disappointment. He had clearly had little success so far.

"Here," Cassie said, "I've got something for you." She fumbled in her reticule.

"No, Cassie, don't give him anything," Flora said. "He's only a common thief. And there are people all round us who will come to our aid if we call."

"Hand it over," the ghost said again. He was fidgeting and looking about him, as though Flora's warning had alarmed him and he expected to be apprehended at any moment.

Cassie had found what she was looking for. "Here it is," she said, holding something out in the direction of the pasteboard mask. It was a bottle, no bigger than her index finger.

"What is it?" the ghost said. "Gin?"

"Better than that." Cassie took off the lid. "Have you heard of frankincense?"

"Gold and frankincense and myrrh," the ghost said wonderingly. Perhaps he had been to Bible classes in his childhood. One or two of the crowd had come a little closer and were peering in the shaky green light, more interested in the bottle than in his luminous bones and skull-face.

"Yes," Cassie continued, "and what they don't tell you is that the frankincense was worth more than the gold and the myrrh put together, on account of the heavenly smell. There must be a hundred guineas' worth in this bottle alone."

"Hand it over, then."

"Don't you want to sniff it first? Wouldn't want you to think we was trying to palm off some cheap scent on you." She pushed the bottle at him, and he finally raised the mask with a resigned gesture, as if he hated this job and all its complications. The face underneath was almost that of a boy, with a wispy ginger moustache. Cassie pushed the bottle almost up his nose. "Come on, big sniff."

He gave a yelp and crouched down, cursing. The onlookers, more interested than ever, bent over him, not at all unsympathetic, to find out what the matter was. "What did you do to him?" a man asked.

"It's only smelling salts," Cassie said. "I like the smell myself." She and Flora moved away before the crowd had time to get indignant with them.


In Parliament Square, more braziers were burning, this time with purple fires as well as green, a combination which diminished the ghostly atmosphere rather than enhancing it. Even without them, it would not have been wholly dark, because the Embankment with its Yablochkov candles was only a little further on; the waltzing violin was just audible in the background above the noise of the crowd. If the Count's purpose had been to frighten people, he, or his henchmen, had gone about it the wrong way, here, at least. It felt more like a celebration, a grand festival of night. All the same, there were shrieks among the crowd from time to time, presumably as the ghosts went about their business.

"Where are we going?" Flora asked.

"Back to the office," Cassie said. "With any luck, Dr. Farthing will still be there. Even if he isn't, we'll have candles, and we can spend the night if we have to."

"What is it?" Flora said suddenly, and Cassie looked at her green and purple face, thinking she had seen another ghost.

A flickering had begun against the wall of the Palace of Westminster. A tall figure of light appeared there, his metal-clad feet not touching the ground, the brown stone of the building visible through his armoured legs. Cassie followed the outline of his body upwards, greaves and plackard and breastplate, somehow knowing what she would see when she looked at the face. The visor was raised, and the figure beckoning them into the House of Commons, though wearing a white beard, was that of a young man. She knew the way he stood, the exuberance of the gesture, those mischievous blue eyes in the unlined face. The ghost on the wall of Parliament was Hastings.

# Chapter 33

Posing in costume with slight changes of position was not acting as Hastings understood it, and he was glad the Count had finished that tedious part of his preparations. But as he lay in the darkness of his room he was beginning to feel neglected. Had the Count forgotten the next stage of the production, or changed his mind altogether? Hastings had gone beyond the joyous sense of being perfect in the play, and was now beginning to be bored with it. Perhaps he should start reciting another one to himself? He was not sure he knew *Macbeth* by heart, but it was amazing what you found you knew when you had nothing to do but think.

The Count had not visited him for several days. Hastings knew this by his meals, which were his only way of telling the time. Three times a day the food was brought to him by a person he could not see and who did not speak, but whose movements he recognized by sound as those of a woman, probably a young one. He invariably greeted her when he heard her enter, which she did without knocking, and was becoming frustrated by his inability to obtain any response. The food was left on a chair beside his bed, simple meals that could be eaten with the fingers: bread, cold meat, cheese, apples, two small stoppered bottles, one for wine, the other for water. When he had finished, he put the plates and bottles back on the chair and the girl removed them when she brought the next meal. He began to speak to her at greater length during her brief visits, asking her how long she had worked for the Count and whether she had ever left Cimmeria to see the outer world, and sometimes it seemed to him that he could detect changes in her breathing and movement that suggested she was listening. *What kind of a man am I*, he thought, *that I cannot persuade a young woman to talk to me?*

He planned his attack for the evening meal. When she arrived this time, he would not be lying in bed as usual, but sitting on it, close to the chair. This was a risk, as he could not be sure that she did not have the night vision the Count laid claim to, but even if she did, his unwonted action might draw some kind of response from her. Having taken up position early he had a tedious wait. This room was always cold, because there was no fire; this was one reason he spent all his time in bed. Now, having dressed already, he pulled all the covers round him, taking care not to swaddle himself so tightly that he would not be able to act with appropriate swiftness, and waited, passing the time by remembering as much of *Macbeth* as he could. When he came to "Is this a dagger which I see before me," he almost thought that he *could* see the dagger, a magic-lantern projection a few inches from his face with blood dripping from the blade. But the spectacle was not a pleasant one, and he did not think the role was quite as suited to him as that of Hamlet. It was easier to think of himself as a young man who could not bring himself to commit a crime than as an older one about to become a murderer.

At last he heard her footsteps outside. The door opened, and she approached the bed. She always put the tray she was carrying on the floor, then lifted the old tray with its dirty plate and cutlery from the chair and laid it beside the other, which she now put on the chair in its place. Finally she would pick up the used tray from the floor and retire from the room. Hastings waited until the new tray had been put on the chair; it was already apparent from the confidence of her movements that she had no idea he was so close. When the tray was safely in position—for he did not want to upset it—he reached out and caught her by the wrist. She gasped and tried to wrench her arm away, but he had it securely and was able to restrain her without effort.

"Please," he said, "I don't mean to hurt you. I just want to talk."

"Let me go."

"Oh, so you can speak. I will let you go, I promise, but I have been so lonely here. It is almost as if I am being kept prisoner."

"Please, sir, I can't talk. I shouldn't have said anything at all. If the Count finds out…"

"Is the Count here?"

"No, sir. He's away often. He didn't come home at all last night. He's a very busy man, especially in the last few days."

"Well, then, he can't know you have been talking to me. I say—what is your name?"

"Susanna, sir."

"Well, Susanna, it feels awkward carrying on a conversation in the dark. You haven't a candle on you?"

"No, sir, I'm sorry."

"The ways of this place are most interesting. You walk from wherever it is, let's call it Piccadilly Circus, with my meals three times a day, and never feel the need of a light to show you the way? I have been training my eyes to the darkness for some time now, but I could no more manage that than I could scamper through the trees like a squirrel. I suppose you have to have done it all your life."

"Yes, sir, I have."

"But it is bright in Piccadilly Circus, or wherever you get the tray from? There must be fire to cook the meat, at any rate, and I cannot picture you doing all your work in darkness."

"I don't know what you mean by Piccadilly Circus, sir."

"Well, whatever you call this place. Cimmeria, perhaps?"

"Yes, sir, that is the name of the house. And it is no use you asking me about what is dark and what isn't. I am blind."

Hastings was the only inhabitant of this wing of Cimmeria. Having an uncomfortable suspicion that others beside himself were being kept prisoner here, he made Susanna lead him all round, opening every room to prove they were empty. Most were not even furnished or carpeted. He tried throwing open the shutters of the first one they came to, but there was no moon or stars, no light from nearby houses to alleviate the darkness. He did, however, feel that it changed its nature, became less oppressive, when he did so. He was no longer clutching

Susanna's wrist but resting his hand lightly on her forearm as she guided him from room to room. Yes, she said, the house was in Hampstead, the very one he had arrived at a fortnight ago, and all the windows in this corridor looked out over the Heath, which must be why it was so dark out. And the reason the rooms were unfurnished was that the Count had not lived here very long. He was a foreign gentleman, very busy with his hobbies, and, yes, he had particularly wanted a blind servant, and had sent to the Home for the Blind for one. She herself had been here no longer than Hastings had, and her only duty was to wait on him, an invalid as she had been told. She was not to talk to him because it would distract him and make him sicker still.

"Are the other servants here?"

"I don't have much to do with them, sir. I am to regard myself as a nurse, not as a domestic servant. Those were the Count's words."

"But you get the trays from the kitchen?"

"Yes."

"Are the other servants there now?"

"Yes, sir, the cook and the kitchen maid."

"Then take me there, Susanna. I feel like a hot supper for a change."

To Hastings's disappointment, there was no gaslight in the house this evening. Susanna, who naturally did not care whether there was or not, told him that the gas had gone off about an hour ago, and the other servants were very put out about it, especially as the main range in the kitchen was gas-fuelled. Nevertheless, as they faltered to the bottom of the staircase that Hastings had fallen down the previous week and through the narrow passage that led to the hall, he became aware of shadows and knew that he was returning to civilization. The hall, lit only by candles, seemed enormous, and he could almost believe he was in a land carved out of the inside of a mountain. But the kitchen, when they reached it, was much as he remembered it from the time of his arrival, with its fire providing most of the light and making it more welcoming than anywhere else in the house. Only when he entered did he take his hand from Susanna's forearm. She was older than he had pictured her, her hair under her cap already greying and her face tense and pale; she wore the smoked-glass spectacles of the blind. "I had to bring him," she said as soon as they entered, but the cook continued her preparations at the table without so much as looking up, while the kitchen maid greeted him with the same smile with which she had served him his breakfast sausages.

"It's boiled fowl," she said simply.

"I could smell as much," Hastings said.

# Chapter 34

The candles were lit in the office. Dr. Farthing had been lying down and rose to greet them.

"Sorry to wake you, sir," Cassie said.

"That is all right; I was not asleep. I was just lying here resting my eyes."

"There are queer things going on outside," Cassie said.

"I suspected there were. Is that why you two ladies are not on the boat train?"

Cassie returned now to her chair, and Flora, after a moment's hesitation, sat in Dr. Farthing's at his desk. "That is my fault," she said.

"Fault's got nothing to do with it," Cassie said. "It isn't anybody's fault. It would have been no use us going to Cimmeria when Cimmeria was coming to us anyway."

Dr. Farthing made a sharp noise which Flora decided must be his way of coughing, and indeed when he spoke there was a touch of hoarseness in his voice. "That is an enigmatic remark, Miss Pine. What can you mean?"

"I don't mean to be ungrateful, sir, for all the book-reading you did for us in Oxford. But we were spared a wild goose chase is all I can say. Hastings, Mr. Wimbury, isn't in Cimmeria, he's here in London. To be more accurate about it, he is on the walls of the Houses of Parliament, or he was when we last saw him."

Dr. Farthing coughed again. Flora continued watching him all the way through Cassie's narrative of the encounter on Victoria Station, the cutting off of the gas supply, her vanquishing of the ghost and Hastings's manifestation, and thought he looked distracted and uncomfortable. Why had he been lying down with such momentous events happening in the street outside, if, as he claimed, he had had some intuition of them?

"Are you sure it was he?" was all he said.

"There was no doubting it, sir. We both know him well, and it was Hastings Wimbury, dressed up in armour, as it might be acting a part in a play."

"Or, um, the psychic residue of Mr. Wimbury, his ghost, in common parlance?"

"Why should his ghost be wearing armour? Dr. Farthing, I've studied the files in that cabinet, and read many reports of ghosts, but I never yet came across a credible story of a person that died and came back dressed up as what they wasn't."

"There are prowling ghosts. You met one yourself."

"And he was a common thief dressed up as a skeleton, with a mask made of pasteboard. I said credible, sir, and credible is just what he was not."

"Then what was it you saw on the wall of the Houses of Parliament?"

"My fiancé," Flora began, then seeing Cassie's sharp look, stumbled a little, "Mr. Wimbury…worked in the theatre until very recently. He was interested in all the equipment there, limelight, chemical fires, magic lanterns—in fact, he, he was suspected of having appropriated some of it to his own use. And now that equipment is being employed all over London. There are coloured fires burning on the streets and the ghost we saw is the projection of one of the stolen magic lanterns."

"It is extraordinary," Dr. Farthing said. "After all Inspector Dollis's talk of a criminal mastermind, it seems he was under our noses the whole time. Or under my assistant's nose, and your own, madam." He gave a slight bow in the direction of Flora.

Flora and Cassie spoke at the same time, "What do you mean, sir?" and "Oh no, sir, it can't be Hastings!" respectively.

"But surely, ladies, making all due allowances for your emotional proclivities, the logic is inescapable. Mr. Wimbury stole theatrical equipment—yes, *stole* is the only possible word— then disappeared shortly before the dramatic goings-on of this evening in which that equipment played so large a part, and, to cap it all, you are both witnesses to the appearance of the man himself impersonating a ghost! Inspector Dollis need look no further for his mastermind. Remember, he is said to be a gentleman."

"You do not know Hastings," Flora said. "He has many faults, I confess, but never in my wildest imaginings have I considered him a mastermind."

"And besides," Cassie put in, "that don't explain the Count. He's the mastermind, if anyone is. The man's a foreigner, too."

"It has not occurred to you that everything you know of this Count, including the description of Cimmeria, came from Hastings Wimbury himself? Miss Pine, you are a woman of some intelligence, but I am afraid when love comes in at the door, intelligence often climbs out of the window." Farthing glanced at the place in the wall where his own window once was.

"It's true," Flora said. "I never thought of it before. He writes, he wrote, the most wonderful letters, full of descriptions of the life of the theatre, of the boarding house in Bayswater where he was living, and, yes, of the Count and of Cimmeria, too. He is an artist, Dr. Farthing, he has always insisted on the appellation, and I naturally assumed he meant an actor. But there are other artists, are there not, those that create, not with their bodies, faces and voices, but with their imaginations? Suppose Hastings meant he was an artist of that kind? And I always thought him somewhat deluded when he called himself a genius! It could be that his delusions *were* his genius, if you understand me. I am afraid I am not a very good companion for a man of that kind, Dr. Farthing."

"Exactly, Miss Burlap. And, if you will forgive me, I think you are well out of the association. Wimbury's delusions have led him to crime, as you yourself admitted."

"But I only meant the petty crime of stealing from his employers. I never dreamed he would be behind all this, whatever it is."

"Well, I don't believe it," Cassie said. "Whatever he's done, I know he was sorry for, and was led into it by others worse than he was. You're not saying Hastings has whole gangs of criminals doing his bidding? He was never much interested in anything but acting."

Dr. Farthing wandered over to where the window ought to be and stood there facing it as if he could see whatever was going on outside. "They are all out there doing his bidding now," he said. "Frightening people in the streets of the city, stealing their valuables, enforcing the rule of Night in the capital of our great Empire. And they say the sun never sets on it! It has set now, has it not?"

Flora shook her head, not in denial, but to clear a fog that seemed to have settled inside it. "I know, I always knew, that he was not altogether respectable, not the kind of man my parents would have chosen for me. Indeed, that was part of his charm. But I never dreamed that he was capable of this." She thought of the darkness they had come through to get here, of their encounter with the skeleton, the braziers of coloured fire, the people dancing to the violin on the Embankment. "But I suppose it is rather beautiful in its way. And really, has there been much harm done? A few people have had their purses and wallets stolen, but that happens all the time anyway. We only have that policeman's word that Hastings has been profiting by it."

"Inspector Dollis never mentioned Hastings at all," Cassie said.

"But he does profit," Dr. Farthing said. "I am not denying that his principal motive is an aesthetic one. He enjoys the chaos he has created and the power that it gives him over the city. But an artist is entitled to a fair remuneration. He has a share of all the thieves' takings, or so Dollis tells me. It must come to quite a bit, even when you take into account the fees he pays to his agents in the gasworks. And in any case the whole thing is underpinned by the Bond Street jewel robbery. Did you not wonder, Miss Burlap, where he got the ruby he sent you, an unset one such as only a professional jeweller would be likely to possess?" He turned back from the window.

"You never told me he gave you a ruby," Cassie said.

"I do not see that it is any of your business," Flora replied. "I returned it anyway, on the advice of a friend. I could not accept such a present, however it was come by, from a gentleman to whom I was not exactly engaged."

"Then you admit it—" Cassie began, but Flora's sudden exhalation stopped her.

"Dr. Farthing."

"Yes, madam?"

"Will you explain to me, please, how you knew that Mr. Wimbury had sent me an unset ruby?"

"Oh, excuse me, clumsy of me!" As he resumed his seat on the couch, Dr. Farthing's knee came in contact with the occasional table and brought it crashing to the floor, together with the candle in a saucer that had been on it. "He told me as much. Mr. Wimbury has no secrets from me."

Cassie got down on her hands and knees and lit the fallen candle preparatory to righting the table. "He told you?" she asked. "When did you meet him?"

Dr. Farthing laughed. "Oh dear, ladies, I'm afraid you have me there! When did I meet Mr. Wimbury? Now, let me see, I'm sure I have it in my files. Do you mind if I just check?"

Dr. Farthing got up again and went over to the filing cabinet, where he stood with his back to them, rummaging through the drawer, muttering, "Wimbury, Wimbury. Ah, here it is. Do you know, ladies, it is difficult to remember sometimes where one is, not just in a filing cabinet, but in the world as a whole, which a well-kept filing cabinet may be said to represent. Indeed, for a moment there, I'm afraid I forgot, not merely where I was, but who." He turned. In his hand he held, not a file, but a small black object that caught the candlelight on its barrel and chambered cylinder. Flora refused to accept it was a gun.

"There must be some mistake," she said. "A gentleman doesn't—" It would be unforgivable of her to accuse him of threatening her with a firearm unless she was perfectly sure that that was what he was doing; on the other hand, the situation seemed to call for immediate action of a sort that was not necessarily compatible with good manners. In her confusion, she turned to Cassie for support, only to find her still on her hands and knees beside the couch. "Cassie!"

"Wait a minute, there's something under here." Cassie pushed her head and shoulders, together with the lighted candle, underneath the couch. She gave a muffled squawk.

"Never mind that now," Dr. Farthing said in an irritated tone. "Come out from there, Miss Pine. I would really rather not shoot you."

Cassie scrambled out as if pursued by something unseen, and got to her feet.

"I am sorry I did it," Dr. Farthing said. "I was given no choice in the matter. The poor fellow was so proud of having found his mastermind, he came round to see me as he always does—I mean, did—to drink a glass of sherry and crow about his triumph."

"What fellow are you talking about? What is the matter, Cassie?"

"It's Inspector Dollis," Cassie said. "Under the couch, where our luggage was."

"He fell just there," Farthing said. "He got up when I shot him and took one pace, then fell. I think having caught me in the middle of a crime, to wit his own murder, his first instinct was to arrest me—indeed, it was his last instinct, too. So he died in the performance of his duty. I had just time to roll his body underneath the couch when I heard you open the door downstairs. That is one thing that can be said for candlelight, Miss Pine: it covers a multitude of sins. No doubt there are several bloodstains if you look for them."

"You are the mastermind," Flora said.

"I am Count Nollo as well as Dr. Farthing. I leave it to you to decide which of the two, if either, is my true identity. The beard is false. When I am the Count I wear a long moustache instead. Like your friend Wimbury—yes, I know him well—I prefer to remain clean-shaven so that I can change my appearance at will. As I say, it is a little confusing at times having to be two people."

"But why, sir?"

"Why am I two people, do you mean? In a word, insomnia. I sleep for perhaps half an hour in twenty-four, and then thanks only to the stillness and darkness of this office, and your own calming presence, Miss Pine. You have some sympathy with me, I think, being a sufferer yourself. You are still at the stage of fighting it, but if the condition develops in you as it has in me—I call it a condition for want of a better word, but I no longer regard it as an illness—you will find eventually that fighting it no longer works. And then you must make some difficult decisions about your life. You will never again know what it is to close down your brain for eight hours and wake at the end of it feeling the world made new. You will always be lonely, knowing that most of the rest of the world has a regular experience which you can never share. You have been singled out, rather as Hastings Wimbury believes he has been singled out—perhaps that is the best way to look at it, as a gift or vocation. After all, we insomniacs may never know peace, but we have something the mass of humanity cannot even imagine, and would perhaps envy us if they could. We have an extra portion of life! All those hours which others waste in dreams and insensibility are given us to do with what we will. Can you blame me that I made up my mind to be two people?

"My first idea was to be the Count at night and Dr. Farthing in the daytime. It is a rather uneven distribution of personalities, however, for the daytime self overlaps the night-time one for most people. There are those delicious hours between six o'clock and midnight when we, at least those of us who can afford it, leave our daily tasks and enjoy our dinner and our wine, go dancing or to the theatre. My daytime self had all those, while the poor Count was confined to the hours when no one was around in the streets but a few drunks and other insomniacs like himself. No wonder he wished to extend his activities. He started by going to the theatre in Dr. Farthing's place, and fell in love with its lights and its phantoms. There is a whole world of night in those palaces of the West End, and the dwellers there, like myself, are not content to be a single person. You should not blame young Wimbury, Miss Burlap. He is not the only one to be seduced by it."

"But what could you possibly achieve?"

"I am making London into my own theatre. Oh, I confess, I do not have much in the way of actors at present, just some pickpockets and common thieves in the prowling ghost disguises I first learned about in my Farthing hours, from the articles I keep in those files. And, of course, Wimbury—I have been training him. If I must stay awake, at least I shall have been entertained, with a play I dreamed up and directed myself, rather than the feeble creations of others. Those who cannot sleep cannot dream either, you see, and you would not believe how much one misses that nightly madness when deprived of it. And then there is simple darkness. I miss that even more. Perhaps one day—one night, rather—when I have enough control over the gasworks, I shall let the dark fill the city and then, finally, I may get some sleep. By that time Londoners will be as frightened of my ghosts as their rustic ancestors were of the will-o'-the-wisps and boggarts they imagined in their lanes and fields, and we can all be benighted together."

"This is nonsense!" Flora said.

"It must seem so to you. To me it seems like a play I have not yet written the end of. Everything up to now has been a rehearsal, you see, and I had hoped that tonight would be the first act, or at any rate the prologue. And then Inspector Dollis came to tell me that his men were even now on the way to Hampstead, to arrest a man known as the Count, and proposing to take me with him to Scotland Yard for the interview. They would find no Count there, of course, but they *would* find Wimbury and the servants and bring them back to give evidence, and I knew I would have to confront them. My acting and costume are not so good that I could hope to deceive the members of my own household— even Wimbury would have seen through me. And I am afraid, in

the stress of the moment, I got stage fright, I dried, as I believe
the actors say. There was simply nothing in my head, not the
Count, not Dr. Farthing, no plausible story, not even a sentence
I could utter to play for time.

"I was standing with my back to him, getting the sherry out
of the drawer, when Inspector Dollis started his crowing, and I
continued to rummage, as though sorting through files, in the
hope that language would come back to me, and a little of my
old cunning along with it. And that was when I saw my gun,
and a simple solution occurred to me. Poor Dollis—I wonder
whether he knew he was dying the death of a werewolf."

"You aren't going to shoot us?" Flora said.

"As I told Miss Pine, I really hope not. I think the best thing
for me is to leave, don't you? Of course, the Count is finished in
London, and Dr. Farthing, too, but I still have some resources
I can lay my hands on, and I see no reason why I should not
stage a similar production elsewhere. The world is full of cities,
and every city has room for a few extra ghosts. Miss Pine, may I
trouble you for the key to the office?"

Cassie handed it over without demur, as she had done Dr.
Farthing's bidding so many times in the past.

"As I told you before, Miss Pine, I shall miss you. If I thought
my life was suitable for a lady to share, I would ask you to come
with me, but—"

"No, sir, never."

"A pity—I thought not. Well, I shall go and enjoy the
spectacle of night while it lasts. I'm afraid I must lock the door
after me, but I am sure someone will be along to rescue you in
the morning. If were you I would take advantage of the interval
to get some sleep. You must need it."

Neither of them said anything after they heard the key turn
in the lock and Dr. Farthing's footsteps descending the stairs.
They sat, one in each of the chairs, trying not to look at the
couch, in the certainty that the shadows cast by the candles
would form themselves on closer examination into bloodstains.
Flora had never shared a room with a dead body before; she

wondered if there really were such things as ghosts, if the dead inspector could rise from his undignified resting place and shake his gory locks at them. But it was impossible to believe that there was a dead man there at all, and she had no intention of peering under the couch to see for herself.

After they had been sitting in silence for a quarter of an hour, they began to smell smoke. The candle under the couch had set light to Inspector Dollis's clothes.

# Chapter 35

The coloured fires are beginning to burn out. As they give their last splutters, they generate more smoke than before so that the spectators splutter, too, and even the prowling ghosts moving among them are coughing. The magic lanterns last a little longer, but before they fade, the novelty of the apparitions projected on historic walls is already wearing off. They do not, after all, do very much, merely make a few gestures and movements and begin again. One can only be startled for a limited period before boredom sets in, and the magic-lantern operators, being petty thieves rather than theatrical professionals, are as prone to boredom as anyone, and tend to leave their posts to look for pickings of their own. The lantern outside St. Paul's, unwatched with the oxygen and hydrogen still feeding the fire of its lime cylinder, goes up with a bang in a great rush of white flame, causing more screams than the original ghost, though no one is hurt. The ghost of Hastings-Hamlet on the wall of Parliament freezes in the midst of its beckoning gesture, which is now comical rather than frightening if you look at it attentively, as many do. *He's only a young man*, some of them think, *got up to look like an old one. And look at the expression on his face, pursing his lips as if he wants to kiss us. Not sure I'd be scared of him if I met him on a dark night.*

Only the party on the Embankment has retained its energy, and added to it as the evening has gone on and more and more people have sought out the light of its Yablochkov candles. The violinist is now competing with an accordionist—after a bad-tempered period when they were close together, the waltzes of one clashing with the polkas of the other, they have mutely agreed to split the territory between them, the violinist taking the side nearest Westminster Bridge and the accordionist nearer to Blackfriars. It is just possible to dance from one area to the other, changing your rhythm as you do so, though you have to cross a stretch in the middle where neither is really audible, and there are a lot of non-dancers to get in your way. What is the point of not dancing on a night like this? There is nothing much else to do except look at the lights of the boats on the river and wait to have your pocket picked.

From Hampstead Hill, the Yablochkov candles of the Embankment are visible as a single light rather than many, compressed into the shape of an earthbound star. Hastings would probably not be able to see it at all if the gaslamps of London and Westminster were burning all round, but it guides his progress as he makes his way down the hill. He knows he will lose it when he reaches the bottom, and will have to be content with the glimmers of lanterns, oil lamps, and candles behind the curtains of the houses he passes. These are enough for him to see by now that his eyes have been sensitized by prolonged exposure to the darkness of Cimmeria, but he is more concerned about the difficulty of finding his way once he is in among winding streets. He is trying to impress that star on his mind so that it will carry on burning inside him even when he can no longer see it, leading him to the centre of the city. He does not recognize it as the place where he stood waiting for his rendezvous with the thieves at the impossibly distant time before his ordeal. For him, it is the star of the Magi transposed to a lower level.

At the corner of Belsize Road, he is dazzled by the lights of a police wagon headed in the opposite direction. It is not going above a trot, and pulls over when he hails it. Hastings wishes a good evening to the constable who serves as the driver and asks for directions towards the centre of London, more because this is the normal thing to do with policemen than because he actually needs help. His star is no longer visible, but its influence is still strong inside him.

The officer gestures along the way his vehicle has come, but seems reluctant to go into details. "If I was you, sir, I'd make my way home. This is not a night to be out on."

"That is what I am doing, Constable," Hastings says, though he has not yet given much thought to his precise destination.

"I live in Bayswater." (Is this still true? His rent must be long overdue, and no doubt Mrs. Makepeace has let his room to another tenant. She will not be overjoyed to see him.)

"Then you're a long way from home, sir. At least on foot. If you was to walk that way into Hampstead you might be able to find yourself a hansom, though there aren't many about tonight. Queer things happening and a lot of the drivers are laying low. Can't say as I blame them myself. It's been a busy night for us on the Force—the evening's hardly begun and the cells are full already. May I ask where you're coming from?"

"Hampstead Heath. Not the Heath itself, a house on the edge of it."

"That wouldn't be Cimmeria, would it?"

"Well…"

"And your name wouldn't be Count Nollo?"

"No, Constable, it certainly isn't that."

"I'd like you to get inside, sir. Never mind the bars and that, they're just a convenience. You ain't under arrest, not yet at any rate." The door at the rear of the wagon opens and two more officers get out, preposterous shadows in their great helmets. "We're going back the way you came, that's true, but we may find it handy to have you around when we get there and interview this Count fellow."

"He isn't there."

"Oh, so you know him, do you? Well, you come with us and we'll find out all about it, and afterwards, well, who knows where we'll take you afterwards? Maybe even as far as Bayswater."

The inspector burns very slowly. Flora has no intention of getting down on her hands and knees to see for herself—if a dead body is a repulsive sight, one that is on fire must be still more so—but she asks Cassie to report on his progress at regular intervals.

"It's reached his knee," she says. "Or at least the right one. The left leg is only just scorched above the ankle. I thought he was going out altogether just now, but then the fire seemed to take heart, so to speak. It has something to do with the air, don't it?"

"What does?"

"Fires need air, don't they? And there ain't much of it in this office, on account of there being no windows and the door being shut."

"Cassie, cannot you put him out?"

"I could if we had some water, miss, but that's down the passage and the door's locked, ain't it?" (Both of them know this from experience, since they have taken it in turns to try the handle, neither having confidence in the other's efforts.) "I could try and smother it with my shawl, or even take off my dress and use that, but they'd probably just burn up with the rest. After all, it's his clothing that's on fire." She exhales loudly. "Don't like that."

"What?"

"One of the flames has been licking at the couch, and a bit of the webbing underneath has caught. There's a tear in the leather, and—there! Smell that?"

An animal stink has pervaded the room. "What is it, Cassie?"

"It's got to the horsehair inside. It's burning like fury, now."

"Move the couch!"

Cassie gets to her feet and tries. "I can't lift it, miss. Come over and help me, will you?"

Flora looks round as if for someone else in the room who could do it for her, then gets up and takes the other end of the couch. With one woman at each end it is just possible to lift it off the floor. "Where are we taking it?"

"Over to the window."

"There is no window."

"The place where the window used to be, I mean. It'll be out of harm's way there." Cassie cries out. "Hurry up, miss, this end is blooming hot. I'm going to burn myself in a minute."

By the time they reach the wall, there are two fires in the room. Cassie's end of the sofa is now being licked by a bluish flame that seems almost on the point of going out, but then comes back more strongly and is soon joined by another. Meanwhile, the corpse of Inspector Dollis has been revealed, lying on his back, his upper person looking very little different from the living man. (From where she stands, Flora cannot make out the bullet-hole, much to her relief.) The lower Dollis, on the other hand, looks far less respectable. It is not so much the flames flowering from his trouser legs that shock her—they look almost natural, like a decorative garment worn in some exotic land—as the fact that most of his shin area has been exposed. The naked flesh is a curious mottled black and white that draws her eyes no matter how hard she tries not to look. At least there is nothing more in his vicinity that he can set fire to, now that Cassie has moved the occasional table.

"Perhaps it will all just burn out," she suggests.

"I don't like the smoke. It can't be doing us any good."

Cassie is right. While Dollis is smoking only lightly, though with a savoury odour that Flora tries to keep from smelling, the sofa is gushing smoke by now. It has formed a rolling layer just under the ceiling that reminds her of thunderclouds. "If only Dr. Farthing hadn't bricked up his window."

"If only he hadn't locked us in."

"Is the key still in the lock, do you know, Cassie? I believe there is a trick you can do of pushing the key out and having it fall on the floor on to a piece of paper, which you then pull under the door."

Cassie goes over and looks. "Yes, it's still there. How do you know about that?"

"I have a brother. It is the kind of thing brothers take an interest in."

Cassie fetches a sheet of foolscap from the desk and Flora takes out a hair pin to poke at the key with. It will not budge. "I don't understand," she says. "It always worked for Algy."

"Did he use a hairpin?"

"I can't remember what he used. Perhaps a pen would be better."

The pen, however, proves too thick to penetrate the keyhole. While they are preoccupied with these efforts, the flames from the couch have found their way to the wall panelling. Neither of them sees the long black streak on the wood, now beginning to grow a crust of red sparks.

# Chapter 36

U nable to find a hansom cab, Dr. Farthing has made his way to the Embankment. His plans are not at all clear to him; he walked out of the office exhilarated at having made a grand gesture to the two ladies, and as he turned the key in the lock and headed down the stairs, he was still repeating to himself his parting words about how he would carry out his plan all over again in another city. He was looking forward to seeing the City of Dreadful Night for himself. As soon as he found himself in John Carpenter Street, however, he became aware of the inconveniences of that city. For all his cultivation of it, he is not much better at getting about in the dark than anyone else. His progress along the street was slow, guided by the railings, and it was a relief to him when he saw the lights and heard the music of the Embankment.

Now he is standing there, an island in a pool of space that has formed around him, as if the merrymakers sense the potent and dangerous presence in their midst. If they only knew that they owe this entire festival to the strength of his imagination. All the same, he cannot help thinking that the result of his scheme is not, after all, as he imagined. What he would really like now would be a good night's sleep, and that prospect is further away than ever. The police will be at Cimmeria by now, so he can never return there. They will find the remaining jewels from the Bond Street robbery, but fortunately most of the proceeds of his crimes are safely deposited in bank accounts under various names. He will write to the banks when he is safely abroad, and meanwhile he has enough in his pocketbook to get him there. Are the trains running? He sees no reason why they should not be: they are not dependent on the city's gas supply, after all. All the same, his heart misgives him at the thought of making his way through the crowds cavorting here.

Lost in his thoughts, he does not at first notice the wolf approaching him on its hind legs. It holds a broad-bladed, rusty knife in its right forepaw, an incongruous weapon for a creature whose yellow teeth in its gaping jaw are so impressive. "Give us your pocketbook, governor," it says.

"What creature of the night says *governor*?" Dr. Farthing replies. "You might make more of an effort to be intimidating."

If the wolf is abashed by his reproof, its motionless features give it no opportunity of showing the fact. After a pause, it simply repeats its demand.

"Do you even know who I am?"

"What's that got to do with it? Hand over the valuables, or I'll rip you."

"I am your employer. You have, perhaps, heard of the Count?"

The beast puts its free paw to its muzzle, and gives a little start, as if taken aback to find insentient fur there rather than face. "You're him? How do I know?"

"Would I even be talking about him unless I were?"

"I don't know. You might be a rozzer."

Farthing sighs, and feels in his pocket for the werewolf gun; here at last is his chance to deploy it appropriately. While he is hesitating, his forefinger comes into contact with something else, and he takes it out. "Here, do you know what this is?"

"Some kind of bead?"

"It is an unset ruby, from the Bond Street jewel robbery. Why would a police officer be carrying such a thing?" He congratulates himself mentally on having forgotten all about this trivial proof of identity till this moment.

"Hold it up in the light," the wolf says. "Pretty. All right, then, sir, I'm sorry, but I didn't know who you was."

"Do you want to make yourself useful? You may take the ruby; I have no further need of it."

"Yes, sir."

"I left two ladies locked in my office in John Carpenter Street, as a precaution. One of them I am rather fond of, and they cannot be comfortable. Will you go there and let them out if I give you the address?"

The wolf nods, its yellow eyes gleaming in the electric light.

"Very well. And mind you do so and don't just make off with the ruby. Come back and find me here, and I will have another present for you, something even more valuable."

As soon as the wolf has disappeared into the throng, Dr. Farthing makes off in the other direction, towards Westminster Bridge and Victoria Station. He has given himself an incentive to move now. Even on this night of confusion, the liberated ladies will, he supposes, find their way to a police station and tell their story. Dr. Farthing, murderer of a police officer as well as chief suspect in the Bond Street robbery, will have the entire London force at his heels. He pulls off his beard as he goes, an action that would have drawn some curious looks on any other night.

Ladies do not faint nearly as often as novels suggest. Cassie and Flora are choking with the smoke from the burning horsehair, their hands and faces glowing with the heat from the room's two fires, but they continue their efforts to push the key through the lock. They are both aware by now that the fire has spread from the couch to the wood panelling, so that the whole of the outer wall is now papered with a moving pattern of flame, but each has decided that mentioning it to the other would only cause despondency. Meanwhile, Inspector Dollis has flared up, and is now making a disconcerting sound which can only be described as *sizzling*, as the fire, hitherto confined to his clothing, discovers an appetite for human flesh. Not only that but little fingers of yellow are beginning to dance around the floorboards, quite innocent-looking at this stage, but it surely cannot be long before the floor itself goes up.

They are taking it in turns: one, presently Cassie, pushing at the key; the other, Flora, on hands and knees peering under the door at the rectangle of paper, willing the key to drop on to it. Cassie is wondering why the simple key is so stubborn—is it something to do with the way the little bays and promontories of metal engage with the lock? Flora is thinking that even when the key finally drops it will almost certainly fall far beyond the paper. "Don't push too hard, Cassie," she says.

"If I don't push as hard as I can, it won't drop."

Neither of them hears the street door below opening or the footsteps on the stairs. The first Flora knows of it is when a shadow falls across the sheet of paper she is peering at. A boot comes into view, then a cylinder made of rusty brown fur; even though it is attached to the boot, she cannot think of it as a leg.

There is a knock at the door.

"Oh, thank God," Flora says.

"You can come in," Cassie calls through the door. "The key is in the lock."

Hearing it turn, Flora gets to her feet and steps to one side, though even this action exposes her to a blast of hot air from deeper in the room. Standing against the wall, her face to the fire, she does not immediately see their visitor. Cassie does.

"Miss Flora," she says, "there is a wolf at the door."

The wolf is nearly seven feet tall and Flora finds herself gazing directly into its open jaws, flinching as if expecting the smell of recently chewed meat to be breathed out from them. What she really sees, beyond the great yellow fangs, are the eyes of a man looking out from the creature's throat.

"Blimey," the wolf says. "If I'd of known it was going to be as hot as this, I never would of come, ruby or no ruby."


All through the interview with the sergeant, Hastings is waiting for the question about his own role in the robbery at the Villiers Theatre, but it never comes. Instead the sergeant, a young man with a luxuriant moustache who yawns throughout as if investigating the crimes of a man who has turned London into a carnival of darkness were an irksome chore, returns again and again to the Count himself and what he has revealed of his past life. "Forget the Cimmeria business. Who was he really? Was he foreign or English?"

"I have no idea."

"I'll put foreign, then. He don't sound like an Englishman."

A frowning young woman is introduced to draw a sketch in accordance with the instructions Hastings gives her: a novel experience for him, and one that fills him with an enjoyable sense of power. "The moustache is not the same as the sergeant's here," he says. "It trails down below the level of the chin. There, that's it."

By the time he is led from the room, Hastings, despite the lack of sleep, feels tight and bubbling with exhilaration, like a bottle of champagne about to shoot off its cork. They did not ask him—he is free to return to his normal life. Not that he knows any more what his normal life is, but he is sure it must be wonderful. And as if in response to this festive mood, there, to greet him at the door are two familiar faces, for both of which he feels a great warmth. It seems right that they should be here at this moment of vindication, though, come to think of it, he has never seen them together.

Cassie sees him first, and starts back. "Hastings!"

Flora's expression is a mixture of pity, discomfort and something that might be love if looked at in a different light. (The gas is still off, and Scotland Yard is lit by oil lamps.) She looks tired and her face is shadowed with what appears to be soot, as Cassie's is, he now notices. "Mr. Wimbury," Flora says. "How curious to see you here!"

"Oh, I see," says the sergeant, who has followed Hastings out of the interview room. "It's all a conspiracy, is it?" He speaks in the tone of someone who has witnessed three conspiracies already that day and has no patience with another one.

"This gentleman is an acquaintance of mine," Flora says, "that is, I suppose, of ours." She nods at Cassie, who sniffs at the belated acknowledgement. "I wonder if we might speak alone with him for a few minutes, officer?"

"I'm afraid not, miss. You're all witnesses."

"Surely half the population of London are witnesses tonight! You cannot stop all of them talking to each other in private."

"No, miss, but I has to if they comes in here."

"Oh, very well. But we may talk in front of you, I dare say? He is someone we have not seen for a long time, and we have been concerned for his welfare. I promise we will not delay our own interview long."

"If you must."

Cassie, Flora and Hastings take seats in the area, half-reception room, half-corridor, outside the interview room. They sit in a row against the wall, Hastings in the middle, while the sergeant stands to one side, shifting his weight from one leg to the other.

"Where have you been?" Flora begins.

"Cimmeria."

"We know all about that," Cassie says. "There's no such place. It was just a bit of make-believe by—"

"Never mind that, ladies, if you please," says the sergeant. "I can't have you discussing the case."

"I wish you would not eavesdrop," Flora says.

"It's my duty, miss."

"Oh, very well. Hastings, I do not know what exactly you have done, and how much you are to blame—"

"Could we perhaps drop this subject?" Hastings looks nervously at the sergeant.

"All right. What do you propose to do now?"

"I shall go back to, to, um." He looks from Flora to Cassie and back again, suddenly aware that their simultaneous presence may not be an unmixed blessing.

"Precisely," Flora says. "You cannot return to Halcyon House."

"Oh, Miss Flora, he can have his old room back again, across the landing from mine. You won't be needing it and I know Mrs. Makepeace won't mind, as long as he's able to pay the rent."

"You cannot return to Halcyon House," Flora says again, "and the mention of rent, at any rate, is to the point. Your employment at the Villiers is over, for which we can only be grateful. I wish you had never gone there in the first place. I take it you have no money?"

He shakes his head.

"Fortunately, we have some with us, the funds for a little expedition we were planning, which are no longer needed. We can lend it to you until you are able to pay us back. Have you given any thought to your future?"

He looks from one to the other again.

"Hastings, it is no use looking at us. Whatever your future is, it is not sitting on this side of you, or indeed the other."

"Oh, Miss Flora!" Cassie says.

"A word with you, Cassie!" Flora stands up, and the sergeant, jerked out of his lethargy, makes a move to stop her. "Officer, this lady and I have spent an hour or so this evening locked up together in a burning office. We have had plenty of opportunity to talk in private already—another few minutes will make no difference." The sergeant slumps back against the wall with a twitch of his moustache, as Cassie rises reluctantly and the two women drift off to the far end of the room. Hastings, watching them, is unable to make out what they are saying. Flora is doing most of the talking, and Cassie's attempts to interrupt her become feebler as the conversation continues. Nevertheless, it seems to take a great deal longer than five minutes, and Hastings is aware of the imaginary champagne inside him beginning to go flat. He would be glad of a little sleep now, but he does not know where he can hope to find it. Women, he reflects as he watches their gestures, are not nearly as enticing when they are covered in smutty stains, though no less mysterious. What exactly were they doing in that burning office Flora mentioned? No doubt he will not be permitted to ask them on their return. Once or twice, Cassie casts a longing look in his direction; is he to marry her, he wonders? Whichever one he ends up with, the decision does not seem to be up to him, which is perhaps just as well.

He is almost asleep when Flora jogs his shoulder. "There, Hastings, it is all settled. Cassie?"

"Here," Cassie says, taking something out of her reticule.

"This is the loan we spoke of. It will suffice till you are able to find employment, and you will need employment where you are going."

"Mr. Wimbury has undertaken not to leave London while our investigations are proceeding," the sergeant says, and slumps back again.

"And you will be needing this." She takes something from Cassie and presses it into his hand. "Cassie assures me that it can still be"—she looks at the sergeant, who is paying no attention at present, and lowers her voice—"*used*. It is the best thing for all of us, Hastings. You cannot go back to Reigate now. Or anywhere that is…" She pauses, struggling for the word. She must be tired, too, Hastings thinks, after whatever has happened to her this evening. "… *decent*," she concludes.

Hastings considers objecting but cannot bring himself to make the effort. Arguing with Flora was always difficult, and he has a feeling he will at least be spared that for the rest of his life. After a glance at the sergeant to make sure that he is still not looking, he peers down at the object now clutched in his hand. Cassie and Flora, their faces close to his as if shielding him, are both studying his face to see what his reaction will be. He can hardly take it in, something he is supposed to read and understand when he would rather not be thinking of anything more, but eventually he reads it and does what is expected of him. He nods, and both of them give the same pained-but-pleased smile, so he must have done the right thing.

The object in his hand is a ticket for the boat train to Calais.

The gaslamps will not come on again tonight. It will be a few days before all the Count's agents in the gasworks are identified, so the city can expect some interruptions to the supply in the nights to come as they continue to follow the instructions of a mastermind who is no longer functioning. The other activities he directed have, however, ceased. The coloured fires have burned out, and the magic lanterns are abandoned—as the police have come to terms with the crisis, one or two of the operators have been arrested, as have some of the prowling ghosts, whose costumes make them a great deal easier to identify than ordinary criminals. By now, both the violinist and the accordionist have left the Embankment, their pockets stuffed with the pennies, threepenny bits and sixpences that have been thrown to them, and the crowd has thinned out. London is almost back to its usual nocturnal state, though darker. It is to the Embankment that Hastings makes his way after he leaves Scotland Yard. He has no thought in his head but sleep, and, paradoxically, a well-lighted area seems the best place to get it. He has had enough of darkness for the time being, and he has no fear of being robbed as he settles down on the bench to pass the few hours remaining till dawn

Dr. Farthing, on the other hand (or perhaps he is the Count, given the absence of beard), is walking up and down the deserted spaces of Victoria Station (now faintly illuminated with long disused lanterns and oil lamps unearthed from their storage cupboards by the employees of the South Eastern Railway), watched sleepily by the same policeman whose presence was so alarming to Flora when she was here several hours ago. Will the constable be replaced at some stage, and will the replacement have news of the death of Inspector Dollis and the hunt for his murderer? It would be awkward being one of the few people on the station available for questioning. Farthing may have to make himself scarce in a hurry. He is reassured by the feel of the werewolf gun in his pocket, and still more by the thought that there is plenty of darkness outside to disappear into if necessary. Whatever happens he must return in time for the first train to Dover at six thirty-five.

The sun will be coming up by then. It has been a cloudy night, but not a smoggy one, and there is some hope that the clouds will give a bit of pink fire to the sunrise, making a fitting second act to the light show earlier in the evening. Hastings will perhaps catch a glimpse of it as he enters the station along with the other early morning travellers. He will be just in time to catch the train, the same one as the Count. Both will travel first-class, but in different carriages. It will not even occur to Hastings as they leave the train at Dover that the nervous middle-aged passenger a dozen paces in front of him, the only other one who has not stopped to negotiate with a porter about luggage, is the man who imprisoned him in the darkness of Cimmeria and coached him to play the ghost of Hamlet's father for a magic-lantern display. On the ferry, Hastings, who has never been abroad before, will spend all his time at the bow, trying to catch his first glimpse of the French coast, while the Count, as he certainly is by this time, is in the first-class lounge nursing a glass of cognac and wondering what the lighting equipment is like at the Paris Opéra. On disembarkation this time, it will be Hastings who is a dozen paces in front of the Count as they are jostled by the throng descending the gangplank. Is there any recognition now? It would not matter even if there were; he is not an actor or the employee of a theatre any more, and hence of no use to an impresario.

And will they meet in their future lives? Europe is a comparatively small continent if you come from Great Britain and are of an artistic or criminal character. Sooner or later every ne'er-do-well from this country who has a modicum of culture or imagination turns up there, writing an endless first novel in a garret on the Left Bank, or lecturing about Botticelli to rich and pretty English tourists among the masterpieces at the Uffizi, or whispering the details of an elaborate financial scheme to a gouty duke at a German spa while a string quintet plays Mendelssohn. Surely any two such unsavoury characters must meet after a while? By then the Count may be a Count no longer (since the title is not so exotic in these parts), and Hastings Wimbury may have changed his name to one easier for foreigners to pronounce. But if they do meet, it will not be recorded in these pages.

*June 1903*

# Epilogue

For reasons no one could remember, the palace of the bishop of Woking was called the Hermitage. It was not in Woking itself, but some three miles outside the town (or, as one should remember to call it now, the city, with the cathedral having been built), in the village of St. John's. Mrs. Pilkins, the wife of the new bishop, was not displeased with the palace itself, which was an old country house converted for the purpose when the new diocese was created in the 1880s, and would be serviceable enough when the gaslights were updated to electricity and new flush toilets installed. But the previous bishop, who had been in his sixties when appointed, had allowed the garden to become sadly neglected. There was the usual Scottish gardener, a man even older than his erstwhile employer, and Flora's first act on becoming mistress of the palace was to give the old fellow a nice send-off with a pair of gold-plated secateurs to mark his honourable retirement and a bottle of whisky to make it more cheerful. He would be perfectly happy failing to tend the little plot at the back of his cottage in Knaphill. She would appoint a younger, stronger man in due course; for the time being, Crawford's assistant, a boy scarcely out of his teens, could trim the hedges into a semblance of respectability and mow the back lawn, the only part that had been kept more or less free of weeds.

These arrangements had sufficed for the garden party that had followed Ambrose's installation, especially as about a third of the lawn was taken up by the marquee erected for the occasion, which was where the guests had taken their refreshments. The obscure logic of workmen apparently dictated that the marquee could not be taken down the next day, so it was still there this next evening, the tables folded up and heaped in a corner and the chairs stacked ready for removal in the morning. Flora liked having a tent full of greenness where she could linger after dinner feeling she was inside and outside at the same time. She had lifted down a couple of the chairs and was sitting on one of them, awaiting her visitor.

Collins announced Mrs. Underhill exactly as he would have done in the drawing room, though, as the entire front of the marquee was open to the elements, Flora had been able to see them approach all the way across the lawn. The famous gardener, though clad in appropriate tweeds, was otherwise not quite what she had been expecting: she was plump rather than wiry, and, far from being a crone, was about the same age as Flora herself.

"I'm so sorry," Mrs. Underhill said, taking her seat on the chair indicated. "I came as soon as I could." The voice was wrong, too; gardeners, when not Scottish, should have a West Country drawl, whereas this one sounded almost well-bred, with a trace of London. But then, Flora reminded herself, Mrs. Underhill was not a gardener in the sense she was used to. Like so many other aspects of life, such people were different nowadays. There was a sort of horticultural aestheticism spreading across the south of England, in which the grounds of one's house were regarded as canvas and the flowers as paint, and its practitioners expected to be treated as artists.

"I understand you are very busy," Flora said. "It is good of you to fit me in."

Throughout the brief interview that followed, Flora was aware of a sense of unreality that made her feel that her chair, rocking on the unstable surface of the lawn every time she moved, was about to take off and float up to the canvas roof. Something about this visitor made her uncomfortable. She got through the details as quickly as she could, her own voice sounding unsteady to her. Mrs. Underhill would arrive on Monday to make an extensive survey of the grounds, which would take two or three days, during which time she would reside at the Hermitage. She would then return to her other tasks and a detailed plan for the work would be delivered to Flora by the end of the month. Work on the redesign was unlikely to begin before August, when the Pilkins family would be on their annual holiday in Scotland, and most of the planting would take place in the autumn. Mrs. Underhill's plans would include recommendations for the number of men to employ on completion of the project to maintain the gardens in perpetuity.

"Perpetuity," Mrs. Underhill said with a giggle. "A nice word for the property of a bishop." What was it about the youthfulness of her laugh that was so disconcerting? It made Flora feel unexpectedly chilly, as if her shawl had been ripped from her shoulders and her summer dress with it. She stood up abruptly, feeling that she could not bear to stay another minute where she was, and Mrs. Underhill took it as a hint.

"Quite right, Mrs. Pilkins, there can't be more than an hour of light left, and if I'm to get an idea of the present state of the garden, we really must have a look at it now."

Flora knew she should be leading the way round the weedgrown borders and scruffy shrubberies, but her knowledge of the layout was only sketchy, and Mrs. Underhill, moving with a vigour that did not seem to go with her substantial appearance, was exploring everywhere, excavating among brambles to point out a half choked peony, scraping blackfly off a rose petal and holding it up on the tip of her finger for mutual lamentation, dirtying her hands in the orangey soil. "Clay, Mrs. Pilkins, clay. Typical Surrey soil, I'm afraid. Nothing grows well in it but roses, which is good, and rhododendrons, which depends on your point of view. Ah, here they are."

They were standing on the edge of a small spinney of holly and birches, its edge so overgrown with rhododendron that it was almost impossible to go further. There were just a few of the sad purple flowers left; they always made Flora think of the mourning decorations in Church during Lent. "I have never liked them," she said. "The flowers are gloomy and those great, glossy leaves…"

"Like I say," Mrs. Underhill replied, "it depends on your point of view. They are a useful shrub for these conditions as nothing much else will grow here, and the flowers make a show in season, which they ain't at present."

Flora started. The word was perhaps an affectation, but it somehow contributed to her sense of unreality.

"Besides that," Mrs. Underhill went on, "there is a new species now that I've heard of that has the most lovely flowers, orange and yellow, and with a sweet smell, not at all your standard rhododendron. They come from somewhere out East, I think."

Flora said nothing. She was very cold suddenly, and staring through the rhododendron leaves into the darkness of the wood was giving her the impression that night was coming on fast. She turned and looked at the woman beside her, whose pale face now looked blotchy in the uncertain light. There was something about it that made Flora uncomfortable; perhaps she would not employ the fashionable bohemian gardener after all.

"Oh, Miss Flora," Mrs. Underhill said. "You don't have the least idea who I am, do you? And I knew you the moment I laid eyes on you."

Cassie had grown used in her career to sitting in her tweeds and muddy boots on the delicate chairs of drawing rooms holding a cup of tea, though after her day's work she would have preferred a drop of brandy. She was especially honoured on this occasion when the bishop dropped in briefly, a tall greying man looking rather stagey, as Cassie put it to herself, in his black and purple. He had obviously been curious to see whom his wife was entertaining at this late hour, but showed not the least interest in the garden.

"Well," he said, "I'm sure it will grow with great vigour under your tutelage, Mrs. Underhill."

"It's growing vigorously now, Bishop," Cassie said. "That's the trouble, really. Still, I shall soon put a stop to that."

"Oh, good." He accepted a cup of tea, and took a sip of it while standing, then drifted off again, apologizing inaudibly as he went.

"My husband has only been a bishop for a few days," Flora said, "and is not yet sure what is expected of him. It is a rather

curious diocese, mostly noted for the extensive cemetery at
Brookwood. In the sermon he delivered at his installation
he remarked that most of his flock were dead. Some of the
congregation thought it in bad taste, and that has made him a
little anxious. He is inclined to work too hard, I think."

"He seems a nice gentleman," Cassie said.

"And what does your husband do, Mrs. Underhill—may I
call you Cassie? I didn't know you at first, but now that I do I
can't think of you as anything else."

"And I can't think of you as anything but Miss Flora, though
Flora is more in my line than yours, you might say. Mr. Underhill
has passed on."

"I'm so sorry."

"Oh, I don't mean he's dead, he's just passed on elsewhere,
to other things, and no doubt other attachments. It wasn't much
of a marriage, but having a Mrs. in front of one's name is an
advantage for a woman in a professional way. It makes you
sound a bit more serious."

"I was expecting someone older."

Cassie nodded. She had heard this remark often, though
usually from her male customers. "And you were expecting a
stranger, like I was."

They looked at each other. "Have you ever—?" Flora began
and stopped.

"Thought back to those nights at Halcyon House, and later
when you was sleeping on the couch in Dr. Farthing's office?
We nearly came a cropper, then, Miss Flora. I think about it
sometimes, but it seems another world."

"After all, it was another century."

"And we had some mad ideas, didn't we? We were all set to
travel off to some country that didn't even exist, just because he
told us it did."

"An evil man, Cassie." Flora shuddered, and Cassie knew
she was remembering the body of Inspector Dollis burning
on the floorboards. The image cropped up in her own dreams
occasionally.

"I know he was, miss, but the funny thing was I liked him. It's strange, ain't it, how you can like a person and they turn out to be capable of something like that? Still, as you say, it was the nineteenth century and I suppose people were more credulous then."

"He only had to turn out the lights, and the whole of London went mad!" Flora smiled.

"And we was rescued by a wolf!" Cassie said. "Sent, if you ask me, by Dr. Farthing, so he wasn't all bad."

"Such things happen when one is young," Flora said. "It is different now. Look at us both, grown women with our own lives and responsibilities. You have no children, Cassie?"

"No, miss."

"I have three. My eldest, Algernon, will be going up to Cambridge this autumn. Before I know it, I shall have lost them all. You can see why I am anxious to busy myself with the garden."

In the carriage on the road to the station, Cassie wondered why they had both avoided the subject of Hastings. Flora had been going to mention him, she was certain, but had checked herself. Surely the memory could not be as painful as that of the burning body in the office? No doubt Flora had been unwilling to spoil the pleasant atmosphere of their reunion by bringing up the rivalry that had once existed between them. For they had been rivals, even when working together; at the very last, as they were arguing at one end of that long room or office or whatever it was in Scotland Yard, Flora had been insisting that Europe was the only place for a man who had committed the crimes Hastings had, while Cassie had wanted him to stay. It was all very well for her to be self-denying, but she had, Cassie felt, no business to be self-denying on behalf of someone else. He could have stayed. He had done no more than filch a bit of equipment from a theatre, and with all the other crimes that had been committed that night, who was to know if the police would even have bothered to investigate? And if he had gone to prison, what then? It would probably have been a few months, a year at the outside, and he and Cassie could have got married. He couldn't have been a worse rogue than Underhill.

What it is, Cassie thought as the carriage drew up outside Woking station and she stepped out into the bluish darkness of a summer night, is that Hastings was right, and a respectable type like Miss Flora could never understand the fact: artists were not like anyone else and didn't have to abide by the same standards. Hastings was an artist, and even the Count was an artist of a sort, although in his case he had taken it altogether too far. And now she was an artist, too.

The train was already at the platform, giving off exasperated puffs of steam, and she only just reached the carriage in time— she was glad she would not have to spend the night in Woking, a town which, like most Londoners, she associated chiefly with death. She had the first-class compartment to herself. As they pulled out into the Surrey countryside, she found herself thinking again of those curious rhododendrons with the orange and yellow flowers and the overpowering scent, like drowning in honey. They would be the only thing for that spinney of Miss Flora's. Besides, she would be able to see the nurseryman again, a man with a foreign name she couldn't pronounce, but the same blue-green eyes and boyish way of looking round the room when he talked, as if in search of someone or something more interesting than you were, that she remembered from twenty years ago. He had had an adventurous life before coming back to England, been all over the place collecting plants, he said, China, Tibet, India, Japan, which accounted for his weather-beaten skin. All the same, she would have known him anywhere, and she was almost sure he knew her, too, though he hadn't said anything yet. Now they had something in common: they both worked with flowers, a slower and more reliable source of colour than those lights he used to be so fond of. Something had stopped her renewing their acquaintance last week, a feeling that it was better to leave those memories untouched, but now having met Miss Flora again after all this time, it seemed as if it was fated somehow. Not that she would tell Flora anything about it—one coincidence would certainly be quite enough for her to deal with. A sprinkling of lights went by outside the carriage window: that must be Weybridge, another place where she had the prospect of some garden designing shortly. It was pleasant being her own boss, and an additional pleasure to think that this time she would have the man she wanted all to herself. She settled back in her seat; she would sleep the rest of the way to Waterloo.

# Acknowledgements

Two books were especially inspirational in the writing of this one: *Theatre Lighting in the Age of Gas* by Terence Rees opened up the world of limelight, sunburners, magic lanterns and chemical fire, while Jacob Middleton's *Spirits of an Industrial Age* introduced me to that most bizarre of Victorian nightmares, the prowling ghost. Thanks to Archna Sharma, Richard Francis and Justin Golding for valuable feedback at a time when I wrongly thought the book was finished, to Neem Tree Press for making it a reality, and to Creina Francis for her support throughout the writing of it.

# About the Author

Matthew Francis is Professor Emeritus in Creative Writing at Aberystwyth University. He read English at Magdalene College, Cambridge University. He writes novels, short stories, and poetry. He has won the *TLS* / Blackwell's Prize for Poetry and the Southern Arts Literature Prize, and been shortlisted twice for the Forward Prize, twice for the Welsh Book of the Year Award and once for the Ted Hughes Award. In 2004, he was chosen as one of the Next Generation Poets. He is a Fellow of the Welsh Academy.

Matthew lives with his wife in Aberystwyth, Wales where he enjoys playing chess, cooking and playing the ukulele.